Merry Christmas, Baby

Merry Christmas, Baby

Donna Kauffman

Nancy Warren

Erin McCarthy

MaryJanice Davidson

Lucy Monroe

Susanna Carr

BRAVA

KENSINGTON PUBLISHING CORP.

http://www.kensingtonbooks.com

CONTENTS

MAKING WAVES

Donna Kauffman

Chapter One

"You did *what?*" Burke Morgan stared in disbelief at his chief crewman—his only crewman.

A broad smile creased Dorsey Apolo's smooth, wide face as he dropped two stuffed duffel bags on the deck next to his feet. "Took a job Down Under, mate."

The sea breeze whipped at Burke's hair, and the Caribbean sun beat down on his neck. Another perfect day in paradise. Until a second ago anyway. "First, I can't tell you how wrong it is for a Polynesian guy to do an Aussie accent. And a bad one at that. But more wrong is you ditching me on the eve of our first tour." He motioned to the bags at Dorsey's feet. "When did you get the offer? When were you going to tell me?"

"I'm telling you now. And I'm sorry, bruddah. Truly."

Burke snorted. Dorsey was all but vibrating with excitement. His dark eyes were gleaming, and he was fidgeting like a toddler. A big man with a graying braid that hung halfway down his back and deeply grooved creases fanning out around his dark eyes, he was seventy-five going on twenty-five. It was one of the traits Burke most enjoyed about him. Not as amusing at the moment, however.

"I've never sailed down there," Dorsey said. "You know I've always wanted to. We're going through Whitsunday, in the Barrier Reef. Brand new, forty-seven-foot Chincogan cat," he said almost dreamily. "One honeymoon couple and I'm captain and crew. Six weeks, then I'll be back."

Burke's eyes bugged. *"Six weeks?* That's mid-February. The season will be half over by then. One hell of a honeymoon."

"Young couple has deep pockets."

"Which we don't," Burke reminded him.

"Yet," Dorsey said with a wink. "You're going to make a go of this new enterprise, I'm sure of it. I've nothing but faith in you."

"I've got faith in me, too," Burke replied. "But that faith was partly based on the fact that you were going to crew for me my first season out." Privately he'd been hoping they'd team up even longer. Burke had been crewing all over the Caribbean and the South Pacific since he'd left home at seventeen. Some kids dreamed of joining the circus, but ever since the time old man Ramsay had taken him out on the Chesapeake Bay fishing, Burke had dreamed of running his own charter. Only somewhere a lot warmer.

He'd hooked up with Dorsey for the first time at nineteen, on a Scandinavian owned charter out of the Lesser Antilles. The two had worked together often in the thirteen years since. The charismatic Hawaiian had been father figure, mentor, compatriot, and brother-in-arms to Burke. He trusted him like he trusted no one else, save perhaps his three brothers.

But his brothers weren't supposed to help him crew the exceedingly wealthy and very well connected George and Tutti Wetherington around the islands from Christmas through New Years. He'd been counting on Dorsey for that. Heavily. He didn't realize just how heavily until now. Burke was a decent people person, but his skills were mostly centered around being the dependable, take charge kind of guy that clients could feel comfortable being captained by. Dorsey was the colorful character that clients loved and remembered. His cooking was out of this world, and the wild and oftentimes ribald tales he told of his fiftysome-odd years sailing the tropics charmed clients no matter their income bracket.

"We've got bookings straight into March, Dorse, and a lot of the word of mouth that got us those clients was as much for your reputation as it was my ability to steer a damn boat. What the hell am I supposed to do?"

"Ah, don't get your trunks in a twist," Dorsey admonished. "I wouldn't leave you in dry dock, you know that. I got it covered. My oldest granddaughter, Kamala, is gonna help you out till I get back. And you might not want me back when you get a taste of her cooking." His grin widened, if that was possible. "She's a hell of a lot easier on the eyes, too."

Burke didn't say anything to that. He'd seen assorted photos of the ever-expanding Apolo clan over the years. They were a hardy, stout bunch, regardless of gender. But her looks didn't concern him at the moment. His eyes narrowed. "I thought none of your kids or grandkids sailed. You bitch and moan about that every time you come back from a visit home."

Dorsey was a wanderer, but as a much younger man, he'd managed to stay in Kauai long enough to marry and have three children with his now ex-wife, Lana. He hadn't been around much for them, or for his seven grandchildren. But now that his older grandchildren were having children, and the years were adding up, he'd started to feel a bit of regret over that. Not that Burke thought for a second that he'd have been capable of staying in one place even if he'd wanted to, but to give the old man credit, since his great-grandchildren had started popping up, he'd made an effort to stay better connected. He went back home when he could, spending longer and longer periods of time there now, during the slow season.

Unlike Burke, who had been home to Virginia only once in the fifteen years since he'd left Rogues Hollow. Escaped, actually. That one visit had been almost exactly a year ago, last Christmas, when his estranged father had passed away. The visit made him miss his brothers more now; seeing them all again had been the only positive part of that holiday trek. The rest he didn't miss at all. To him, the holiday season meant steady work. Work that he loved. And this Christmas, he'd given himself the best present of all: realizing his dream of captaining his own charter. That was about as sentimental as he got.

"Yes, I know," Dorsey was saying, unable to hide his unending disappointment. "Two sons and a daughter. Seven grandchildren." He sighed heavily. "Not a seafarer in the bunch. Where did I go wrong?"

"We are not going there, okay?" Burke had heard this rant more times than he could count. "Besides, I figured if you were going to ditch me, it would be to head home and hold the newest great-grandbaby of yours."

Dorsey shook his head. "I'm no good with diapers and bottles, *brah*. I'll wait until they're walking and properly housebroken. Old enough to take out on the water and teach them to sail."

"You don't give up, I'll give you that," Burke said, fighting the smile that was always near the surface when Dorsey was around. "You Apolos don't believe in waiting too long to start up the production, do you?" They didn't believe in waiting long to get married either. Dorsey's youngest granddaughter, the one who had just given birth, was barely past her twentieth birthday. "Didn't Malani just get married earlier this year?"

"What can I say?" His eyes crinkled at the corners when he smiled. "We're a passionate, impetuous lot."

"If that's your way of saying horny and impatient, with no apparent access to birth control, then I suppose you're right."

Dorsey just laughed. "Well, we may start young, but the Apolo family is strong. Lana sees to that. I'm the one disgrace to the family tree, and you'd best believe she won't tolerate another."

Burke had never met Dorsey's ex-wife, but from the tales he'd told, he didn't doubt for a moment that Lana was a clan matriarch of the most controlling order. "I'm surprised she's agreeing to Kamala coming all the way down here, and over the holidays to boot."

Dorsey's smile tightened a bit, and he looked out across the water. "Yes, well, Kamala is a grown woman, almost thirty. She can make her own decisions."

"Then she takes after her grandfather." Despite the tension in Dorsey's tone, Burke heard the underlying thread of pride. There was more to that story, he was sure, but he wasn't going to press. The only important thing was running his trip as planned. "So you say she's a good cook?" Traditionally, small charters like his, which boarded at most four guests at a time, attracted their following by offering as much luxury as possible while tooling around the islands. And top on that list was a competitive gourmet menu. Dorsey's menus weren't so much haute cuisine as they were innovative, but his charm and presentation went a long way toward making his meals memorable occasions. If Burke were left in charge of the galley, they'd all be eating scrambled eggs and peanut butter and jelly sandwiches. He suspected that wouldn't cut it with the Wetheringtons.

"Oh, she's more than that," Dorsey said, his smile one of pride. "She's trained and worked in some of the best restaurants in the islands. L.A., now."

"She's stateside? I thought Lana liked to keep her flock close."

"That much is true. But Kamala, well, she has her own ideas about things."

Burke wondered just what he was getting himself into here. A sturdy Polynesian babe wielding sharp knives and an attitude wasn't exactly painting a positive picture. Nor was it conducive to providing the atmosphere necessary to charm the customers.

"She's saving up to open her own catering business," Dorsey went on, conveniently glossing over what Burke suspected was a rift in the Apolo family.

Which was none of his business. Lana and the rest of the outspoken, opinionated clan were thousands of miles away. Hardly a concern of his. And, as Dorsey said, if she was staring at thirty, Kamala was certainly an adult, able to make her own decisions. "How is it she has six weeks free?" Burke frowned. "Wait a minute, how much did you tell her I was paying? Because it's one thing for you to take your cut, with your experience. But—"

Dorsey waved him silent. "She gets my cut," he stated flatly. "If you don't think she's worth it by the time I get back, I'll make up the difference myself."

Burke started to argue, but there wasn't much he could say to that arrangement. He didn't like being put in the middle of a family situation, which he suspected was exactly where Dorsey had plunked him, but he wasn't exactly in a position to refuse his offer either. Which, he also suspected his old friend had thought out in advance. Dorsey was as wily as he was charming.

"Well, don't think that just because she's related to you I'm going to go easy on her," Burke warned him. "She has to pull her own weight, same as anyone."

"She'll do fine," he said, quite confidently. But then Dorsey was the most optimistic man Burke had ever met. Which, in the past, had complemented Burke's somewhat more pessimistic views quite nicely. Dorsey winked at him. "I'm leaving her in good hands, after all."

"We'll see," was all Burke said, ignoring the first niggling suspicion that threatened to form. Dorsey, better than anyone, understood the nomadic ways of a sailor. No way would he play matchmaker, especially with one of his own. "When is she supposed to arrive?" Burke asked. "For that matter, where is she supposed to arrive?" They were docked in Antigua, which had a decent airport, but they were supposed to be under way early that afternoon, heading toward Barbuda, where Burke's very first private charter guests awaited. They were slated to set sail tomorrow, for a ten-day trip through the Lesser Antilles, ending back here just after the new year.

Dorsey lifted one duffel and heaved it onto the pier. "She's catching a prop job in from Miami, due in an hour or so from now. I figured we'd meet up at the airport and I'd send her on to you from there." He heaved the second bag onto the pier, his massive brown shoulders barely flexing under the burden, then tossed a gleaming smile over his shoulder. "Unless of course you'd like to come with me, send me off in style. I could introduce you in person."

Burke shook his head, ignoring the twinkle in Dorsey's eyes. "You know we have—or should I say, *I* have—" he corrected pointedly, "too much to do before heading out." He hoped Kamala didn't mind jumping right in. It was going to take another set of hands if he was going to get them under way on time.

Dorsey levered his huge body effortlessly onto the pier, next to the bags. "Understood." He brushed off his Polynesian print docker shorts and planted his beefy hands on his waist. He was a smooth-skinned giant in a tie-dyed T-shirt, smiling in the face of Burke's doubtful expression. "Don't worry so much, *kaina*. She'll be a good fit for you. I promise." He lifted one duffel over his shoulder, then bent to pick up the other. "Who knows," Dorsey added with a wink, "she might be the second best thing that ever happened to you."

The knot in the pit of Burke's stomach tightened, and the idea that there was more going on here than giving his granddaughter a simple temp job was growing increasingly hard to ignore. But he did a good job of it. "Yeah? And the first best thing?"

Dorsey headed off the docks, toward the gravel parking lot where an island taxi waited. "Why, me of course," he called back, as expected, his rich, booming laugh filling the warm December air. *"Aloha `oe!"*

Frustration and dread notwithstanding, he was smiling as he waved his friend off. *"Mahalo,"* he called back. Such was the life they led, he supposed. A wanderer by nature himself, he could hardly expect any different from somebody who was just like him. The timing sucked, but he didn't hold it against Dorsey. They were all rainbow chasers.

He turned back and ran his gaze critically over the polished rails and newly refurbished rigging. His rainbow ended right here. Fifteen years of longing, of saving every extra dime. She wasn't brand new, or the latest model, but she was all his. *Making Waves,* owned and captained by Burke Morgan, was ready for service.

Or would be, he thought, his smile fading. As soon as his first mate arrived.

It didn't occur to him until a few hours later, when the sound of crunching gravel had him looking up from tweaking with the electric mainsail winch, that he'd never gotten a clear answer from Dorsey on whether she'd ever sailed.

He wiped his hands on the rag stuck in the waistband of his faded khaki shorts. Surely Dorsey wouldn't have sent her here if she didn't know her way around a boat. Then again, once they were under way, it wasn't as though she really had to do anything other than cook and hostess the guests, follow the occasional simple direction. But it would make him feel a hell of a lot better if she had at least a working knowledge of sailing. Just in case.

He was already making a mental list of who he could get to replace her after this trip was over—he didn't care who she was related to, or how much she needed the cash; if she couldn't pull her weight, she was gone ten days from now—when the cab stopped at the end of the pier and the rear door opened.

And a pair of endlessly long, tanned and toned legs emerged, followed by snug white shorts and a belly-baring red top that hugged a body the way God had certainly intended a body like hers to be hugged. When she finally straightened and shook her long black hair back over her shoulders, Burke realized he'd been right about one thing. Sturdy she was, indeed. There was definitely a whole lot of Apolo currently striding toward him. Only in Kamala's case, every bit of it was packaged in a way that would drive any man with a pulse straight to his knees, in ready begging position.

He automatically moved toward the side of the boat, thinking maybe he was a bit more sentimental about Christmas than he'd thought. "Thank you, Santa," he murmured in abject appreciation.

And to think, he hadn't even been a very good boy this year.

He only hoped he'd read that twinkle right and Dorsey meant it when he'd said she'd be in good hands. Because the next couple of weeks were going to be pure hell if he had to keep his off of her.

Chapter Two

Kam climbed from the stifling heat of the taxi and gazed out over the small island harbor. It had been quite a while since she'd looked at this kind of view. She'd left Kauai to go stateside five years ago. As she watched the masts sway, she wasn't quite sure if that had been long enough.

It was thoughts of her alternatives that had her straightening her shoulders and lifting her chin. She'd burned her bridges at her last job. And though she loved *Kapuna wahine* Lana with all her heart, going home again wasn't an option. She knew her grandmother wanted only the best for every member of her family; however, Lana's idea of what was right for Kam and Kam's own ideas were worlds apart. She'd tried it Lana's way, working close to home, embracing the boisterous bosom of the Apolo clan, but as much as she also loved her large and rowdy family, they suffocated her with their vision of her future. The core of which, of course, revolved around her settling down with an appropriate young man—meaning one they hand selected—so she could add to the assembly line of Apolo grandbabies her sisters and cousins were producing with alarming frequency.

L.A. had been both her haven and her land of opportunity. And the only long-term partnership she was interested in was the one she was struggling to form with her bank, in the manner of qualifying for a small business loan so she could open her own catering business. So far, her desires had gone unrequited.

After spending a couple of years working her way up to assistant head chef in a trendy Santa Monica restaurant, scraping every dime while fending off the unwanted attentions of Octopus Steve, the owner, she'd begun to despair of ever meeting her goal. She didn't want to start over somewhere else, but she wasn't sure she could make it another year and a half without finally snapping and using one of the many sharp implements at her disposal on Steve's much vaunted appendage.

Add to that the approaching holidays and the serious pressure from Lana and Co. to fly back to the islands for the duration, and she'd all but leapt at the opportunity Dorsey had dropped in her lap. Her grandfather was one of her favorite people in the world, and the only Apolo who understood her. He'd been the one who'd stood up to both her parents and the formidable Lana, defending her right to find her own path, do things her own way.

Dorsey's offer was the miracle she'd been praying for but never believed would happen. Crewing on his best friend's new cat charter around the islands over the holidays—thereby not only putting her far out of Lana's reach, but also providing the promise of the much needed final capital investment for her business loan—well, she'd have been an idiot to turn it down. It had given her the nerve to walk out on her grab-assy boss and take her first step toward becoming an entrepreneur in her own right.

Yes, she'd heard about Burke Morgan, reliable captain and the islands' perennial eligible bachelor. Probably some of it was just Dorsey being his larger-than-life self, telling his heavily embellished stories. But if she could handle Octopus Steve, surely she could fend off any untoward behavior from one aging island *haole* for a month or so.

Of course, there was one other teeny tiny hitch in her miracle solution, but the payoff was too big, the timing too perfect.

With no other solution in sight, she'd calculated the risk . . . and taken the leap. Then immediately scheduled an appointment with her doctor.

Just thinking about that made her stomach pitch as the horizon stretching out far beyond the clear turquoise harbor seemed to bob up and down along with the boats. Turning away as the cabbie scrambled out of the front and hurried to the back to help her with her bags, she told herself it was just anticipation of this new adventure that had her feeling unsettled. Still, when she tucked her hair back, she surreptitiously checked the tiny patch she'd stuck behind her ear, praying her other miniature miracle lived up to her doctor's hype.

"You want me carry bags to boat?" the cabbie asked with what could only be described as a beaming smile, despite numerous missing teeth.

She had six inches and a good forty pounds on the guy. "No, no, that won't be necessary." She pulled out her wallet and paid him, tipping him as much as she could afford, wishing she didn't have to pinch every penny. She was tired of pinching.

As the taxi pulled away, she turned her attention to the boats themselves, although yacht might be a far more appropriate term for the sailing rigs lined up along the docks. Big and pricey was her first impression. That she couldn't tell one from the other was her second. Thankfully, while Dorsey might not be able to describe what a person wore or what color eyes they had, he could remember every detail of every boat he'd ever sailed.

He'd described Burke Morgan's catamaran in exhausting detail, his tone so affectionate you'd almost think it had been his. Most of his talk of mainsails and beam width and twin diesels had gone in one ear and out the other. But she'd retained what she thought were the basic identifying marks that even she could manage to find. She was looking for a white forty-five-foot cat with a mainsail sporting alternating aqua and dark blue stripes. Which would be great, if any of the boats actually had their sails up. Which, being docked, they didn't.

That left her looking for a big white catamaran.

"Gee," she muttered, propping her hand to her brow as she looked along the piers, "that really narrows it down." Maybe she should have taken better notes. She patted the backpack she'd slung over her shoulder, glad now she'd packed the sailing guides she'd picked up at the used book store. Maybe they'd make more sense once she was actually on the boat. Figuring she'd just wander the docks until she found a cat named *Making Waves,* she bent to swing the strap of her duffel over her other shoulder when she heard a man call her name.

She lifted the bag, then turned toward the voice, but surprise kept her from responding right away. Dorsey might proudly stuff his wallet with the snapshots his family sent him on a regular basis, but the man was hopeless when it came to recording any of his own life on film. Her own wallet bore only a single photo of her grandfather that was several years old, and she was thankful to have that much. He was a great one for telling stories, though, and while she'd never seen most of the places he'd been, much less the people he'd shared the better part of his life with, he used such vivid detail and spoke with such enthusiasm that she'd always felt as if she'd traveled the world right there with him, and that his friends would be instantly recognizable to her, were she to bump into them on the street.

"Another reality altered," she murmured beneath her breath, even as her pulse bumped up another notch. Because if the man presently striding toward her was who she thought he was, she was going to have to dramatically retool every tale Dorsey had told that had featured his best pal, Burke Morgan. And God knew, that was going to take some doing.

When Dorsey had spoken of his younger vagabond protégé, Kam had pictured a man a couple decades younger than her grandfather. Which was why she'd imagined Burke Morgan to be in his fifties. A dashing man, to be sure, given Dorsey's many tales of Burke's exploits with members of the fairer sex. She'd heard all about the wide grin, the sun-burnished good looks, the aggressive charm, but she'd been thinking *fun traveling companion, easy on the eyes.* Not *studly island hunk, hell on the sex drive.*

She stood in mute silence as he strode off the pier and up the short hill toward her, all dazzling teeth and sparkling eyes, like a pirate having come ashore to claim his share of the loot. And knew her long neglected sexual needs had just come out of dry dock.

She swallowed against a suddenly dry throat as she thought about the skimpy clothes she'd packed, her backup game plan. Insurance, really. That's all it had been. She'd dazzle them first and foremost with her cooking, but when necessary, she had no qualms about distracting them from her possible other shortcomings with a bright smile and a little cleavage. This trip was too important to her future not to use whatever tools she had at her disposal to insure everyone had a good time.

Only nowhere in her game plan did "good time" encompass anything more than becoming part of the attractive native view. Easy on the eyes, but out of reach of the hands. Not that she'd worried about that. After all, she'd assumed it would just be her, a couple of old guys, and a matronly socialite.

"Kamala?" Burke closed the distance between them, extending a hand toward her. "A pleasure to meet you."

Wide hands, she thought, her entire game plan dissolving in an instant, *and muscular arms.* The sleeveless white T-shirt he wore played up the broad shoulders and chest, the thick neck, along with the taut belly and trim waist. But it was the look in his eyes that had her quivering just a little. Intent and focused. Not likely to overlook flaws of any kind.

And while, at the moment, all he probably saw were the genetic gifts she'd shamelessly played up, she knew all about the flaws she'd cunningly hoped to cover up. *Well,* she thought, *too late to back out now.*

She extended her hand, brazening it out. She'd be doing a lot of that for the next six weeks. That was if she made it through the next six minutes. "Call me Kam," she told him. "And the pleasure's mine, Mr. Morgan. I've heard so much about you."

He laughed as his hand engulfed hers. "It's Burke. And I swear at least half of those stories are lies, and the other half have probably been grossly exaggerated."

His voice was a deep rumble, and though that, along with his touch, was more than a little unnerving, when coupled with his easy smile and comfortable laugh, she found herself loosening up without realizing quite how he'd done it. "Yes, but which half is which?" she heard herself ask. *Jesus, Kam, don't flirt with the man.*

But he just laughed again and released her hand as he reached for her duffel. "I'll let you be the judge," he said with a wink.

It was all very congenial, though, and she realized he was a man who smiled often and probably flirted as easily as he breathed. A part of that natural charm Dorsey had talked about. Nothing personal in it, she thought with relief, hoping he'd assumed the same about her flippant comment.

He slid the strap of her bag from her shoulder, his knuckles barely brushing her skin.

So why that sent a little ripple of awareness skating all the way through her body, she had no idea. He might be used to exuding his laid-back island charm, expecting nothing but a laugh or roll of the eyes in return, but it seemed she was going to have to work some on that return part.

He transferred the weight of her duffel easily to his back, then turned and gestured for her to go in front of him. "We're the third dock on the left, last one out, second slip."

She looked past him at the solid central pier . . . and the

boats that bobbed on the gentle swells wafting through the quiet cove. And froze up. She'd been fine up until that moment. Well, mostly fine.

"I, um . . ." she paused, feeling her throat begin to close over. She yanked her gaze away from the rocking boats and looked back to him, not entirely sure connecting her gaze to his made her feel any more grounded or secure—but looking at him didn't make her want to throw up, so she went that direction. She patted her backpack, and stalled. "After talking with Dorsey, I prepared some menus ahead of time, and I was hoping I could pick up a few things from the local market before we took off." She tried to smooth the edge of panic from her voice, but she knew she'd rattled that off way too fast to sound casual.

His gaze didn't change, however, but it did remain intent on hers. Unsettling, but not nearly as much as the prospect of stepping on the swaying deck of his boat. She was going to have to face that, but if she delayed the moment of truth a bit longer, maybe the patch would have a chance to completely kick in. Because surely it was supposed to work better than this.

"There's not much here, I'm afraid," he told her. "But we're heading over to Barbuda just as soon as we get your gear stowed, and they have a great open market. Small, but well stocked. We're not meeting the Wetheringtons until after dinner tonight, so you'll have plenty of time to shop for whatever you need. And you don't have to worry about preparing anything other than maybe a light evening snack tonight. First full meal will be tomorrow morning, before we get under sail."

Under sail. Just the words made her stomach roll. How in the hell had she ever thought she could pull this off? Was she so desperate to finally realize her dream that she was willing to hurl her way through the tropics to do it?

Of course she was, or she'd have never agreed to do this.

No more working for Octopus Steve, she reminded herself. No more sweating laborious long hours just to increase someone else's bottom line, to make a name for someone else's venture. No. Six weeks from now she'd finally have the rest of the backing she needed to become her own boss, to sweat laborious long hours for her own bottom line, to find out once and for all if she could make a go of her own venture. What fool wouldn't have jumped at that opportunity?

The fool who believed that a stupid patch could cure her of being seasick, she thought acidly.

"Shall we?" he said, sweeping an arm in front of him.

She tried to gulp down some air, thankful for her natural, olive-toned skin. It masked the pale, pasty look she knew would be obvious otherwise. She took her first tentative step toward what would likely be her doom.

His hand came up to steady her elbow, and the warmth and sureness of his touch so distracted her that she was halfway down the pier before she realized she'd taken more than a step.

"Here she is," Burke said, a smile and more than a little pride in his voice, "the first lady to ever completely claim my heart."

Startled, Kam's gaze jerked from her feet—where she'd kept it carefully aimed the entire time—to a beautiful, stunningly white catamaran with blue trim. It took her a moment of not seeing an equally stunning woman standing on the deck of the boat to realize that the lady Burke spoke of was the boat itself. "She's gorgeous," she said, quite sincerely. "If only I could admire her from afar," she added under her breath. *Like, from Miami.*

Burke tossed her gear bag so it landed on one of the cushioned benches in the rear well, then hopped the short distance from pier to boat deck as easily as a cat might leap from sill to counter. The force of his landing barely made the boat bob, a piece of news she tried her best to latch on to. The boat might be steadier than it looked. *Maybe it won't be so bad.* She repeated that phrase over and over as Burke braced his foot on the side rail and reached his hand up to help her make the hop.

If he only knew how big a leap this really is for me.

Then her gaze shifted to his face, to that easy grin, and the light that seemed to perennially twinkle in his gray-green eyes. If she could just focus on them, on the steadiness and enjoyment that seemed such a natural part of him, maybe, just maybe, she could pull this off without completely humiliating herself.

She ignored the other boats chugging into the small harbor, the bobbing horizon and ebb and flow of the water moving beneath the pier, and the boat itself, and reached for his hand. His skin was so warm, his palm so wide as it encompassed her own. Steady, natural, easy. She could do this.

Unfortunately, ignoring all the moving parts of this scenario proved to be a gross oversight on her part. She'd no sooner gone to step from the pier when the ripples created by the incoming boats caused the catamaran to dip and sway, making her miss her step completely and launch forward with a startled squeal, arms flailing, into thin air.

Instead of landing in a bruised heap on the deck, a sturdy pair of arms came around her waist. Her legs and arms wrapped instinctively around him for support as he staggered backward, stopping only when they both crashed into the bench seat lining the opposite side of the rear well.

She struggled to scrape her hair from her face, then tried to disentangle herself from him immediately, but he only tightened his hold.

"Wait, just wait a minute." He sounded as though he'd had the wind knocked out of him. Or worse.

But as she managed to take a breath or two herself, and the panic, fear, and mortification receded . . . her other senses kicked in. Like how sturdy and strong he was, and how even a woman of her height and size—and she was all Apolo—didn't seem too heavy a burden. And the fact that those wide palms her hormones had all but salivated over earlier . . . were now very deliberately clamped on her backside. She was sure it was only because that had been the only thing he'd had to hold on to, but when she turned her head at the same time he did, and their gazes clashed, she swore she felt his fingers tighten just a little. And his body felt a little harder, and, for a moment anyway, a tiny bit less steady.

"I'm so sorry," she managed, her body flaming with more than embarrassment.

"Don't worry," he said calmly, though his jaw appeared a bit clamped. "You're in good hands." Keeping his gaze on hers, he shifted forward just enough to allow her to unlock her ankles and unwind her legs from his waist. She wasn't sure if the boat was still rocking, or if it was just the impact of all that raw masculinity making her feel so totally aware of her own femininity, but as soon as her feet hit the deck, her knees wobbled. The sudden motion made her tighten her hold around his neck . . . and made him tighten his hold on her backside.

She gasped. And when the full length of her body matched up to the very full length of his, she might have moaned. Just a little.

Good hands, indeed.

Chapter Three

It was that little moan that did him in. Sure, she'd been a one-two punch to his libido from the moment she'd stepped out of the cab, but that didn't mean he'd planned to manhandle her from the moment she stepped foot on board. He had more finesse than that. Or at the very least more self-control.

He'd even managed to deal with the sudden impact of all that sizzling stimulation being dumped quite literally right in his lap. Instant lust was in the eye of the beholder, after all. He would have controlled the response. Where he could anyway. But that one little quiver, followed by that gasp and moan combination, and well, he was only human. His fingers pressed more deeply into the sweet abundance of her backside, and he shifted his head so his mouth was directly aligned with hers, all before he'd even thought about what the hell he was doing. Or who he was doing it with. But she was angling her mouth, too, so he was having a hard time remembering why that mattered.

His lips were a breath from hers when she blurted, "I thought you'd be much older."

That jerked him out of whatever fog it was he'd wandered into. "What?" This close and her eyes were still so dark he couldn't distinguish pupil from iris. But he could see the color warming the natural deep hue of her skin.

She glanced away then, shifting her weight off of him, pushing at his chest as she moved out of his embrace. "Nothing. I'm sorry," she said, though for what he had no idea.

So far, he had no regrets. Except perhaps not being a bit quicker following through on that chance kiss. He might have regretted it afterward, he thought, watching her move carefully across the deck to sit on the padded bench next to her bag, but it would have been worth the risk anyway. He stayed where he was, however. Folding his arms, he studied his newest crew member. She looked like every man's wet dream, and yet she'd been all business with her menu talk, then confusingly awkward when she'd stumbled her way onto the boat, then pow, right back to the wet dream with that almost kiss. So which was she? Calculated vamp or serious chef? Straight talker . . . or endearing klutz.

He was going to have a couple of very interesting weeks, in very close quarters, to figure it out. It was a distraction he definitely didn't need during this all important first trip, and yet there was no denying he was anticipating solving the puzzle that was Kamala Apolo almost as much as he was anticipating proving himself an able charter captain.

However, professional obligations would always come before personal interests. "Let me show you where to stow your gear; then we can get under way." He moved toward her, intending to grab her gear bag, but she hoisted it to her shoulder first, clearly preferring to keep some distance between them.

He swallowed the urge to smile. Maintaining distance was going to be a challenge. For both of them, he thought, given how she was wielding her duffel like a shield. Sparks were sparks, and he wasn't imagining the ones that had just exploded between them. They might be able to pretend otherwise for a little while, but a ten-day trip was a lot of hours in tight spaces. And if she lasted the whole six weeks . . . well, he didn't even dare go there.

"There are two cabins fore and two aft," he explained as he stepped down into the circular central salon, which doubled as both lounge and dining room, though most meals would be served under the awning in the rear cockpit well. "The Wetheringtons will have the larger fore cabin at their disposal," he said, motioning toward the narrow passage to the right of the navigation deck. He turned and angled past the galley, motioning to the narrow doorway on the other side. "I have the rear right and you'll have the back left."

He turned, expecting to find her right behind him, but she'd stopped in the galley area.

"Will you need me on deck? If not, I'd like to familiarize myself with the galley here." She was opening the latched cupboards, peeking under the counter. And carefully not looking at him.

"No, take all the time you need."

"Great." She nudged her duffel toward the passage door to her cabin and stowed her backpack in an open space under the counter. "Thanks."

Burke didn't leave right away, although he understood he'd just been summarily dismissed. If she was trying to indicate that there would be no repeat of the spontaneous combustion of a few moments ago, she was doing a damn fine job. Yet he couldn't help but wonder how long that would hold up.

He needed to stow his tools and get them under way. It was going to take a couple hours to get to Barbuda, and he wanted to dock with plenty of time to load up on supplies before meeting their clients. His first clients. He'd sailed with the Wetheringtons before, but never as both captain and charter owner. Burke enjoyed the little twist of anticipation in his gut. Sure, he was a little nervous. Any captain would be a fool not to be, what with the capriciousness of Mother Nature. But he'd done his homework; he had all his charts and reports. By all accounts, it should be clear and calm sailing for the duration of the tour.

In this case, the nerves were more personal. Working for others, he'd always given his best, earning the respect of clients and employers alike, but ultimately not caring a great deal what others thought of him outside his work ethic. This was different. For the first time, there were distinct will-they-like-me butterflies in his stomach. His head told him he was being ridiculous. He knew what he was doing, and so did the Wetheringtons. But his heart wasn't as easily persuaded.

Which confused him as his heart was rarely ever in the equation.

Maybe that was why he didn't head out, but instead leaned his weight against the counter a foot or two behind Kamala and folded his arms. "Dorsey already has some things stocked, though I couldn't tell you what."

She was peeking in cupboards and unlatching drawers, poking in the deep cooler. "Mmm hmm," was the sum total of her response.

He did grin now. So aloof. "Why did you think I was older?" he asked, deciding not to let her put space between them after all.

She lifted a casual shoulder. "Dorsey said you were younger, so I knocked off a couple of decades." She crouched in front of the lower cabinets. "I was thinking mid-fifties."

Her new position tugged down the waistband of her snug white shorts in the back, exposing more smooth skin and just a hint of—Jesus. He swallowed hard. Dental floss thong. He had no idea how women tolerated them, but at the moment he was mightily grateful that they did.

So, he thought, dragging his gaze unwillingly away, she'd expected him to be old enough to be her father. And had been distinctly unsettled to find out otherwise. He assumed she'd known something of their clients from Dorsey, which meant she thought she'd be in the company of a bunch of old farts. So, either she always dressed with the intent of bringing a man to his knees regardless of his age, or . . . Well, he wasn't sure. Maybe she was the type who needed constant reassurance that men found her attractive, but was also the type who didn't actually want anything more.

But something about the honest surprise he'd seen in her eyes along with the impossible-to-hide animal attraction made him think she was nothing so shallow as a self-centered cock tease. The question was, then, what exactly was she? And why in the hell was he standing here wasting time he didn't have wondering about it?

He was just about to mumble something about getting under way and leave, hopefully salvaging what was left of his common sense while doing so, when she huffed out a sigh and levered herself to stand. And he wasn't going anywhere.

"Listen," she began, turning to face him, "about what happened on deck. We should probably—" The boat tipped as a wake from another boat rippled beneath it. Whatever else she'd been about to say was lost as she froze and grabbed the counter. His gaze went from her white-knuckled hands to the less-than-healthy-looking tone of her skin.

"Are you okay?"

She nodded immediately, but he wasn't buying it, or the light laugh she used to cover the moment.

"The motion just caught me off guard." Possibly noting his skepticism, she ducked her chin for a moment, then looked back at him, her smile somewhat rueful now. "Okay, confession time." She took a short breath, then blew it out, apparently nervous, but holding his gaze readily enough. "I don't suppose Dorsey mentioned that I don't exactly have a ton of experience sailing." She finally let go of the counter, but only after bracing her legs as if expecting the boat to get hit by a ten footer. "In fact, I don't really have any."

Before he could respond, she lifted a hand, and despite the fact that the color hadn't exactly returned to her cheeks, her expression was resolute and quite serious. He respected that much.

"I also don't know if he told you how important it is to me that I do this job," she said. "I might not be experienced on the water, but I promise you I know my way around the kitchen. Galley," she immediately corrected. Her lips quirked slightly, but didn't detract from the earnest look in her eyes. "The menu will be one of the most memorable island dining experiences your guests will have had the pleasure of partaking in. And as for the sailing, I'm a quick study. If you need help, you only have to tell me what to do and I'll be glad to pitch in."

Burke didn't say anything right away. There was something more going on here than she was saying. He didn't doubt she couldn't sail. She had no sea legs whatsoever. But that didn't trouble him too much. They had nothing but gorgeous weather ahead, and he doubted he'd need much in the way of helping. He also knew George Wetherington prided himself on being something of a sailor himself, and Burke had already planned on letting the older gentleman help out to whatever degree he wanted. Anything to make the client happy.

He also didn't doubt Kamala could cook. Not that he was simply taking her word for it, but Dorsey had given his word as well. And Burke put a great deal of stock in that. So what it was that niggled at him, he wasn't quite sure.

"Don't worry about steering the boat," he told her, "that's my job. If you can cook as good as you claim—"

"I can."

He grinned. He admired her confidence, and though personally he could be perfectly happy eating peanut butter sandwiches, he found himself looking forward to sampling her creations.

Almost as much as he looked forward to tasting her.

"Dorsey told me you're planning to open your own catering service," he said. "I assume you need the paycheck here to make that happen." Now it was his turn to lift a hand and stop her response. "All I ask is that you make George and Tutti happy at mealtime, and clean up after, and we'll get along just fine."

She nodded firmly. "I won't let you down." Then those soft lips of hers quirked again, but when he noticed and smiled himself, she quickly smoothed it away.

"What?" he asked.

"Nothing. You'd better get on with what needs doing and I'll get on with putting the galley in order."

He stepped closer before he knew he was going to. "I don't know what Dorsey told you about me, but I'm a pretty easygoing guy. I've even been known to have a sense of humor. I don't want you to feel like you have to watch every word or censor yourself. I know in essence I'm your boss, but I usually look at crewing as more of a team effort, a partnership. So, just be yourself. Say whatever is on your mind." His smile spread. "Just use discretion in front of the clients."

"Okay," she said, the smile peeking out again. "Thanks. I appreciate the openness."

"Great. So why don't we begin with you letting me in on what that little smile was about before?"

Her lips quirked right away. It made the exotic slant to her eyes even more pronounced. It made him want to kiss that mouth. Badly. It was insane, in fact, how he couldn't stop thinking about it.

"It was nothing really," she said, hopefully oblivious to his all but drooling lust for her. He didn't like feeling so out of control. It wasn't how things usually played out.

"And totally inappropriate given that my own name is somewhat unusual," she went on. "But . . . Tutti?" She laughed. "Sounds like a flavor of ice cream. Where do the social elite come up with these nicknames anyway? And how come the guys don't get stuck with lapdog labels?"

"For the record, the men of George Wetherington's social standing and income bracket do sport a few eye-rolling names themselves. I've personally chartered boats for a Biff, Corky, Moose, and a Boog. Not a one of them a day under seventy."

"Dear God. Suddenly Kamala Ooh Lala doesn't sound so bad."

"What?" Burke asked, on a sputtering laugh.

She flushed a little, and he liked seeing the color come back in her cheeks. "A schoolyard nickname courtesy of Tamo Hakuna and his other fifth grade buddies. I, uh, developed a little early."

"I hadn't noticed," Burke said, with such a deadpan delivery it made her laugh, as he'd hoped it would.

"I should explain," she said, "about the clothes. I don't normally dress quite like this. And I'm afraid most of what is in that duffel is more of the same. I'm ashamed to admit it now, but I was desperate enough to keep this job that I figured maybe you'd—"

"Overlook your lack of sailing skills if you added something appreciable to the scenery?" He grinned. "I'm all for it, personally. I'm sure George won't mind either. Just don't elevate his blood pressure too high, okay?"

"I didn't mean to give you the wrong impression before—"

Burke stepped closer. "Listen, if what happened on deck made you nervous, I'm sorry. It was an honest male reaction to a very beautiful woman suddenly landing in my lap. And I'm not going to lie to you. I'm attracted. Probably would be no matter what you were wearing. There's a lot more to you than nice curves and tight shorts."

Her smile spread slowly. "You use that line a lot?"

His look of surprise was sincere. "That wasn't a line."

She gave him a little eye roll. "You don't even know me. Right now I'm not much more than ample curves and stretch fabric. How could I be? But," she said quickly, when he shifted closer, "you are right. I am more than that, which you'll see."

"So, do I have to wait until you think you've proven yourself before I act on the attraction?"

Her gaze narrowed. "Is this part of my job description?"

He didn't blink at the intended insult. He'd earned it, but he'd also decided if plain speaking was to be the rule of the day, they might as well put it all on the table right now. "Not even remotely. I told you, you cook and clean and make the clients' tummys happy, and you'll get your paycheck. Are you seeing someone, otherwise attached?"

"What? No, but—"

"And are you unattracted to me?"

She looked flustered, but she answered squarely enough. "I wasn't expecting—you."

"No, you were expecting someone old enough to be your father, I get that. Someone safe." He moved just a hair closer and was deeply gratified when she stood her ground. "I can be safe."

She just snorted.

"Honestly. I'm not so hard up for attention that I force it where it isn't wanted. I'm a big boy; I can take a no and simply enjoy the view for the next month or so. No problem."

"I appreciate that," she said, though rather than cop an aloof air, she was eyeing him somewhat consideringly.

He took that as an encouraging sign. "However, in the spirit of that straight talk I was advocating earlier, I decided it best to admit I am attracted to you up front. All the facets of you I've seen so far. And you might be surprised to know you've revealed a few things that have nothing to do with the clothes you are or are not wearing."

She tilted her head, but didn't comment directly to that. "It's a small boat," was all she said. "And we're hardly going to be alone."

"I know. And yet that doesn't particularly dissuade me."

"So, is this standard procedure, then? Do you always come on to your crewmates?"

Burke laughed. "Nah. But then Dorsey isn't really my type."

"And the clients?" she asked, striving to remain serious, but her mouth was already wobbling with the effort to keep from smiling. "What will they think?"

He lifted a hand, let his fingers trail ever so lightly along the silky length of her hair. "They'll think it's pretty natural, given that most charters down here are operated by couples who are either married or otherwise committed to one another."

She smiled dryly. "Yet, somehow I doubt those couples are chasing each other all over the boat, screwing each others' brains out at every opportunity."

His grin was slow and wide. "So, you're picturing that, too, are you?"

Rather than shove him away, her dry smile merely extended to include another eye roll. He was glad she could give as well as she could take, and that she didn't take anything overly seriously. She confronted things straight on, much as he did, but had a sense of humor as well. She was a good match for him in that regard.

Yet, teasing aside, for some reason he couldn't explain, he needed her to know that he wasn't just some island playboy looking to nail anything in his path. "I take my job very seriously, Kamala."

"Kam," she said.

He nodded. "This boat is to me what your catering business is to you, something I've worked very hard for and plan to make a success of. This is my first charter on my own boat, and nothing is more important than making sure it goes well. I didn't plan on you, much less this . . . whatever it is we're doing. I've been a ball of nerves all day, and that was before you came on board. I'm excited about this first trip, determined to make it go well, and anxious to get under way."

"So why are we still standing here?"

He tucked his fingers through her hair, cupped the back of her neck. "Because I can't stop thinking about what your mouth would have tasted like if you hadn't stopped me earlier." He shifted closer, until his body brushed hers.

Her eyes went a bit heavy lidded, but she didn't react in any other way. She didn't touch him, nor did she back away. She merely held his gaze, almost as if she was challenging him in some way. Letting him take the risk of making the first move.

Perhaps undecided on whether to explore the sizzle between them . . . or possibly knee him in the balls.

For some completely inexplicable reason, that only aroused him further. Charting the unknown had always been an aphrodisiac for him. "So," he murmured, "tell me now just how safe you want me to be. Right now. And I promise I'll behave." He lowered his head. "Because otherwise, I have a feeling we're headed for some pretty dangerous waters."

Chapter Four

What in the hell was she thinking, letting him just move right in like that? She never jumped first and let later take care of itself. She certainly didn't let the guy jump first either. In fact, she was so used to pushing men back a step, she had no real reason for why she hadn't kneed Burke Morgan across the cabin by now. Just on principle alone. They'd known each other a grand total of an hour or less, and he thought she was going to allow him to take charge? Take her? Just like that?

So smooth with his lines about how serious he was, how dedicated. It was obvious he'd honed it down to a fine craft by now, because she'd admit it was damn effective. Jesus, with moves like that, he probably had a throng of panting women in every port. But surely she wasn't about to become one of them. She saw right through him, after all.

He'd taken one look at her, or more likely one look at her tightly clad butt, and thought to himself, *Well now, right there is six weeks of casual sex on a platter.* And she couldn't blame him. To a point.

But she certainly had no business leading him on for one second longer. Right this instant was the time to put him squarely in his place. And add a couple of shape-devouring muumuus to her shopping list.

So what in the world possessed her to slide her hands up

those perfectly developed arms of his and allow him to tip her head to the side so he could angle that perfect mouth of his across hers, she had no earthly idea.

His lips were warm, his kiss sure. He held her just where he wanted her, and damn if she had even the tiniest inclination to thwart him. Because whatever spark there might have been between them earlier had now exploded into a shower of heat and sizzle so all encompassing that from the moment his mouth had claimed hers she wanted to do nothing more than let him take her just like this for as long as it was humanly possible to sustain it. Rational thought was highly overrated when you were staring primal lust incarnate in the face.

Her fingers dug into the hard muscle of his shoulders as a moan built in her throat. Her hunger was like a wave of pure carnality rolling over her senses as he continued his absolute seduction of her mouth. It felt wild and dangerous and all too tantalizing. Allowing a man she'd just met to take her like this, to accept him with absolute abandon for no other reason than it felt so damn good. And as the hunger built, layer upon layer, want upon want, her body alternately tightened with need and felt so boneless she was certain she'd sink to the floor in a pure puddle of pleasure.

He pulled her feverish, clamoring body against his rock-solid frame as he continued to plunder her mouth. Pirate, indeed. And she was his ill-gotten gain. But it was the throaty growl she got from him when their needs collided that sent her careening in a new direction. In that instant she could no longer simply be a willing recipient, though there was nothing remotely simple about the conflagration that this endless kiss had provoked. It was too tempting all of a sudden, the idea that she could participate, that she could—perhaps had—create a similar tidal wave of raw need and desire in him.

It didn't require thought, only the guts to go with the instinct, to dive in. To challenge as he was challenging her, to meet confidence with confidence, demand with demand. She was fisting her fingers in his hair, turning his mouth so she could dominate, so she could tangle her tongue with his, before she even realized she'd taken that running leap.

And then the growl became a low, rumbling hum of pleasure, deep in his chest, and the next thing she knew his hands were on her hips, lifting her onto the narrow galley counter and pushing her back—or was she pulling him in—so fast, so needy, her head rapped against the cabinet door. She didn't care. He didn't stop. His mouth left hers and branded a hot trail along her chin before moving lower. His hands were already ahead of his mouth, his wide palms covering the tight shirt that was now causing excruciatingly exquisite friction against her tautly budded nipples.

He solved that problem in one yank, the flimsy front clasp of her bra going down in defeat an instant later. She arched into him with a shameless demanding cry, as his hot, wet mouth closed over one nipple, then the other. Her fingers were twisted tightly in the thick waves of his hair as she directed him back and forth, wishing for nothing more than that tongue of his could be in two places at one time. Or maybe three.

There was no ability to think, much less make even the feeblest attempt to rationalize what in the hell was going on here. Nor did she much care at the moment. She'd completely given herself over to the moment. She'd rationalize later. Or not. It simply wasn't an issue right now. When his hands fumbled with the waistband of her shorts, her mind nimbly and fearlessly leapt ahead, already feverishly embracing the idea of the two of them doing the only thing possible to extinguish this out-of-control fire of need blazing between them.

She'd had a grand sum of five lovers in the past four years, and each one of them had gotten her naked only after careful consideration and full medical discussions. And yet, here she was, on a boat of all places, half naked and clamoring to be taken and taken hard by a virtual stranger who, for all she knew, could have banged half the female population in the Caribbean. And still she didn't care. All that mattered at the moment was putting out that raging, rabid, all-consuming fire. Mother of God, why didn't he hurry the hell up?

She was clawing at his shirt, ripping it up and over his head even as he jerked her shorts down her hips. Both were panting heavily, between grunts and groans, moans and gasps. Mouths never left hot skin; tongues left damp trails; fingers explored, caressed, slipped, and slid.

Just as he grabbed her thighs to yank them around his waist, the boat pitched violently, thudding hard up against the pier with a resounding smack. The sudden motion threw her from the counter onto Burke, who toppled back, slamming into the opposite counter before spinning both of them toward the navigation deck. His hip banged against the counter as she flung a hand out to keep them from hitting the instrument panel.

"What in the hell?" Burke said, continuing to swear as he righted both of them, keeping his hands on her hips to steady them both until they got their legs beneath them. The boat was still pitching hard, and the thud and scrape against the dock continued. "Wait right here," he instructed her, jaw set, eyes blazing, but letting her go only when she gripped both counter and console board for balance.

He yanked his shorts on and took off, going out the back toward the cockpit in less than a few long-legged strides—apparently having no problems with balance despite the constant pitch and slant of the floor beneath their feet. Kam could only cling white-knuckled to the counter and console as the fever of desire abruptly abandoned her . . . and nausea from the matching pitch and roll of her stomach rolled in to take its place. She'd barely gotten her wits about her, fighting to recover from her totally uncustomary and complete loss of control under the onslaught that was the absolute temptation of one Burke Morgan, when she immediately realized she was not going to be able to steady her stomach as quickly as she had her heart rate.

She managed to get her shorts pulled up, then looked wildly around for the bathroom—head, she corrected herself, remembering that much from her book on yachting basics—desperate to do anything to take her mind off of what she'd just done with Burke . . . and what she was about to do as the contents of her stomach pitched viciously up against the back of her throat. Clutching her shirt and unclasped bra across her breasts, she dove through the narrow passageway to the cabins, flinging herself toward the narrow, sealed door just to her right, barely wrenching the handle open and dropping to her knees in front of the small toilet before her stomach gave up the battle with one violent wrench.

"Damn," she swore under her breath, as soon as she was done. She felt a bit shaken, but better. Definitely better. Praying she stayed that way, she clambered up on still shaky legs and began cleaning up. Clutching the tiny sink, she splashed water on her face with one hand, then thankfully found some toothpaste and mouthwash in the medicine cabinet. After a quick brush and a rinse, she clasped her bra shut, and realizing the buttons on her shirt were no longer there, she gave up and tied it in a knot between her breasts. She began to feel marginally human, until she stared at her hollow-eyed expression in the tiny mirror. "Well," she said dryly, "this is all working out great so far, don't you think?"

With a wince and not a little disgust, she ripped the patch off from behind her ear and tossed it in the trash. Maybe the doctor had screwed up, and instead of a motion sickness patch he'd given her a sex stimulation patch or something instead. Because that was the only possible explanation for what had just happened between her and her new employer—excuse me, teammate—out there in the galley. "Jesus," she swore again. She couldn't believe she'd just gone at him like that. Or how desperate she'd been to have him touch her. Talk about being a team player.

The boat was still pitching, and her stomach twitched

enough that she shifted back toward the small head. She was debating crouching again, just in case, when she heard Burke come below deck.

"It was just some idiot kid in his daddy's new speedboat," she heard him say, "trying to impress his girlfriend by doing doughnuts in the no wake zone. I hope his dad is impressed with the repair bills that might be coming his way. Fortunately, no damage to—Kamala?" He found her a moment later. "Kam, are you all right?"

Her mortification now complete, Kamala knew she should square her shoulders and do her best to appear as if she were perfectly fine, but the combination of the boat rocking and being caught dead to motion-sickness rights was too much to overcome. Her face flushed, and her stomach clutched, and all she could think was that she'd quit her job to come down here and make a fast paycheck, and inside an hour she'd already blown her last hope all to hell.

"I'm okay," she muttered, forced to brace her hands on the wall and lean over the toilet, knowing she was moments away from being sick again. Angling her back to him, she fought the disappointment, the anger with herself for not being able to handle this better. "Just—why don't you get under way," she forced herself to say, a last ditch effort, though the mere thought of them moving at all was almost enough to tip her stomach back over the edge. "I'll—I'll be okay." Which was such an obvious lie that even Burke had to see right through it.

He proved that to be true when, instead of leaving, he stepped into the tiny compartment and crouched behind her. She stiffened, already embarrassed beyond belief. If ever a first impression could go horrifically awry, this one had, and she had only herself to blame. First she'd admitted she couldn't sail. Then she'd all but thrown herself at him, not that he'd been complaining, but still, that was not part of her game plan. And now this. How To Crush Your Dream In Three Easy Steps. She let her chin drop. "I'm sorry." Any hope she might have had about brazening this out and somehow finding a way to salvage the situation vanished when her stomach decided it wasn't done torturing her, and she once again lurched over the edge of the toilet.

To her stunned surprise, Burke merely stroked her hair back, holding it out of the way, steadying her balance by bracing his knees on either side of her.

"So sorry," she managed, moments later. It had been a false alarm, or maybe there was simply nothing left to heave, but it didn't really matter that she hadn't actually puked in front of him; her pride was totally beyond redemption anyway.

"Don't be," he said, and she heard the underlying humor in his voice. "Admittedly, it's a bit hard on the ego to discover that instead of getting you all hot and bothered, I actually made you violently ill."

She snorted a laugh despite herself. "Trust me, this wasn't your fault."

He smoothed his wide palm up and down her back in slow, soothing strokes. "Well, that's a relief, then." He steadied her with his hands as he pushed to a stand behind her and reached in a latched cabinet for a small cotton hand towel. He got it wet and handed it to her. "Here." She took it, wobbled a bit, making him grab at her elbows. Carefully, he helped her straighten up, but just enough so he could close the lid. "Why don't you sit down. You still don't look so hot."

Gratefully, she sat, knowing whatever color might be in her face was from sheer embarrassment at this point. "Thanks."

He took the towel from her and handed her a dry one, then crouched in front of her. When she averted her face, he tipped her chin back around, so she had to look at him. "What happened?" he asked gently. "Are you sick?"

"In the head maybe," she said, before she could censor herself. Hell, at this point why bother anyway? He'd said he wanted straight talking. Well, he might change his mind after he heard what she had to say. She was well past the point of believing she could pull this off, so best to end the charade, what was left of it anyway, right now. She sighed a little, then looked at him. "I have another confession to make. I have a little problem with motion sickness. Okay, maybe not so little a problem."

He'd been a champ all through her being sick, but that bit of news sat him literally back on his heels, his easy smile becoming an easier frown. "You took a six-week job on a sailboat and not only can't you sail, but you get seasick?"

There was nothing to do but nod. "I get queasy watching *Love Boat* reruns."

"Then what in the hell made you think—?" He broke off, shuffled back so he could stand up, then paced out of the small bathroom, bracing his hands on the narrow hallway wall. "What was Dorsey thinking?" he said, only she wasn't sure if he was addressing her or if the question was rhetorical at this point.

"He doesn't know," she offered. "Well, he knew I didn't know much about sailing, but he assured me that my cooking skills were the commodity you most required. I can cook, by the way. I didn't lie."

He turned, braced his legs, and folded his arms across his still bare chest. It shouldn't have been turned on, not in the middle of her most shameful moment, but weak stomach notwithstanding, there was no denying the bump in her pulse rate. And to think she'd had that body, those hands, so close . . .

"No, you didn't lie," he said, apparently not as caught up in hormonal overload as she was. Not that she could blame him. "But you withheld some pretty serious information," he added. "I know you said you needed the infusion of cash, but how did you think you'd pull it off?"

"I saw a doctor about it, and he prescribed this patch thing. He swore it would work. I thought it would, too." She lifted a shoulder. "Maybe it was nerves. Or . . ." Her gaze shifted past the door, out toward the galley counter, where he'd pinned her against him. Visions of what they'd been doing to each other—what they'd been about to do with each other—flashed through her mind. She forced herself to meet his gaze again. "Honestly, I don't know what the hell I was thinking. I've worked so hard to get this far, I wouldn't have risked everything on a gamble if I wasn't pretty damn sure I could handle it. I certainly wouldn't have quit my job, no matter how bad things had gotten there."

"Bad how?" he demanded, surprising her.

Given how angry he likely was, she didn't challenge his right to know; she just told him. "I was assistant head chef at Shoop, a celebrity hot spot in Santa Monica. My boss thought I'd welcome an increase in pay in exchange for putting in some overtime. Only, turns out most of that overtime was going to involve the two of us and very little clothing." She raked her hands through her hair. "Given what we were just doing a little while ago, I can only imagine you think I'd given him good cause to believe exactly that. I assure you, I didn't, but I don't expect you to believe that. Nor do I expect you to believe that I've spent a large amount of my time playing down the physical attributes so my professional skills would be taken more seriously. But that obviously wasn't working out too well, so when Dorsey offered me this job . . . ."

She trailed off, looked away. Listening to herself, she was even more disgusted. "I guess I gave in. I figured if I couldn't beat them at their own game, I'd join it." She lifted her hands, let them fall in her lap. "No one is sorrier about that lame decision now than I am. But I swear I believed the damn patch would work, or I'd never have considered taking Dorsey's offer. I suppose I should have tested it out, but this all happened rather suddenly. I was lucky to get the appointment before I had to fly out."

When he still didn't say anything, she looked at him again. He was studying her in that intent way of his, but she pushed on despite feeling more exposed and vulnerable now than she had when he'd been tearing her clothes off. "And though this likely doesn't mean much to you at the moment, despite the fact that I very purposely dressed to distract, I had every intention of earning my keep here as a cook and hostess, and only as cook and hostess."

He kept his arms folded, kept his gaze on her. "So, what happened in the galley, was that another calculated distraction?"

She knew she more than deserved his skepticism, or worse, but that he thought so little of her, despite knowing she'd earned nothing more, still stung. "No," she said straightforwardly. "I honestly have no idea what came over me." She waved a hand. "Maybe it was the nerves, my stomach still being twitchy despite the patch. Then finding out you weren't twenty or thirty years older than me but instead a very attractive guy I was immediately attracted to, and that made me feel more than a little awkward about—" She stopped, motioned to the clothes, or lack thereof, she was wearing. She looked back to him. "I know how important this cruise is to you, how important you are to Dorsey. He's very important to me, and I'd never intentionally embarrass him like this."

When he still said nothing, she tossed her hands up. "Okay, so I have no good explanation for what happened out there, but I can promise you that I can and will be the consummate professional if you'll just give me another chance to prove myself."

"So," he said, pushing away from the wall, "you still want to give this a go? What about . . ." He nodded toward the toilet she was sitting on.

She huffed out a sigh of defeat. "Right. That. I guess neither of us is going to want to rely on another patch."

He walked over to her and pulled her to a stand, wrapping his arms around her when she wobbled a bit. She tried to stiffen and stand on her own two feet, but he continued to hold her.

"Burke, really, I meant what I said about not trading favors. Even for a second chance I wouldn't—"

"I know that. And I believe you." He stroked the hair back from her face. "I'm not looking to strike some kind of sexual bargain with you. But I'd also like to believe you were honest about what happened out there not being calculated."

"It wasn't," she assured him. "I don't know what that was."

He pressed his fingers across her lips, then slowly drew them away, making her sigh just a little as her body instantly forgot all about being queasy and leapt right back to being jumpy, but for an entirely different and far more enjoyable reason. "Me neither. You might not believe it, but I generally keep business and pleasure completely separate. And I certainly didn't intend to tangle myself up with someone who is related to a person I care a great deal about. And yet, it's all I can do to keep my hands off of you."

She couldn't help it, she smiled. He made it very easy. "Which still seems to be a bit of a problem for you." She shifted beneath his hands. Hands she was perfectly content to leave right where they were. Since he was being open about it, she was as well. "Not that I'm complaining."

His smile grew. "You know," he said, drawing her closer, "I've been a sailor for a long time. And I've had more than my fair share of seasick clients. I've got a few tried and true methods that I've picked up over the years."

Skeptical, she arched a brow. "You really think you could cure me?"

"I think we should give it a try."

She cocked her head. "And in return?"

"In return you'll get your chance to prove to me just how great a chef you are. It's what I hired you for, and as a captain with clients waiting, it behooves me to do whatever I can to make sure you can fulfill that obligation. But that's all you owe me."

"And this?" she asked, shifting slightly in his arms.

Now he smiled. "This part is all up to you."

"So, are you giving me another chance just because you

need a chef, or because you want to explore whatever this is we're doing with each other?"

"Since we're being blunt, I'll have to say both."

"And if I say I'll cook, but no thanks to anything else?"

"Then I'll spend the next couple of weeks taking a lot of cold showers."

The open, guileless smile he was offering her made her laugh.

"I'm a big boy," he said. "I can handle it."

She snorted out a laugh, saying, "I bet you are, and I bet you can," at the exact time he realized the double entendre and choked on a laugh of his own.

"Yes, well, that's not what I meant, but—"

She cut him off by cupping his backside and jerking him up against her. What the hell, right? She was already wet and clenching again, which beat all to hell how she'd been feeling just a little while ago. If seduction was one of his miracle cures for motion sickness, she wasn't exactly opposed to giving it a shot. God knew, it had been working pretty damn well so far. Careful planning hadn't gotten her very far, so what the hell, why not just throw caution to the wind and go, as they say, with the flow. "But," she finished for him, "you have yourself a chef. And . . . whatever else we decide goes with that."

He immediately turned them both around, lifting her over the raised threshold and pressing into the narrow passageway. Her back against the wall, he nudged himself between her thighs, making her sigh and sob a little with need.

"One thing," she croaked out. Dear God, the man was like human catnip or something. "If this interferes with our ability to do our jobs, or if for any other reason it's just not working, we can say stop and we stop. No harm, no foul."

"Agreed." He slid his hands to her waist, then began sliding them upward.

"After all, a month or so from now," she panted, dying for his fingers to just get a little closer to the throbbing tightness that was her nipples, "I go back to L.A., and you go wherever your next cruise takes you."

"That is true." He made a groaning sound in his throat when she pushed her hips against his.

"So . . . about that cure for seasickness," she persevered, deciding there was something quite erotic about trying to carry on a civil conversation with someone who was doing some very uncivilized things to her person. "Maybe you should share one or two before we get under way."

He paused with his fingertips a mere wisp away from where she needed them most, making her wish she'd just shut up and let him play. "Let me ask you something."

"Okay." She had only herself to blame for stopping him. She tried not to squirm.

"At the moment, how is your stomach?"

"Jumpy, but only because you stopped what you were doing."

"And when we were in the galley earlier, were you feeling queasy in any way?"

Her lips twisted in a wry grin. "So, is this how you 'help' your clients get over their seasickness?"

His smile held no guile whatsoever. It was a large part of his charm. "I never mingle with the guests. Not that way. Besides, septuagenarians usually aren't my type. But you had a point earlier, about the usefulness of distraction."

"I'm admittedly intrigued by the premise. But glad," she added with a wry smile, picturing the aging Dr. Wilson, "that my physician didn't think to try something similar."

Burke grinned, and slipped his fingertips just a bit higher. "Me, too."

"However," she managed, struggling not to just grab his hands and put them where she needed them, "using this method of distraction could become a problem when the guests are on board."

"We can worry about that later," he said, leaning down to drop a kiss on the side of her neck, making her gasp when he nipped her earlobe.

"Don't we need to be getting—oh. Yes." She moaned deeply

when he finally slid her nipples between his fingers. She was officially all done with the civilized part of this exchange.

"We have some time," he murmured against the damp skin of her neck. "I have another idea that might help speed up the recovery process."

"I'll bet you do."

Chapter Five

Burke rolled to his back, splayed her across his body. "Let me go cut us loose; then you can help me steer the boat out of here."

The minute he suggested leaving her, even for a moment, panic flashed across her face. "That's your idea? To go straight to sailing? Maybe I should come topside with you. I'm good with knots."

"Lesson one," he whispered, running his hands down her arms. "Trust me. Lesson two, relax. Don't tense up. Here, let me show you a little trick."

She shot him a dry smile, but he just shook his head. "Not that kind of trick."

"Can't blame a girl for hoping."

He laughed and cocked his head. "You know, you're not like anyone I've ever met."

"You mean women don't usually rip your clothes off five minutes after meeting you, then run to the bathroom and lose their lunch? Imagine that." She braced her hands on the wall on either side of his head and shook her hair back. "So glad I could be the first," she said in an exaggerated, breathy voice.

He grinned at her little performance, but pulled her hands from the wall and put them very definitely around his neck.

"What I meant was that you have this interesting combination of easy confidence and a sharp mind, without being pushy or arrogant about it—which is intriguing in and of itself." He started backwalking her out of the passageway, back up to the cockpit. "But wrapped up in all that are these little moments of insecurity, and rather than try and pretend otherwise, you just own up to them, put them out there to be dealt with. Most people aren't like that. They don't want to broadcast their vulnerabilities."

"Interesting analysis," she said. Then, weaving her fingers into the waistband of his shorts, she added, "So, are you the type who likes to keep his vulnerabilities under wraps, then?"

"I never thought about it, but probably. Yes. When you're running a crew, captaining a boat, you don't really want to project any weaknesses." He smiled. "Makes the guests jumpy."

"I wasn't talking about job confidence. I meant just in general."

"You know," he said with a fast grin, "we really should be getting under way."

She smiled at his rather obvious attempt at derailing the current conversational path. "You started this, you know. But fine, go untie the boat or whatever needs doing. Just know that I'll expect an answer later." Her lips curved in a deep smile. "Or maybe I'll just make it my mission to figure it out for myself."

"See? Confidence. Very arousing."

She tugged him closer. "Why yes, yes it is."

Just then the two-way radio on the console crackled to life, startling them both. "Burke?" came a woman's voice, the island flavor clear if a bit raspy. "Burke, honey, you there or what?"

"Now what?" Burke mumbled. He braced her hips. "You, don't move."

"Oh, trust me," she assured him, "I'm not doing anything that involves motion unless absolutely necessary."

"Hmm," he said, a conspiratorial smile curving his lips. "A challenge."

She just lifted a shoulder. "Take it any way you want."

"Okay, now you're just begging me to do something rash."

Now it was her turn for a conspiratorial smile.

"Burke?" came the squawking voice again. "Honey, pick up. It's important."

"It'd better be." Burke debated risking that the moment he took his hands off of Kam, she'd come up with some reason why they shouldn't be doing . . . well, everything they'd been doing. Or worse, that he'd come to his senses and realize he had a whole lot more important things to be devoting his single-minded attention to. And none of them involved getting Kamala Apolo naked.

Which was a damn shame, really.

He leaned over and snagged the radio mike. "Hiya gorgeous, what you want with me?"

"Gorgeous" was Maybelline Concha, who ran the hotel on Barbuda where many of the charter guests booked a night's stay before or after their cruise. She was somewhere between sixty and a hundred years old, and a sharper businesswoman he'd never met. She was one of the many inhabitants of Montserrat who had fled a decade earlier after volcanic eruptions had buried two thirds of her island home under a lava flow.

She'd ended up on Barbuda, starting up a new place there, catering to the sportsmen and eco-tourists who flocked to the mostly deserted island for the excellent birding, snorkeling, and fishing it offered. She ran a tight ship and had turned not only her small inn into a profitable venture, mostly by hooking up with the island charter services to offer joint promotions, but had largely been responsible for the new boom of economic growth the island was now enjoying. His respect for her was enormous. She'd also flirted shamelessly with him from the moment they'd met. He'd always liked that about her, too.

"You don't wanna know the things I could do to you, child. Now listen, you under way yet?"

"As a matter of fact, not yet. Dorsey's off to Australia as it turns out, and I had to wait for my new crewmate to arrive."

There was a pause, then, "Something tells me there's more to that story than you're tellin' me. You'll fill me in later."

Burke smiled at her confidence. "Maybe I will, maybe I won't," he teased.

"Oh, you know I have my ways," she shot back. "And speaking of ways, you can take your time making your way over here. Your guests have had a sudden change in plans."

Burke's smile fled. "What? What happened?"

"It's all good, so wipe that frown away, hon. Mr. George and Miz Tutti got a nice little surprise Christmas present is all. Seems their granddaughter phoned to announce she was pregnant. They decided to fly back home and spend the holiday celebrating a new life on the way. But don' you worry none, they left me a little something for you. Paid for their trip in full, they did. I'll keep it safe until you come for it."

Burke let out the breath he hadn't been aware of holding. "Thanks, May."

"My pleasure. So you got a little Christmas present, too, I guess. A couple weeks off. And nothing better to do than get to know your new crewmate, eh?" Her cackle filled the small room, then abruptly cut off when she clicked off.

"No clients?"

Burke turned to find Kam firmly bracing herself, using the wall and anything within reach to keep herself as steady as possible, despite the fact that the boat was hardly rocking. He was going to have his work cut out for him, he thought, then smiled when he realized he was going to have time to do a whole lot more than cure her motion sickness. "Yep. But don't worry, we got our fee anyway."

"What happens now?"

She was still just a bit green looking, and despite all the new plans forming and shaping in his mind, he knew he had to do the right thing. "You know, I can still pay you your cut and you can just head back to the States. I'll have enough time now to find a chef before my next run. I know it's not the full amount you were hoping to earn down here, but—"

"Are you firing me?" she asked point blank, though her tone was easy, not accusatory.

"No, not at all. Just giving you an out. If you want to take it."

"And if I don't?"

"Then I guess you cook for two for the next couple of weeks."

"And after that?" When he just looked confused, she said, "What I mean is, if you can really miraculously cure my sea-sickness, and maybe I can barter a few sailing lessons off of you over the next couple of weeks, then is there any reason I can't finish out the season as originally planned?"

He hadn't been aware of just how much he'd hoped she'd want to do just that, until she said it. "No reason at all."

She took a careful step forward, held out her hand. "Why don't we make a deal," she offered. "Give me these next two weeks to prove I can cook and learn the sailing basics. Give you a chance to prove you have the miracle cure. If either of us fail, then I take my fee and go home. I know that wouldn't give you a lot of time to find a replacement." She smiled as she folded her hand in his. "But I'm banking on the hope that you won't have to. Deal?"

He tugged gently on her hand, sliding her into his arms. "Deal." Christ, the instant her body molded to his—and damn if it didn't just fit right where it needed to— his brain switched off and his body switched on. Not that it had ever turned completely off. He wasn't sure it ever would as long as she was nearby.

He ran his free hand up her arm, slid it beneath that water-fall of silky black hair, and shifted her head to the side so he could nibble once again at the delectably soft skin of her neck.

"I was about to start that first sailing lesson right now, but suddenly I'm not in any real hurry to go anywhere."

She ran her hands up his back, folded her arms around his neck. "Funny," she said softly, "I was thinking the same thing."

"Sailing can wait," he murmured, trailing little kisses along her collarbone.

She just nodded. "Sailing can definitely wait."

"What do you say we begin with a little motion practice instead?"

She shifted her head just enough to shoot him a wry smile. "Is that what they call it down here in the tropics?" Then she sighed a little as he slid his hands down her hips. Her sigh turned to a soft moan when he cupped her up against him. "Just promise me I'll make it through the practice without humiliating myself again."

He glanced up. "You feeling queasy again?"

She shook her head. "I think I'll be fine, as long as you don't stop doing that."

"This?" he asked, pulling her hips more firmly against his, fitting the bulge that was his now throbbing cock, between the perfect softness at the apex of her thighs.

"Yes," she said, the word more a growl. "Definitely this." She leaned back against the console, so his mouth dropped lower, shifting so his lips brushed over the nipple pushing at the tight, stretchy fabric of her shirt. "And maybe a little of that." When he pulled her nipple into his mouth, she jerked, and moaned deeply. "Okay, a lot of that."

"You know," he said, dying slowly by inches . . . some of them more painful than others, "as much as I would like to take you right here against the wall—and in fact, I think we should definitely keep that in mind for later—I think there's a much better place for this."

"I don't know, the place you're in is feeling pretty damn fine at the moment."

He grinned, then gripped her hips and settled her into the

soft leather of the captain's chair, which sat high off the ground, like a well-padded bar stool. "Change of plans," he said abruptly.

"Huh?"

"I might hate myself for this later, but if we're really going to make a go of this joint venture—"

"First it was motion practice and now it's a joint venture," she teased. "Boy, you have some interesting euphemisms for sex."

"Har har. As much as I want to rip off what little scraps of clothing you're wearing and have my way with you right here, right now, I have an idea that might serve us both better in the long run."

"You're full of ideas. I was hoping to be full of something—oh." She slid forward when he spread her thighs and stepped between them, the chair at just the right height to make for a perfect fit. "Well, then. Okay. Good idea."

"Close your eyes," he murmured. "Just relax, deep, even breaths." He kept his hands on her thighs; long, slow, smooth strokes, up and down that satiny skin, until he felt the tension completely ebb out of her. "Don't move," he murmured. "Stay just like that." Her eyes opened, but he shushed her back when she started to sit up, continuing to touch her, stroke her, until she was pliant and relaxed once again, and her grip on the arm rests was no longer white knuckled and tense.

He slowly let his hands drop away, then turned and started up the motor. At the sudden purring thrum, she jerked her eyes open. "What are we doing?"

"Finding a little privacy," he told her.

"It seems pretty private right here."

He grinned over his shoulder. "Not for what I have in mind."

Her eyes widened a little, but rather than challenge him, he saw a little spark come to life. Curiosity. Another adventure to embark on. Apparently they had a few more things in common. It made him feel good when she let her eyes drift shut and he saw her work on smoothing out her breathing. She was going to trust him.

He headed out and untied the boat in record time, determined to make sure her fledgling trust was well earned.

Chapter Six

"I can't believe you're letting me steer your precious new baby," she said, fifteen minutes later.

Burke stood right behind her, his body tightly aligned with hers, his knees pressed into the back of hers, cradling her backside between his hips. It was a miracle she could concentrate at all. But he was intent on keeping her relaxed, and for that she was eminently grateful. Staying calm while sitting in the chair hadn't worked too well once they'd started moving, so he'd pulled her in front of him, placed her hands beneath his on the wheel, and kept his body in full contact with hers. The physical distraction worked for keeping her mind off her stomach, but considering the growing bulge she'd felt pressed against her backside, she thought it lucky they hadn't rammed a half dozen other boats on their way out of the harbor.

He rested his chin next to her ear now. "It's not like there's anything for you to run into out here."

Once around the small outcropping of rock and trees that marked the edge of the inlet, he helped her direct them toward two tiny atolls about a half mile out. So small, they were more like outcroppings of rock than anything, but beautiful in their desolate abandonment all the same.

"It's just gorgeous out here," she said.

He continued running his hands slowly up and down her

arms, pressing his knees forward every time she started to lock up her own. His body framing hers kept her loose limbed and as relaxed as possible. It was strange, but as long as she was behind the wheel, and they were making steady forward progress, her stomach was fine. It was like driving a car, which she handled just fine. It was being a passenger she couldn't stomach. Literally. The water was so calm, slicing through it wasn't much different than it was winding her way through freeway traffic around the highways of L.A.

Of course, she knew it would be entirely different when they were under sail instead of motor. All the pitching and rocking, dipping side to side—she cut those thoughts off, focused instead on the stunning view. The rest of her attention was on the feel of Burke's body cupping hers, so pliant and flexible, yet providing the rock steadiness she needed. "This is truly amazing."

"The boat or the view?"

"Both. But I meant the thrill of driving her."

He gripped her hips, pulled her back slightly, making her gasp as she realized just how aroused he was. "I know what you mean."

She laughed, surprising herself with how at ease she felt, pushed so far outside her comfort zone. She credited all of that to Burke.

"Okay," he said, covering her hands with his own once more. "Just around this outcropping. There." He pointed past her shoulder, and she saw the narrow passageway between the two tiny islands. "We're going to duck in between them, then slip inside the lagoon of the one on your right." He helped her steer through the skinny passageway, and when they passed through the coral rock, she gasped at the lovely, perfect cove created by the two atolls.

Angling starboard, they slid carefully into the lagoon at the center of one of them. Deep, crystal clear turquoise water, white sandy strips of beach, completely shielded from the view of the rest of the world. It was like a little pocket of paradise inside an already exotic, perfect world.

Burke cut the engines and dropped anchor, parking them right in the deepest part of the almost enclosed inlet.

"It's one of my favorite spots," he told her.

She turned in his arms. "Is it, now? I can see where this would be a perfect place for . . . what was it you called it? Motion practice?"

He grinned easily at her teasing. "It's perfect for fishing and snorkeling. The atolls are more coral than rock really." He tugged her closer. "We'll see how motion practice stacks up against that. You have a bathing suit tucked in that bag?"

"We're going snorkeling?"

"If you want." He dropped a kiss on the curve of her shoulder. "Later. Right now I have a different idea in mind. But it does involve getting wet."

She could have told him just how wet she already was, but that gleam was in his eyes, the sparkle of fun and play that appeared to be such a natural part of him. Fun and play. Two concepts she'd admittedly had little in common with of late. "Okay, I'll go change."

As soon as she stepped out of the protective circle of his arms, she hadn't gotten halfway to the galley before she was swaying and grabbing for the nearest handhold, her stomach swaying right along with her. She made a disgusted noise and paused, trying to get control of herself. "I was perfectly fine all the way out here," she grumbled.

And then Burke was there. Big, warm hands smoothing down her sides. "Not as much rocking when you're moving across the water like that. Come on, forget the suit. There's no one around." He took her hand and led her to the back deck, holding her steady but making direct progress all the way to the set of steps that led down each pontoon, directly into the water.

She gripped the railing. "Wait. We're going in?"

"The water is warm. Don't worry about your clothes, just come on in." He slid in front of her, went down the steps first, then reached up for her hand. "You've trusted me this far."

She took his hand and sighed as the warm water lapped at her ankles.

"Can you swim?" he asked.

"Like a fish," she assured him, then made the plunge. Once free of the rocking boat, she felt instantly better, calmer. Controlling her own motion in the water was entirely different from being on something that controlled the motion for her. She slid through the warm water, following Burke's languid, sure strokes, until they reached the shallow water near a sandbar.

"Careful of the coral," he warned. "Don't stop until you're over the sandbar." Once the water was shallow enough for them to stand, he stopped, reaching easily for her and pulling her into his arms. "How does someone who moves like a mermaid have such problems with seasickness?"

"It's different. When it's just me in the water, no problem. It's the bobbing on something else on the water I have a hard time with."

"Well," he told her, "we're going to fix that."

"How? The boat is back there."

"I want you to lie on your back, and float."

She had no idea where he was going with this, but she did as he asked. Only when her body began bobbing with the gentle current did she realize he was emulating the bobbing of a boat, using her body as the vessel.

He stood next to her, one hand braced gently beneath her to keep her anchored. "How do you feel?"

"Fine," she told him.

"Stomach fine?"

"Yes, of course."

He smoothed his free hand over her stomach, then down one leg, then the other. "That's because you're relaxed."

She could have told him it was because she was in control of how the motion affected her, but at the moment she couldn't think of anything else but his hands on her. She was too caught up in the sensations of the water lapping at her skin, and his wide palms running all over her body, to say much of anything.

"The human body is mostly made of water," he told her, continuing his soothing, yet stirring strokes along her skin. "As long as you stay relaxed, your body will maintain the rhythm of the water, inside and out."

Rhythm, she thought, humming a little breath of approval. Inside and out. In and out. Over and over. That was the kind of motion practice she could get excited about.

"As soon as that rhythm is thrown off, you have the inside and outside clashing against one another. It's natural to tense up when you don't feel right, thinking you can control queasiness by making your body as still as possible, but you're only stilling the shell, not what's rocking inside it. That's exactly what upsets the rhythm." He kept his hand running along her arm, her stomach, her legs.

She'd long since stopped thinking about relaxing or ever being sick again and was now praying only that his hands would move where she needed them most.

"Let yourself float like this on the boat, and you'll be fine."

And then he was lifting her from the water, pulling her effortlessly into his arms, and his mouth found hers. She wrapped her legs easily around his waist, growling in her throat at the rigid length of him that pressed so hard and tight between her thighs.

"You're like some kind of siren song," he said against her mouth. "Come on." And then he was dragging her back into deeper water.

"Wait, what—"

"Lesson four," he told her, and they began swimming back to the boat.

"I was rather liking lesson three," she called out, but he was already pulling away.

They paddled up to the rear steps, and Burke climbed out first. "Grip the railing," he instructed.

She wanted to be frustrated with his constant change ups, but as she pulled herself out of the water, he was pulling a huge terrycloth beach towel from a compartment tucked inside the rear deck. She'd thought he was going to hand it to her to dry off, but instead he climbed up on the wide mesh trampoline that stretched across the space between boat and pontoon. He was like a cat on the netting, perfectly balanced.

While she stood in the stairwell, feet still in the water, gripping the railing like it was her last lifeline. Surely he didn't intend for her to climb out on that open-weave net. But then he was flicking out the towel, expertly knotting the little corner ties to the net before crawling across the mesh to the edge and beckoning to her with a curled finger.

"You must be joking," she told him. "Five minutes of floating therapy is not going to cure me. And that—" She pointed to the towel and net.

"Is like a huge, gentle hammock." He reached for her hand. "Come on. If you hate it, we'll go right back in the water. Or we'll take the dinghy to the beach and do some snorkeling. Whatever you want. Just come up here, give this a try." He smiled. "Have I steered you wrong yet?"

Her body clamored for him still. Frustrated by the drawn-out foreplay, she was jumpy and edgy, though if she was being truthful, none of it had much to do with motion sickness at the moment. She really didn't want to change that dynamic. But there was absolute promise in his eyes. So confident and sure. And then there was that hand he was offering, the one she wanted very badly to feel on her body again.

So she kept her gaze on his and reached for him.

As it turned out, the mesh was more solid than it looked and supported her weight without much give. Of course, she was on her hands and knees, crawling, so balance wasn't really an issue. She sighed in relief when she reached the towel, rolling onto her back and letting the sun seep into her skin, praying she could handle this latest maneuver of his without embarrassing herself.

Burke knelt beside her on the blanket, but didn't stretch out next to her. Blocking the sun with one hand, she peeked up at him. "Now what?"

He laughed. "Don't sound so enthusiastic."

"I was enthusiastic when we were docked. I was enthusiastic back there in the water. You know you could have had me right there."

His eyes went dark, and she saw a tick in his jaw and realized that despite his fun and light demeanor, his need for her was every bit as tightly wound as her need for him. For some reason, that gave her a much needed edge, and though the desire didn't lessen, her tension and nerves did somewhat.

"If I'd remembered these, we'd still be out there," he told her, then pressed a square condom packet into her hand.

She blushed a little, but somehow what should have been an embarrassing or awkward moment wasn't. If she were ever to imagine herself having wild, passionate sex with a virtual stranger—which she hadn't—she'd have thought it would be one of those carried-away-in-the-heat-of-the-moment kind of things. But this had long since gone from "carried away" to "absolutely deliberate." And the fact that they both accepted this and had no problem being direct about it was frankly even more stimulating. She took the condom, curled it into her palm. "And now? What exactly is lesson four?"

"Tuning your body with the rhythm of the water when it's not in the water."

"And we couldn't have done this when we were inside, back at the dock?"

He shook his head. "Too sturdy, too confining. Out here is more flexible, easier to feel and see the water itself."

"This oversized hammock was available back at the pier as well," she reminded him.

Now he grinned and stretched out next to her. "I know, but I didn't think you'd be all that fond of being naked in front of whoever happened to be on the docks this afternoon."

Her eyebrows lifted, questioning his confidence, but the very idea that he planned to do just that provoked a definite yay response from the rest of her body. "Oh, so you think you'd have gotten me naked, do you?"

He rolled carefully over her, straddled her waist. "Let's just say I had high hopes."

She wanted to arch beneath him, feel his weight centered over her, pinning her down, keeping her steady, safe. That and she ached to have him inside her to the point of actual pain.

He leaned down over her, worked the knot in front of her shirt free, then pulled it up and off her arms in one smooth motion. Then, with her arms still stretched out over her head, his hands were on her breasts, and she gasped a soft moan as he peeled the wet fabric of her bra away and tossed it to one side. The sun immediately felt warm on her damp skin, but rather than touch her now bare and very hard nipples, he skimmed his body down hers, peeling her shorts and thong off as he went. She made no effort to stop him. His touch was so sure, his hands so warm and steady, she lifted and let him strip her without a whimper of protest. After all, this was exactly what she wanted.

Once her skin was bared to the sun and sky, she was amazed at how absolutely freeing it was. Never in her life had she done anything like this. It felt wonderful. On the one hand, she felt insignificant beneath the wide canopy of sky and vulnerable, out here in the middle of a smooth, deep pool of water. Yet when Burke moved his weight back to the straddle her hips and she saw his hunger for her written so boldly across his face, she felt inherently female and immeasurably powerful at the same time. It was heady, and it served only to fuel her need for him to greater heights.

He took the condom packet from her hands and tucked it in the waistband of the shorts he still wore. Then he took her hands and leaned over her, extending them farther above her head, past the edge of the towel, until her fingers tangled in the nylon cord that tied the trampoline to the framework of the boat.

"Hold on," he told her. His gray-green eyes all but glittered out here in the sun, and she found herself willing to do absolutely anything he told her to do, as long as he fulfilled the promises she saw in them.

She curled her fingers into the webbing, and Burke slowly slid down her body. "Close your eyes," he told her.

"But I'm rather liking the view," she replied. Burke looking like a shining sun god, all burnished skin and bunching muscles. And, for the moment, he and all his godliness were completely and totally hers.

"Humor me."

She arched a brow. "I would say I've done that and more."

His smile grew to a grin. "And how're you liking it so far?"

She could only laugh. And close her eyes.

He surprised her by shifting his weight off of her, but she kept her eyes closed, her arousal spiked by the idea of anticipating the unknown. She shivered when his voice whispered near her ear.

"Feel the heat of the sun."

She nodded. "It's incredible. Wonderful."

"Let it feel like it's soaking into you, through your skin. Concentrate on the warmth of it, seeping through your muscles, into your bones. Let it make your body pliant, languid."

She could have told him she was already all those things, but the combination of the sun and his velvet murmuring in her ear felt pretty damn good. Lulling. So she let herself drift away.

She felt herself grow drowsy, but as she let herself go, she also began to feel the bob and flow of the boat, the gentle movement of the water beneath her. Instinctively, she tensed her abdomen, her legs.

"Shh," he said, so completely in tune with her. Somehow

that made her feel far more vulnerable than her nakedness. "Languid, pliant. Let the sun soak into every pore. Drift away, Kam. Just drift. Like you're floating in the water. Let the motion roll through you, not over you."

She took a slow breath, and released it even more slowly, focusing on letting the tension go with it. It was harder than she'd thought it would be. Partly because he had her very highly sensitized at the moment, and it bucked up against the instinct to fight the tightening in her gut by freezing up. Then she felt his hand stroke along the flank of her thigh, then up over her hip, along her rib cage. And just like that, the bad tension shuddered out of her. And the good tension rolled in to take its place.

She wanted to open her eyes, watch him watching her. But she knew that would bring in the visual aspect of the motion, the horizon. Better not to go there. Better still to just do what Burke said. And feel whatever it was he chose to make her feel. The visuals that idea brought with it were decidedly more fun. Anticipation sent delicious, pleasurable shivers skating over her sun-warmed skin.

"I wasn't going to touch you," he said, stretched out next to her, his hand still lightly stroking her skin.

"It soothes me. Smoothes me out."

"I want to teach you how to do that on your own."

"I guess I'll need remedial training." Her lips curved, but she kept her eyes closed, concentrated on the heat of the sun, the heat of the wide palm presently stroking her stomach. "Darn."

He groaned a little, then nipped her earlobe. "You drive me crazy."

"Then we're even. Except next time I get to tie you up in the mesh." She grinned when she felt his body twitch against her thigh. "My my." The next instant she was gasping and arching like a finely tuned bow string when his hot mouth closed over her nipple with no warning. When his other hand covered her remaining bare breast, rubbing softly over her tight nipple, her responding moan was a low growl of stunned pleasure.

"Lesson over," he said, his voice strained, a little rough. Then he slid his body over hers and down, leaving her breasts covered with his wide palms as his tongue trailed a direct line down the center of her torso.

Her fingers tightened in the mesh as she arched up to meet his seeking tongue. Between the heat of the sun and Burke's extended foreplay, she could do nothing now but respond and respond fully. She'd never made love outdoors, certainly never splayed herself like this, like some kind of pagan sacrifice to the sun gods. The very notion was intoxicating, especially when she cast Burke in the role of sun god. Every touch further swamped her senses, electrified her every nerve ending.

As his hands teased and taunted, his tongue brought her slowly to the brink, before backing away, plunging deeply into her, then moving once again to where she was knotted with need. Driving her so close, so close. She sunk deeper and deeper into the waves of pleasure steadily washing over and through her, and slowly became aware, on some level, of the motion of the water beneath them. The rise of each gentle swell, the dip of each trough, and how Burke's clever ministrations worked in absolute sync with them both. Up and down, faster, then slower, higher, then lower, he continued to wrench one exulting wave of pleasure after another from her, rushing her toward that seemingly unreachable horizon until she was whimpering with need, so close to begging. And would have, if she could have found her voice.

Finally, blessedly, he drove her and every last drop of cascading bliss up and over the edge. She arched and bucked, unaware that she, too, was now in complete sync with the rhythms of the sea. Her cries of absolute ecstasy were carried away on the gentle breeze that teased her oh-so-sensitive skin as his fingers and mouth left her. "Burke," she said, half sob, half demand.

But he was already sliding out of his shorts, sliding on the condom. When she finally opened her eyes, she let go of the anchor of the mesh without a thought, instinctively reaching for the man who'd been the real anchor to her every need. He blocked the blinding rays, casting himself in a golden halo. Sun god, indeed.

She welcomed him into her arms and rose to meet his body. The weight of him on top of her, as he pushed fully into her, pinned her down tightly. She felt safe, secured. Anchored. As long as he was there, inside of her, filling her up, steadying her as she wrapped so completely around him.

He drove into her again, then when she met him, more forcefully, rocking them both. She lifted to meet every thrust, their motion so fluid and smooth and perfect, she felt she could drown in it, in him, and never miss the ability to breathe again.

She felt him gather, stroke deeper still. They were bucking wildly now, the up-and-down motion of the water serving only to lengthen every thrust. She clung to him, exulting in the sizzling pleasure rocketing through her, through him, willfully driving him higher, harder, faster. She could no longer comprehend a moment when she wouldn't be in complete sync with him, with the rhythm of the water beneath them. Sun and sky, water and motion, heat and Burke, pumped into her, poured through her, filled her to a point beyond pleasure.

And when he came, she matched his shout of complete and utter vindication.

Chapter Seven

Somehow, Burke managed to heave the absolutely satiated weight of his body off of Kam, but he couldn't leave her altogether. After quickly disposing of the condom in the shorts he didn't intend to don again anytime soon, perhaps the next millennium, he pulled her close, tangled his legs with hers. She murmured something as she easily rolled toward him, but her voice was so drowsy, he couldn't make it out.

So he lay there, in this perfect pocket of paradise, with what just might be the perfect woman sprawled across his body, and let himself, and the tangle of thoughts trying to push their way to the surface, drift blissfully away. Plenty of time for that later. He let the motion of the sea work its magic as he slowly stroked his fingertips the length of her spine.

He'd thought her asleep, but she surprised him by lifting her head just enough to prop her chin on his chest. He tilted his face to hers, surprised to discover he could actually feel even better than he had a moment ago. The contentment and honestly joyful expression on her face when he opened his eyes was a punch to a system already battered by pleasure so shocking and complete, he wasn't sure what to do about it.

"Hi," he said, his voice a gruff rasp.

"Hi yourself. Miracle Man."

His mouth spread into a lazy grin. "I can assure you, that last part wasn't in the original lesson plan."

"Well, I think you should consider adding it to the curriculum. In fact, you could probably do away with lessons one through four and go directly to five and be perfectly satisfied with the results."

He rolled to his side and cupped his hand to her cheek. He couldn't seem to rid himself of this constant need to be touching her or stroking her. She said he soothed her, but he wondered now who was soothing whom. He'd never considered himself particularly unsettled, but something inside of him was decidedly smoother than it had ever been before. Another notion to contemplate. Later. Much, much later. "I rather liked all the steps," he told her, wanting to taste her again, and deciding not to deny himself. He lifted her mouth to his and took what he wanted, quite pleased to find her needs once again matched his.

Her mouth was an endless pleasure that he'd only begun to sample. Funny how, having had her, rather than feeling satisfied, even temporarily, he only hungered for more. So much more.

"So," he said, drifting from her lips to her chin, then along the line of her jaw. "Tummy still okay?"

"I don't think there's a part of me that could be tense at the moment." She turned his mouth back to hers, kissed him slow and deep, rousing him up all over again. Making him wish he'd tucked more than one condom in his shorts. "I suppose the real test will come later, when we set sail."

"We don't have to go anywhere, anytime soon, if you don't want to."

She smiled at that. "I think I'm up for the challenge. Besides, if I begin to feel the least little bit woozy, we'll know exactly what to do about it, won't we?" Her grin turned decidedly devilish as she rolled him to his back and slid her body over his. "We've got several weeks to run a thorough check on just how cured I am."

He gripped her hips, amazed at how easily they moved with each other. In sync, as he'd always felt out here on the water. That was when he was most at peace. She made him feel much the same way. "I think I can safely say this will be the best Christmas I've ever had," he told her, wanting to laugh at the sheer joy of it, the surprise of discovery, of her, wanting to shout to the world how great he felt at the moment.

She settled her body over his, just enough to stir him further, but also somehow settling him when she tucked her head beneath his chin, weaving her legs with his and draping her arms over his shoulders, plunging those long fingers of hers into his hair. He made a little moan of pleasure as she gently raked his scalp. "Do you always spend your holidays at sea?" she asked him, as the warm air brushed their skin, the sun keeping their bodies warm.

"Mostly."

"No family calling you home?"

He shook his head. "I have three brothers. We're close, but we're scattered all over the globe. Home was something we pretty much avoided at all costs." He sighed, not sure why he was telling her any of this. He didn't normally talk about himself, his past. "I don't know, that might change a little now. My father passed away around this time last year."

Her fingers stilled and she lifted her head. "I'm so sorry."

He covered her hand, brought it down to rest on his chest as he shifted his gaze to hers. "Don't be. He was the reason we escaped." He fiddled with her fingers, wove his through them. "Now that he's gone, my youngest brother, Jace, has moved back home, taken over the family spread, as it were. He reunited with his high school sweetheart during a huge blizzard we had at home this time last year. They're planning a wedding, rebuilding the homestead. Who knows, maybe a new generation can breathe life back into the place and cast out all the old ghosts along with it." He glanced away. He didn't spend much time thinking about Rogues Hollow, the Virginia land he'd been raised on, and had escaped at his earliest opportunity, as had all three of his brothers. But more and more now, when his thoughts turned to his brothers, they also turned to memories of home. And it wasn't as repellant as it had once been.

"What about your other two brothers?" she asked, sliding down so she could prop her chin on his chest. Their fingers remained in a woven tangle over his heart.

"Tag, my oldest brother, is presently on a dig in Scotland. He's an anthropologist who specialized in Mayan history, but recently shifted gears to do a little digging into our own heritage." He smiled. "A Highland snowstorm and a certain Maura Sinclair had a little to do with that change of direction."

"Ah, so two of the four Morgan men have lost their hearts recently."

"Actually, three of the four. Austin, who is second oldest, is a fashion photographer. He's presently somewhere in Europe with a woman he also met, oddly enough, last Christmas, on a snowed-in train."

Kam smiled. "Well, if I had to get stranded with a Morgan brother, I'm glad I got the one that resides in the tropics." She shivered. "I'm not much for snow."

Burke laughed. "We agree on that, one hundred percent."

"So, you're from a whole family of vagabonds, then."

"The 'rogue' part of Rogues Hollow came from an ancestor of mine. Maybe there's a little of that still in all of us."

"Maybe that's why we connect so well."

"Ah yes," he said. "Dorsey alluded to your black sheep of the family status. Apparently I'm not the only one who ran away from home."

She smiled. "Yes, but I didn't manage that feat until I was in my twenties." She sighed a little, but the smile remained. "I love them all dearly, but their ideas of how my life should be are dramatically different from my own."

"I've heard a lot about Lana. She sounds like something of a dragon, if you don't mind me saying."

"I don't mind at all. She is all dragon, though a beloved one."

"And your parents? What do they have to say about your desires?"

"They are pretty much cut from the same Apolo mold as my grandmother. My mother married quite young and centered her life around taking care of her husband, house, and children." Her smile turned dry. "Often in that order." She lifted a shoulder. "And there is absolutely nothing wrong with that. I've got dozens of aunts and uncles, nieces and nephews, all blissfully happy with their lot in life, to prove that point. Only I wanted something different. Not that I'm averse to marrying, or raising my children. But that's something that for me, you can't plan for. It either happens, or it doesn't. So I had other goals."

"Why a catering business?" he asked. "Why not your own restaurant?"

"That was my first dream. I'm from a family of wonderful cooks who truly appreciate the art of a finely prepared meal. I caught the bug early, only I wanted to do more with it than make dinner on Sundays for the clan get-togethers. But after college, followed by some specialized training, then finally climbing the ranks to cook in one of the best places around L.A., I realized that if I ran the restaurant, I'd be management, not the chef. But at the same time, head chef in a successful restaurant was too intense and political for me."

"So you decided to scale it down, cook for a smaller audience."

"Exactly. I started doing some small functions on the side for friends, dinner parties and such, so I already have a burgeoning client list. But to go full-time I need dedicated space, more equipment, a promotion budget, and I'll need to hire on a few people at least part-time. I've been saving for what seems like forever, and I'm close. Another eighteen months or so at my last job and I'd have probably made it."

He tipped her chin. "But? Oh, right. Heavy-handed Steve."

"Yes, the lovely Steve March, golden son of the very well known and wealthy March clan."

"It was harassment. You should have nailed him, no matter how powerful he was."

"I know. And trust me, I thought about it. It was a game to him, and all in all, relatively harmless. Annoying and tiresome, but I wasn't in fear of attack or being fired for repeatedly rejecting him."

He tipped her chin to him. "If you didn't welcome the advances, it was harassment. Bastard should have his balls in a sling."

She just smiled at that. "Well, I had an arsenal of sharp knives at my ready disposal, and I'm pretty sure he knew that push come to shove, I wasn't afraid to use them. That kept him just on the other side of the line. Besides, I'd worked too hard to start over again, and if I'd gone the legal route, I wouldn't have felt comfortable staying there, no matter the ruling. I knew it was only a matter of time before I could get out."

"Then Dorsey called and made you an offer you couldn't refuse."

"My best Christmas present ever," she agreed. "I leased out my place in L.A. to a friend, and without that overhead and no living expenses here, my cut from this will take care of my financing in six weeks instead of another year or so. Plus there was the bonus of getting out of going home for the holidays and suffering through God knows how many blind dates."

She gave a little shudder, but Burke grinned. She might have been complaining, but it was clearly a sort of exasperated affection. It was obvious she loved her family very much.

"Enough about me," she said, settling herself across his chest. "Do you get to see your brothers often?"

"We keep in touch, but no, we don't see each other as often as we'd like to."

"Now that you're all settling down, maybe it will be easier for you."

"Settling down?" Burke snorted. "Jace maybe, but the rest of us, not hardly."

"I didn't necessarily mean it like that. But, well, you said all three of your brothers are now involved in long-term relationships. That's settling, to some degree. And you bought your boat." She propped her chin on his chest again, smiled into his face. "So, in a way, over this past year you've all taken on a responsibility to something other than yourself."

"I never thought about it like that, but I guess you have a point."

"I'm probably way out of line here, but maybe losing your father was a more life altering thing than you're making it out to be. All four of you have made a pretty major life change in the year since then."

He didn't know what to say to that, didn't want to think about that time a year ago and all the memories it had dredged up—many of them bad, but some of them surprisingly good, most of those having to do with his brothers. He'd been glad to see them again, and he'd thought he'd come to terms with the guilt that came from being more relieved than grief-stricken over his sole remaining parent's death. "Seeing them again has made me miss them more. And I am planning on taking a trip to Scotland this summer. We all are." Now it was his turn to shrug. "So, who knows, maybe you're right. Maybe we will make more of an effort now." He pulled her up so their bodies were fully aligned, her face close to his. "Probably think you're pretty smart, figuring me all out," he murmured, brushing his lips across her chin.

"Smart, no. Intrigued by you? Definitely yes. A man who's made his own way, on his own terms." She smiled against his lips. "That's a man after my own heart."

It wasn't until she spoke the words that he realized that maybe, just maybe, his heart might be in jeopardy here. Even more startling was the notion that he might be okay with that. Of course, she was heading back to L.A. at the end of the season. But that was a long way off. And a lot could happen between now and then.

He rolled her to her back, surprising a laugh out of her. "What if I was?" he asked, having no idea the words were going to pop out until they did.

"What if you were what?" she asked.

He leaned down, captured her bottom lip, then took her mouth completely. He pushed his hands into her hair, pulled her to him, and rolled them to their sides, as she was already wrapping herself around him. So easily. So naturally. So . . . rightly, was all he could think. It should have terrified him, the feelings and ideas that began forging a life inside him. And it did, but not in a bad way. He'd never understood how his brothers, dedicated bachelors all, could have fallen so swiftly, and so certainly, for the women in their lives.

Only now did he begin to think that maybe, just maybe, it was a genetic Morgan trait.

When he finally lifted his mouth from hers, he shifted just enough so he could look into her eyes. Dark eyes, already glassy with desire, with hunger. For him. He could get used to that, he decided, knowing she was likely seeing the same thing in his eyes. "What if it turns out, somewhere down the line, that I'm a man after your own heart?"

The idea obviously surprised her, but the smile that lit her face couldn't be faked. "I don't know," she said, her eyes lighting in consideration. She toyed with his hair, then ran her fingertips over his mouth, then along the line of his jaw. "I suppose we're going to have some time to figure that out."

"Might complicate things," he told her.

"Might," she said, then surprised him by rolling him to his back. Grinning, she pinned his hands over his head, pushed his fingers into the mesh. "But that's what makes life interesting."

"You're something else, Kamala Apolo."

"Yes," she said, wiggling her eyebrows, "yes, I am. I hope you know what you're getting into."

"I haven't a clue. But, like you said, that's half the fun." He laughed with her, but it abruptly became a gasp, then a moan, when she began trailing wet kisses down along his chest, taking her sweet time as she moved lower. And lower still.

Fun, indeed. A lifetime of this could be downright intoxicating.

"You know," she said conversationally, "I've never been someone's Christmas present before, best or otherwise."

He growled just a little when she ran her tongue below his navel. An instant later he was gripping her head, and it was his back arching now as she took him in her mouth. "Lucky me," he ground out. "You're the gift that keeps on giving." But taking wasn't enough. With Kam, he didn't think it ever would be. So he nudged her with his legs, until she turned around. He slid her legs over his shoulders, bringing her right where he wanted her. As he slid his tongue deep inside her, her throaty groan vibrated along his cock.

Mutual satisfaction. Body . . . and, he somehow knew, heart and soul.

That, he hoped, would be their true gift to each other. And a lasting one, if he had anything to say about it.

"Merry Christmas, baby," she breathed, her voice a soft sigh of wonder as he grew hard once again.

"Ho, ho, ho," he murmured in response, deciding right then that having a few Christmas traditions wouldn't be such a bad thing.

Starting with this one.

Epilogue

One year later . . .

"Great trip, Morgan. We're booked again for next year?" George asked, grinning when Burke nodded. "Maybe we can try the Curacao run."

"The food was simply out of this world," Tutti exclaimed, for what had to be the dozenth time. "I'm going to have to work extra hard to fit into that New Year's gown now." She sighed. "But it was so worth it." She clasped a heavily jeweled hand to her plump bosom. "I'll be sure to spread the word."

"I'm so glad you enjoyed it," Kam replied. "*Mahalo,*" she called out, waving as the Wetheringtons made their way down the pier.

"You'd better hold on to her, Burke," Tutti called back to them. "Her ceviche alone will have you booked two years in advance. You mark my words. Aloha, you two!" She wiggled her fingers and clattered on down the pier in her impossibly high heels.

"I'll take that into consideration," Burke called out, grinning as he came up behind Kam and wrapped his arms around her waist. He turned her in his arms and immediately began having his way with her mouth. A whole year later and he still hadn't gotten near enough of it.

"Burke," she protested, "they haven't even left the parking lot yet." But she wasn't exactly pushing him away. She rarely did.

"I'm just following the client's wishes."

She snaked her arms around his shoulders. "Like you could get rid of me if you wanted to. Where would Morgan Charters be without the incredible talents of the Caribbean's number one chef?"

"It's a good thing your grandfather isn't here to hear you say that."

Her grin was saucy. But wasn't it always? "Why do you think I dared to say it?"

He laughed, pulling her against him and swinging her around. "Have you heard from him? I was disappointed when he couldn't meet up with us in Nevis last week."

She shook her head. "He's probably still somewhere off the coast of Melbourne. But Lana swears he's going to be home over the holidays. I guess two new babies and another on the way make it worth missing a week or two of high season."

Though Kam was smiling, Burke didn't miss the fleeting wistful look that crossed her face. She hadn't been home to see her family in close to six months. Though it had been rocky for her the first couple of weeks until she'd finally gotten her sea legs under her, she'd been doggedly determined to conquer her seasickness and make a go of it. And Burke couldn't be happier that she'd stuck with it. And him.

Their first season together had gone so well, the bookings had come flying in. Dorsey had fallen in love with Australia and had decided to stay down there for as long as his infatuation lasted. They'd hoped he'd be back in the Caribbean by now, but apparently he wasn't quite done Down Under.

But Burke knew that Tutti wasn't far from wrong with her claims. Not only was Kam's cooking everything she'd claimed it would be, but her confidence and charm won over even the most nitpicky of clients. Catering to small, intimate groups was what she'd always wanted, so this suited her perfectly.

And though she wasn't exactly her own boss, she shared the role with him, which, along with the lack of management headaches, more than made up for the compromise.

Last summer when he'd gone to Scotland, she'd gone home to L.A. to settle things, with a short trip to Hawaii to see her family. He'd been head over heels by then, and though neither had been looking forward to the brief separation, it had been even harder than he'd expected. Somehow the man who'd spent his entire adult life living on his own terms had swiftly grown used to waking up to her sleepy smiles in the morning and having her warm, sweet body tucked under his every night.

And now another six months had zipped by, and he still couldn't believe how completely his life had changed. For the better.

He took her hand and tugged her to the control deck.

"Burke, we have to be in Barbuda by nightfall. I've got to get to market early if we're going to be prepared to pick up the Markhams by noon."

"We're not picking up the Markhams tomorrow," he told her, backwalking her to the captain's chair. "I'm going to go untie us. Steer us out, okay?"

He was gone before she could protest or ask questions. With a private smile, he cast them off, then came back to stand behind her as she expertly maneuvered them out of the harbor. She didn't need him to settle her nervous tummy any longer, but they'd long since grown used to doing this part together, like they had the first time, whenever they could.

Only, this particular trip, it was his tummy that was a bit jumpy. He pressed the occasional kiss on her hair as anticipation grew along with a bit of nervousness. Only when she was angling past the twin atolls did he reach past her and change their course.

She glanced back at him, her smile knowing. "Okay, what's going on?"

He nudged her out of the chair so they stood in front of the controls, her body pressed back against his. "You'll see." They motored in silence until they reached the center of the cove. Their cove, where they'd spent many a spoiled, lazy afternoon when they'd had the time off. He cut the engine, and they dropped anchor. Then he turned her in his arms. He'd been planning this for what seemed like a lifetime, but now that the moment was finally here, that didn't stop the nerves from jumping along under his skin.

"One year ago today I got the best Christmas present of my life. In a way, I feel like it's been Christmas every day since."

"Burke—" she began, her voice going soft, her expression even softer.

"There is no booking the next two weeks."

"But it's high season and—"

"And thanks to a certain chef I know, we can afford the break." He tugged her closer. "Happy anniversary."

She threw her arms around his neck. "You mean it? Ten whole days, here in the cove, just the two of us?"

"Not exactly. We only have until tomorrow."

"But I thought you said—"

"I did." He pulled the envelope from the back pocket of his shorts. It was slightly crumpled from having to hide it from her when Maybelline had smuggled it to him earlier today. "But I thought you might like to spend part of the holiday with your family. I, uh, I was hoping I could meet them, too."

Her mouth dropped open as she pulled the plane tickets from the envelope. Her gaze flew back to his. "I'm going home? And you're coming with me? Oh, Burke, are you sure?"

"Of course not," he laughed, already dreading his meeting with the infamous Lana. "But it's important to me." Because he knew life with him would keep her even farther away from her family than before, he wanted to make sure he did the right thing by them and make his intentions known. Which gave him the next two days to figure out how exactly he wanted to make them known to her.

"If I didn't already know I loved you, there would be no doubt now." She kissed him hard and fast on the mouth, but it quickly took another turn, as it tended to with them, and Burke was glad he'd waited until they got to the privacy of the cove to tell her.

"I hope you don't mind, but there's more." He took the tickets out of the envelope and fanned them out. "My brothers are heading to Rogues Hollow this Christmas. Apparently Jace and Zanna have an announcement. I'm pretty sure it involves the next generation of Morgans." It surprised him, how powerful the very idea was to him, a man who'd forsaken family so long ago. He suspected a certain Apolo was responsible for that. "I thought it might be a good time for you to meet them."

Now her eyes went glassy. "Really? You want me to meet your family?"

He rubbed his thumbs across her lips. "Of course I do. This way we won't have to chase them down around the globe." When a single tear tripped over her lashes and spilled down her cheek, he knew he was a goner. The words just tumbled out. "I was planning to have you naked on the trampoline out there, weak from multiple orgasms, before I sprung this on you, but now I can't seem to wait." He knew it was the right thing, had been planning this moment, it seemed, since shortly after he'd met her. The miracle, really, was that he'd made it this long before blurting it out. And yet his stomach clutched as the words stuttered on his tongue. "I, uh, you and I—"

"Are you okay?" she asked, sudden concern furrowing her brow.

"Of course I am," he said automatically, abruptly feeling anything but.

She dabbed at the sweat that had popped out on his forehead, stroked cool palms over his damp cheeks. "You're looking a little . . . peaked."

"I wanted this to be special, perfect." His heart was pounding, and he actually felt a bit woozy. Determined, he stammered his way through it. "I was wondering if, while we're meeting families, what you'd think if I—oh shit." And with that he broke off and ran to the head, barely making it in time.

"Are you okay?" Kam asked from the doorway behind him.

He managed to nod, feeling like a complete idiot. He'd never once gotten seasick in his entire life. But then, he'd never proposed before either.

In a complete reversal from a year before, it was Kam now, crouching behind him, stroking his forehead. "What happened?" she asked gently. "Did you come down with something?"

"In a manner of speaking." Shakily, he pushed to a stand, then took his time at the sink, cleaning, brushing, rinsing, getting his act together. She was right there the whole time, rubbing his back, stroking him, soothing him. Right by his side. Always. Which, he knew without a doubt, was right where he wanted her to be.

Calm now, ready, he dried his hands, then turned to face her. "It might have been right in this room that I knew I was going to fall for you. Seeing how badly you wanted to do things on your own terms. Your strength, your determination. I think I've been a little in awe of you since the start."

Her smile was full of light and love. "And here I thought that was just the tight shorts and skimpy top you were in awe of."

He grinned. "That might have been a small part of it." Then he took her hands between his own. "So maybe it's prophetic this should happen right here." He knelt. "It'll be a good story to tell our kids."

She gasped, tightened her grip. "Burke," she breathed.

"I want my family to meet you because I want you to be part of that family," he told her. "I want to meet your family, because I need to ask them for your hand. But first, I need to ask you. Will you marry me?"

She was already tugging him up, even as she crouched

down to meet him on the way up. They collided, sending them both sprawling back out of the head, where they banged up against the passageway wall. "We seem to make waves, even when there aren't any," she said, laughing.

Laughing with her, he held her tight until they got their balance. "So . . . is that a yes?"

"Yes," she said instantly, beaming with happiness.

"Thank God." The boat bobbed gently as he turned her face up to his. "Because I plan to be making waves with you for the rest of my life."

LET IT SNOW

Nancy Warren

Chapter One

"And it's a wild one tonight," Marisa Langley yelled into her microphone over the howling gale that swooped through Chicago like Old Man Winter throwing the hissy fit of the century.

Keeping her demeanor chipper in front of the WLPX camera wasn't easy since her teeth, exposed by her bright smile, were chattering, her hair felt as if it was being yanked off her scalp by frigid fingers, and her jaunty red wool coat—the cashmere one which had cost her an absolute fortune—sported a thick dandruff of snow.

She was freezing. Her cheeks were numb with the cold, her nose felt like an icicle, and she wished she dared sniff before the icicle dripped. Of course, she couldn't sniff during her live weather report. The best thing she could do was to get through her spiel as soon as possible.

"I'm up here on the roof of the W building," she said as she did every night at this time. "I know it's Christmas Eve, but if you can stay inside tonight, do it. Bundle up in front of the fire and get cozy. The forecast is that tonight's freezing temperatures and high winds will give way to a big snowstorm." She gave her trademark weathergirl see-I-told-you-so grin and held up her hand to the white stuff. "We're predicting ten to twelve inches more snow in the next twenty-four hours."

She tried to keep her smile fresh and stop herself from squinting as she looked into the camera. Holding the hand-cam, Rob Sheridon looked only marginally warmer than she. With no audience accustomed to seeing his face, he'd been free to wear a parka with a big hood that all but obscured his features. She had huge parka envy right now. Behind the bright light trained on her, he was like an overdressed angel, and when the wind picked up both he and the camera wobbled.

He made a wrap-it-up gesture with his fist, and she couldn't wrap it up soon enough. Management insisted she do the evening weather forecast out in the open, but she'd never entirely understood why. Would the people of Chicago believe it was raining only if they saw water dripping off the end of her chin? Would they accept a tornado warning only if they saw her rise in the air like Dorothy? At least Dorothy had Toto and a pair of killer shoes. All Marisa had was her camerameanie. If Oz included him, she'd throw herself back into the eye of the twister.

"Santa and the reindeer will encounter some stiff winds tonight," she chirped, blinking to make sure her eyeballs hadn't frozen solid. "Because we can expect more—"

The world plunged suddenly into darkness.

The camera's light extinguished like a candle in this storm. Then, after wondering for a split second what had gone wrong, she became aware that it wasn't only the camera that had been snuffed. All around her, the high-rises of Chicago disappeared from stacks of brightly lit windows to nothing.

Blackness and silence stretched everywhere.

"Shit!" Rob yelled, his voice a whisper in the wind, and she heard the scrabbling of his boots running across the roof of the building.

Though they were transmitting live on the six o'clock news, the sky was so heavy with snow clouds that the daylight was a dark, smoky gray, so she could barely see Rob, barely see the microphone she still held in front of her face, barely see the freezing flakes that fell thick and fast.

Squinting, no longer caring that her eyes were starting to spill over in response to the biting cold, she watched Rob run, looking like a slow-motion mime as he scrambled across the roof.

What on earth?

Her own gasp was swallowed by a cold gust as she realized the cameraman was racing for the door that led off the roof, as though it might be . . .

"Shit, the lock's engaged," Rob yelled.

"You mean the door shut on us?"

They came up here all the time. Lots of the staff did. The roof was used not only for on-the-spot weather forecasts but for lunches, smoke breaks, coffee breaks. The inner fire door had to be pushed open, but the outer one was always open. It must be locked at night, but she assumed maintenance took care of that.

"How could it have locked?"

"Automatic safety precaution," he shouted over his shoulder. "When the power goes out it shuts and locks. If you were inside and there was a fire, you could get out." He yanked on the door and swore some more, but it was clear to Marisa that that door wasn't going to open.

"And if you're already outside?"

The look he sent her over his shoulder pretty much answered that question.

As if she hadn't already been cold enough, an iciness that had nothing to do with the weather chilled her bones. "How long will it be until the door opens again?" she shouted over the worsening gale.

Her cameraman shook his head, a sharp back and forth of the parka hood, looking like an irritated polar bear. "Not until the power comes on. Or somebody remembers we're up here."

"Are you saying we're . . ."

"Stuck," he yelled back.

Stuck? Out here in the middle of a storm? With Rob?

If she had to get stuck, why couldn't it have happened when she found herself sharing an elevator with Hugh Jackman when she was in New York that time?

Or why hadn't she been marooned at Club Med in Mexico when Antonio Banderas was spotted at a nearby villa? Why, oh, why, if she had to be stranded alone with a man, did it have to be in the middle of a ferocious storm and with Rob who despised her?

He turned around and as usual refused to make eye contact.

She had the urge to push him off the roof, except the wind was doing a pretty good job without her help. Besides, she wanted that parka.

She looked around in the darkening gloom. The case wasn't hopeless, she reassured herself. They weren't stuck at the North Pole for goodness' sake, for all it felt isolated and cold up here.

They were in the middle of one of the largest cities in North America, surrounded by people, five-star restaurants, cars, hospitals, food, and emergency crews. Of course, at this moment, they might as well be at the North Pole.

They couldn't get off this roof, and she had an awful feeling they'd be forgotten as everyone panicked at the power outage and then gave in to the inevitable and went home. However, the roof of W had at least one thing that as far as she knew, the North Pole didn't. A smokers' corner. When the smokers had complained about the wind up here, the station owner had glassed in a shelter. Closed in on three sides and roofed, it would offer her and Rob shelter from the storm.

This wasn't a disaster, she reminded herself with determined cheer. It was a temporary annoyance.

If she tried really, really hard, she could even call it an adventure.

Rob walked back to where he'd left the camera, hoisted it onto his shoulder, and slogged his way to the shelter. Clearly he was more interested in the camera's safety than her own since he didn't offer to help her or even glance in her direction. Typical. Still, she kept her gaze fixed on him so she could see where she was going. His big white jacket and his rolling, athletic gait were something to focus on.

He seemed huge in the uncertain light and kind of scary. She smirked to herself. The abominable cameraman.

When he reached the shelter he ducked inside only long enough to place the camera on the wooden picnic table. Then he emerged once more, hauled the metal trash can into the shelter, and popped out again, advancing purposefully on the second wooden picnic table, the one exposed to the elements, where employees ate their lunch or sat and smoked on sunny days.

At last she reached him, conscious that she'd chosen the bright red cashmere for style over substance. Rob paid as much attention to her safe arrival at the shelter as he did to the random snowflakes that landed on his big shoulders.

For once, she decided, he was not going to ignore her.

"All right." Marisa drew in a deep breath and nearly got frostbite of the lungs. "All right." She would keep calm. "Everything's going to be fine." She put a brave smile on her face and tried to mean it. She'd taken a few acting classes back in college. She knew all about projecting a character. Right now she was feeling calm. Secure. Confident. Optimistic. "We've got the shelter so we can keep warm. We'll be rescued before we know it," she said.

Her plan worked. The little pep talk did get his attention.

Rob stared at her a moment, then shook his head so cozily ensconced in the warm hood of the parka. "Well, that's good. We wouldn't want any bad news."

With a scowl he turned away from her, did some kind of martial arts kick, and snapped the weathered wood of the old picnic table's bench seat.

The snap of the wood startled her as much as the violent action. "You're so damned perky," he said as though he were continuing a discussion she didn't recall starting, "if you were going down with the *Titanic* you'd be trying to organize a skating party to the iceberg."

"I would not!"

Another couple of kicks and some jumping up and down on the bench and he had freed a plank which he handed her.

Gee, thanks.

"You're so busy looking on the bright side, you are missing out on reality."

Irritation swept through her, and she welcomed it. At least it warmed her.

"Yeah? Well, I faced reality and it sucks," she said. "Reality is that we're trapped up here for God knows how long in a blizzard." Even saying the word made her feel cold. "I purchased this coat more for its looks on camera than for warmth. I'm starting to get hungry, my feet are frozen, I'm stuck with a man who despises me, and I'm a little bit scared." Her voice wobbled, and it infuriated her.

"I wish you hadn't brought up the iceberg because that's sort of how I feel up here. Like I'm stranded on one." She drew a shuddery breath, feeling colder than ever. *And with one.*

He didn't comment, but bashed more wood into pieces. As irked by the fact he was back to ignoring her as she had been when he'd belittled her, she went on.

"I'm not an outdoor wilderness enthusiast like you. I don't want to sleep in a snow cave and climb mountains and defy nature. I want to be in a nice warm restaurant ordering off the menu right now. Is that real enough for you?"

"That's plenty real," he said, finally making eye contact.

Oh, good. When she was strong and making the best of things he ignored her. But the minute she babbled through everything that was bad about their situation and drove herself close to the border of hysteria, she got eye contact.

She felt like Polyanna trapped with Eyeore.

"Hey, relax," he said. "The power outage won't last long."

She eyed him and the pile of lumber at his feet. "What are you planning to do?" she asked. "Rub two of those sticks together and make fire?" If he didn't want perky, then fine. She could also do sarcastic. And he could deal with the consequences.

"Somebody left a pack of matches inside." He motioned with his head toward the shelter. The chances that the matches were dry and still flammable struck her as slim to none, but if he wanted to bash a picnic table to bits, she wasn't going to stop him.

She turned and trudged over to the shelter.

"While you're in there, go through the trash can," her companion ordered.

Oh, this was getting better and better. "What am I looking for, dinner?"

"Paper. Anything that will burn. Dump everything else out and crumple the paper."

She turned back. "It worked."

He glanced up at her, his green eyes squinting against the wind. His cheeks were ruddy, and she noted that he needed a shave. "What worked?"

"Your plan. I am no longer perky."

Chapter Two

Shrugging deeper into her coat, she walked a few steps along the now snow-covered roof and ducked into the shelter.

For a moment the world seemed amazingly quiet without the howling in her ear.

The last glow of the day's sun was dying fast, but not so badly that she didn't see the book of matches lying on the picnic table along with the sports section of a paper and a take-out coffee container knocked onto its side. Honestly, couldn't people clean up after themselves?

She reached for the matches. They were the kind you paid a couple of cents for in a corner store or got free at restaurants. This matchbook advertised a local pizza place. She opened the dented cardboard cover, and inside were three matches that looked pretty fresh.

Maybe they had a chance at a fire after all.

She glanced over at the trash can and then out at Rob, who was now viciously attacking the second bench of the picnic table. She was certain that he'd got the best end of the deal in their division of labor.

Wrinkling her nose, she approached the trash can. The smell of stale coffee and banana peels sat like top notes above the aroma of garbage. She could tell Rob to do his own filthy garbage duty, but the way the light was going it would be dark soon, and even the possibility of warmth and fire outweighed her squeamishness. Still, she wished she could see more clearly what was inside.

No way she was sticking her hands in there. Instead, she bent down, lifted the can from the bottom, and upended it.

Her leather gloves were the exact shade of her coat. It had taken her days of shopping to match them. For what she'd paid for these gloves, Rob Sheridon could have a whole new wardrobe with money left over for a haircut.

She glared at the karate kid out there and grit her teeth, hoping she'd kept the receipt for the gloves so she could find the store again and replace these that she was pretty certain she'd never wear again after she'd used them to sort through refuse.

There was a lot of paper and other combustibles in the resulting pile. She pulled out the least gross of the crushed paper sacks, old newspapers, and the take-out cups that seemed to be made of cardboard rather than Styrofoam.

Soon she had a nice pile of crumpled papers, including the sports scores she'd found near the matches, and wilderness man was stomping her way with a stack of wood formerly known as picnic table.

"There's the paper," she said, pointing to her handiwork.

He grunted.

Her smile was so brittle she almost cut herself. "And it was such fun rooting through filthy garbage to collect it, too."

"About time you got your hands dirty," was all he replied.

Her arm banged down so hard on the still-whole picnic table that his camera rattled and rolled to its side.

"What is your problem?" he said, righting the camera.

"Why do you despise me so much?" she snapped. It was a strange question; but this was a strange circumstance, and the normal rules of social interaction—where she would pretend not to notice that he couldn't stand her—temporarily didn't apply.

She was a nice person. Friendly, competent, easy to get

along with. She didn't mess up on camera more than anyone else—in fact, she thought she did a pretty good job making Rob Sheridon's job easier. And he acted as though she were beneath his notice.

They were stuck together, and she was already sick of the company.

Her question obviously startled him. He glanced up, actually engaging her in momentary eye contact. All right! Progress. And then hunkered back down and continued arranging pieces of wood and paper in some complicated arrangement she suspected he'd learned while lighting bonfires atop Everest.

She waited for him to deny that he loathed her or make up some phony excuse, and was already sorry she'd asked the question when he said, "You're a tootsie."

Her mouth fell open, and she waited for more, but that appeared to be the sum total of what he had against her.

"A tootsie?" she finally asked. "What on earth does that mean?"

"You're all perkiness and sunshine, the good news only girl. I swear to God, when you have to report that it's raining, it's like you can't even bear to say the words. You only want to have the sunshine."

"You've been rotten to me since I started here, and that's it? That's the reason? Because I'd rather report sun than rain?"

There was a tense silence when the howl of the wind echoed her own feelings.

"You asked me for the reason. I gave it."

Except that she wasn't nearly as shallow as he seemed to think. Or as stupid. In fact, she wasn't stupid at all. Sure, she was a determined optimist, but she was also smart about people. And there was more to this. Something he wasn't telling her.

She kept silent while he worked, then handed him the matches, not at all surprised when the first one he struck instantly blazed its little red heart out.

And, naturally, even the garbage sprang into flame at his

touch. She ought to be pleased she'd have a fire to warm her, but perversely, his competence annoyed her.

As soon as it was obvious the wood had taken its part in the trash can conflagration, Rob eased away and sat on the bench.

Silence.

They had who knew how long up here, and the silence was deafening. It wasn't as though there was anywhere to go, or anything to do.

The hell with it. "A tootsie," she said. Already the shelter was warming up, even though mountain man had placed the can near the open doorway—for ventilation, presumably, since he didn't bother explaining anything he did to her. The crackling flames sounded far too cheerful for the company. "I'm not sure I understand what a tootsie is. I've seen Tootsie Rolls. Those are candies. And quite delicious."

The glance he shot her, devilish in the dancing red light, told her candy was not what he had in mind.

"Or I get the image of a kept woman when I think of a tootsie, but surely you don't think—"

"I was thinking of something light and frivolous. That's all."

"Light and frivolous? I'm a journalist."

He rolled his eyes so eloquently she was afraid his eyeballs would get stuck in reverse and he'd spend the rest of his life staring at the inside of his skull. "You're the weathergirl."

"What about my feature on single mothers?" she said in outrage.

He snorted. "You mean the one where they started their own business, opened a coop baby-sitting service, and all lived happily ever after?"

"Okay, so it was an uplifting story. Sue me."

Silence reigned once more.

"I'm not saying being a tootsie's a terrible thing," he said at last, surprising her by being the first one to speak. "But I'm a realist. Eternal optimism gets on my nerves."

She tapped her gloved fingers against the tabletop. He leaned over and fiddled with the camera. His hood was still up over his head, even though the shelter was already warming. She suspected the hood was yet another barrier to prevent eye contact. "Then why don't you refuse to work with me any more?"

"I'm assigned to you. It's my job."

Now it was her turn to snort in disbelief. "If you can't stand me so much, you could be reassigned. In fact, I'll help you do it. I'll ask for a new camerameanie."

He blinked, looking even more devilish. "What did you call me?"

Damn. Her private name for him had slipped out. There were times when dignified silence was the best course of action. This was definitely one of them.

"A camerameanie?"

So much for dignified silence. "You're a camerameanie. I'm a tootsie. Clearly we should be reassigned."

"Fine. Tomorrow morning we'll get that done."

"Tomorrow's Christmas."

"Consider it your present."

He glanced up at her, a furtive, quickie glance, almost as though he were gauging how she'd taken his words, and in that second when their eyes almost but not quite connected, she had it.

The gleam deep in his eyes was one she'd seen often enough when a man looked at her, but never from him. Of course not! Now that the truth was before her, she wondered she hadn't thought of it before. No wonder he wouldn't make eye contact with her. How he must hate the truth.

"You're attracted to me," she said. Suddenly his unwilling crush was as clear to her as the flames in the rusted metal garbage can.

He gave a crack of laughter and turned his back on her.

Okay, she could be wrong, which would be awfully embarrassing, but she could also be right—and every instinct in her body was telling her she was. Her camerameanie had the hots for her.

She felt oddly breathless as she stared at the broad expanse of his back, so muscular and solid, as he tried to turn away from her and the truth.

"That's why you won't even look at me. You wish it wasn't so, but it is. You're attracted to me."

He didn't answer. The glass panels of the shelter were steaming up, so she felt encased in a cloud, eerily remote from reality as though she weren't even tied to the earth. The normal rules didn't seem to apply.

Rob might try to turn his back on the truth, but he wasn't turning his back on her.

She rose and walked around the picnic table, sitting on his other side so she was once again confronting him. He didn't move, and the heat she saw blazing in his eyes confirmed her suspicions.

"That's it, isn't it?" she said, her voice a little husky. "You're attracted to me. You wish it were some Amazonian woman who kayaks up the river to spear breakfast, but face it. You've got the hots for a tootsie."

He opened his lips as though he'd say something, and then closed them.

She looked at him, really looked. His hood had fallen away, revealing his dark brown hair in its usual state of disarray.

The planes of his face were sharp, the jut of his chin pugnacious; even his nose was beaky, his cheeks stubbled as though all the hard angles and surfaces could protect him. But she had only to look into his eyes to see the longing and the kind of warmth that made their trash can fire pale in comparison.

And at the heat in his eyes, something caught fire inside herself.

How long had she been harboring a secret crush on the man who spent so many hours on the other side of the camera from her and not so much as a minute talking to her or smiling at her or even looking at her?

"You barely look at me, never talk to me, and you won't even smile at me."

He raised his brows as though she'd said something really stupid. "Not smiling at you is your evidence that I'm secretly in love with you?"

Her breath hiccupped a little in her throat. "Who said anything about love? It's a little crush. It's okay. Lots of people get them."

"Don't you think if I had a 'crush' on you that I'd smile?"

She'd seen his smile. It was a killer.

"You smile at the receptionist, even tell her jokes. You smile at our coworkers—even strangers on the street. But you never smile at me, or tell me a joke."

"You wouldn't think my jokes were funny."

"See? That's just another defense."

"You are really starting to get annoying."

Maybe he wouldn't smile at her, but she could smile at him, and she did, a smug tootsie smile that would drive him nuts. "I'm annoying because I'm right. Admit it," she said. "You want me."

For a long moment he said nothing. The fire popped and shushed itself, but she barely heard it. For a guy who'd never looked at her, he was making up for it now, staring deep into her eyes. "And if I do? If I admit I'm crazy about you?"

She drew in a shuddery breath and for a second wished she'd kept her mouth shut.

He leaned a little closer. "What then?"

Chapter Three

If he sat here one more second, Marisa was going to kiss him. She broadcast her intent by the darkening of her eyes, the way her lips slipped apart and she leaned closer.

Every fiber of his being tingled with wanting. But if he tasted her, it would only make his problem worse.

He stood so abruptly he nearly lost his balance. Behind him a small groan told him his companion was as frustrated as he.

"What do you want, Marisa?" he asked in desperation, poking around at the fire in a lame attempt to pretend the blaze needed his attention.

"I thought that was obvious," she said.

"I mean professionally. What do you really want? More features? Your own talk show? To report hard news? Be the next Diane Sawyer? What?"

She paused long enough that he wondered if she'd answer at all. Finally she said, "I want to be visible."

"Visible?" No wonder she drove him nuts. He tried to have an actual conversation, and she said something ditzy. "You're on TV. How much more visible can a person get?"

"I'm the weathergirl. No one ever sees me. Not really. They see the perky blonde who gets rained on a lot."

"I see you," he said, realizing he was already lost. Maybe he could have stayed away from her as he'd planned if fate hadn't thrown them together like this and she wasn't sharper than he'd realized—or his unwanted obsession were less obvious.

She leaned her head to one side. "You see me because you're paid to look through your camera lens and make sure I'm in focus. Big deal."

"No," he said, feeling as if he was battling whitewater and it was winning. "I see you."

She looked at him, long and steady, and he got the feeling his opinion mattered to her. "What do you see?"

He smiled as though this were a quiz show and he had the answer before the buzzer. "I see *you*. I watch your face, all the moods and expressions. You may be interviewing someone or reporting the weather, but I'm always there, watching."

She looked at him as though she were really seeing him for the first time. "What do you see?"

Oh, hell. She'd already figured it out. He might as well admit the truth. "I see a desirable, warm, and fascinating woman I want to make love to."

She choked, torn between a laugh and a moan.

"Really," he insisted. "Go ahead and test me."

"Test that you want to have sex with me? No. Thanks. I'll take your word for it."

"Not that," he said. "Test that I really am watching you. Ask me anything about what you've done or said or worn in front of the camera since the day you started." He'd never have believed in love at first sight. It was the sort of soft, romantic notion that a perky, good-news-only gal like Marisa would fall for. Not a man who'd seen and done the things he had.

It had happened, though. Maybe not the very first time he'd seen her, but he still remembered the way he'd felt, as though he'd been hit in the chest with a cannonball when they were introduced. The way her blue eyes had sparkled at him as clear and sunny as a summertime brook. Her hair was as richly blond as sunshine. Her teeth whiter than snow. Her whole appearance was a goddamn weather report.

Even in his irritation at her sunny beauty he'd known deep down that he was in trouble. Months of staring at her through a camera lens had only deepened his awkward and wholly unwelcome infatuation.

Maybe he was tired of hiding from the truth. Maybe he was hoping she'd slap him for his impertinence, or sleep with him so he could get her out of his system, but something had to change, and tonight change was in the air.

"Okay," Marisa said, responding to his challenge, but with no idea how to go about this. She glanced at him, glanced at the camera that chaperoned them still, and pulled a date at random. "Last Friday."

He closed his eyes for a moment, then opened them, so darkly green she was reminded of the rain forests he loved to hike. "Last Friday," he said. "You wore black pants and the same red coat you're wearing now. You had a silver pin in the lapel shaped like an angel. On the evening news you forecast sunshine."

How was she supposed to know whether he'd guessed correctly? Even she couldn't remember what she'd worn, or what weather she'd forecast. When they got off this roof, though, she was going to check.

"Was I right?"

He smiled at her. For the first time he actually smiled right at her, and she knew what she'd been missing. When she caught him grinning at other women, she'd seen the warmth and attractiveness, but when he turned it on her, she felt the warmth of that grin right down to her toes. "Thirty percent right. There was a little sun mixed in with the rain and the wind."

Since she couldn't check whether he was making this stuff up or not, she allowed herself to feel flattered. This was either the biggest con since Orwell told America they were being invaded by extraterrestrials or one of the most effective come-ons she'd ever experienced.

Because just thinking of him watching her that intently from behind his camera, and with carnal thoughts on his mind, made her feel kind of flustered. No. Not flustered. Warm. Damn it, the very idea made her hot.

And right now, anything that made her hot was a good thing.

For a guy who'd had trouble making eye contact before, he now seemed unable to tear his gaze away. And she was as bad.

"Then you were off for the weekend," he said, moving closer. "Monday, you predicted a cold front. You had a black coat on and a yellow scarf that kept flapping in the wind."

"You snarled at me and tucked it into my lapel," she recalled. His hands had barely touched her, but she'd felt their strength.

"Tuesday you had a big blue sweater on and big blue ear-rings."

"I was freezing in that sweater," she said, recalling how the wind had whipped through to her very bones.

"It was the exact color of your eyes." He looked suddenly embarrassed, as though he'd been caught doing something he shouldn't. "And your forecast was bang on accurate." He gestured to the thickly falling snow. "The cold front came in, along with the snow."

She shivered, and not from cold. "Why are you telling me this now?"

"I thought it would pass," he said, stepping toward her. Instinctively she rose. "We've been working together for three months now, and I want you more every day."

She couldn't help the smile that pulled at her lips. "You have a funny way of showing it."

"I didn't want to want you. I still don't, but you're like malaria. Once you get hold of a man, you don't let go."

She blinked, then crossed her arms across her chest in a gesture even he ought to figure out meant stop right where you are. "Malaria? I'm like malaria? First I'm a tootsie, which I still don't completely understand; now I'm like a tropical disease?"

"Don't kid yourself. I'm not happy about this. If a dose of quinine would get you out of my system, I'd be guzzling the stuff." Then, before she could protest, or even unfold her arms, he pulled her to him and kissed her.

Soft down seemed to envelop her as he wrapped his arms around her, but it was the only part of him that was soft. His body was muscular and taut; even his lips were firm. He had the kind of mouth that demanded rather than requested. Yet something about the way he kissed and the way he held her made her want to give in to his demands.

She opened her mouth to him, slipped her arms out of their locked position and around him.

If he'd been resisting her for months, he no longer was. His tongue was hot and insistent in her mouth, dragging a response from her, making her weak at the knees. Literally, so weak at the knees she'd fall if he let her go.

His hands ran down her back; hers did the same to his. He left her mouth long enough to trail kisses along her cheeks, to her ear, down her throat to where her coat was buttoned to the neck, and back up to her lips.

She whimpered as lust slammed through her as potent and sudden as any storm she'd ever forecast. They were all over each other. With so many layers of clothes between them they were like two suited-up astronauts going at it.

"Why couldn't we have been trapped in the elevator or a broom closet or something?" he whispered with frustrated urgency. "Somewhere where I could undress you and make love to you properly."

She'd caught his excitement and shared his urgency.

"I want you, too," she gasped. "So much." She was astonished how strong her desire. She wanted to be naked and wrapped around him so much she could hardly bear the suspense of waiting.

His thoughts seemed to be keeping track with hers, for he chuckled softly. "We'd freeze our asses off if we got naked."

Right. Not naked, but maybe . . .

She felt his hand fumbling at the buttons that covered her chest. He pulled off a glove with his teeth and then slipped that hand into the opening he'd made in her coat. He hit sweater.

"Today, you dress for warmth," he grumbled, tugging the thing upward.

"As you'll recall, I forecast that the frigid temperatures would continue until Christmas day," she reminded him snootily. "You were obviously listening." Him in his parka, she thought jealously.

She didn't have the heart to tell him there was more than sweater he'd have to contend with. She kind of liked his eagerness. Sure enough he made his way under the sweater pretty fast, and she felt his fingers moving around.

"What is this? Thermal underwear?"

"T-shirt."

He grunted.

"The thermal underwear's underneath . . . then bra, then me."

"This is like searching for the Holy Grail," he complained, though he didn't slow any.

After a little more burrowing, she heard his grunt of satisfaction and her own soft sigh of pleasure as his fingers finally hit her flesh. They were a little rough, a little hard. The hands of a man who climbed mountains and kayaked oceans. The hands of a man who didn't love easily, she sensed, or casually. That's why he'd tried so hard to fight his attraction.

"Are you sure about this?" she whispered, even as his hand closed over her breast, and she knew there was no turning back, not when he could make her feel like this under the least romantic circumstances in which she'd ever been.

"No, I'm not sure about this. I already told you. I don't seem to have a choice."

She stifled a chuckle. "You are such a sweet talker."

"Hey," he said, so she tilted her chin and looked up at him. "I'll never lie to you. Or play word games. I want you so much it's killing me. But I wish I didn't."

She ought to be angry, but she understood. Frankly, she felt the same way.

Still, they didn't have to get married. They were both young, both single. So they had different beliefs and ideas about life. So she was an optimist and he was a card-carrying pessimist. So what?

This was sex. Uncomplicated, well, marginally uncomplicated, healthy sex between two consenting adults.

In a snowstorm, on a roof, during a power outage.

Okay, so it was wildly complicated. And one of the main complications hit her now.

"I'm not trying to spoil the romantic mood, but I don't suppose you carry condoms on you?" she asked.

"You don't suppose right."

She sighed. Still, all was not lost. If he could dig beneath her clothes to reach her breast, then . . .

Chapter Four

Rob felt Marisa's fingers trailing downward, over his belly, following the length of his jacket to the thigh where it ended. Then her hand snuck underneath and began inching upward with obvious erotic intent.

He quivered with anticipation, even as he stopped her with a hand on her wrist. He didn't want this, he realized. He didn't want some furtive making out on the corner of a rooftop.

"I want our first time to be amazing," he whispered in her ear, feeling the soft fall of her hair against his lips, smelling roses and almonds from whatever fancy shampoo she used.

He kissed her cheek. "I want to spread you out on my bed and touch and taste every inch of you. I don't want to be trying to reach you through your jeans. It's too much like high school."

Her hand didn't stop its journey, but she didn't try to unzip him either, merely caressed him through his jeans which was a decent cross between heaven and hell. As his cock began to take over from his brain, rooftop groping looked better by the second. "So, what are we going to do then?"

"We could talk."

"Talk." Her voice was husky and sexy.

He tried to think. "You could tell me something you've never told anyone."

"That's pretty intimate."

"Not as intimate as what I plan to do to you when we're alone in my bed."

They settled with him sitting on the bench and her in his lap. By tacit agreement, there was no more delving beneath clothes, but they kept each other on simmer all the same. A rub here, a caress here, a kiss there. It was like *uber*-foreplay.

Rob promised himself that for every hour they spent up here torturing each other, they'd spend two in his bed bringing each other pleasure.

"What do you want to talk about?" she asked him.

"What did you do for your last holiday," he asked her.

"I went to Paris."

Oh, that was so typical of little rich girl tootsies. "To buy shoes?"

There was a moment's rigidity from the woman in his lap. Then he felt her shrug. "Sure. Shoes and other things. You?"

"I flew to Ecuador to help build a well." God, could he sound any more nauseatingly smug? The big eco-philanthropist. Besides, his trip hadn't been all unselfishness. "And I hiked an ancient Mayan trade route I've always wanted to hike."

The flames flickered, but not so high anymore. He'd used up all the wood from the rotting table outside, and this one hadn't been sitting out in the elements. It seemed remarkably strong to him. Still, if worse came to worst, he'd do his best to break it up. It was going to be a long night.

"I guess we are pretty different," he said, rubbing his hands over her chest, teasing himself with the mounds he'd soon be seeing and tasting. So she flew to Paris for shoes. Everyone couldn't be Mother Teresa.

"Maybe we're not so very different," she said slowly. "I really went to Paris to nurse my grandmother after she had a stroke. That's why I quit my last job."

"And when you came here three months ago?"

"She died," she said simply.

"I'm sorry."

She shook her head. "Don't be. She had a wonderful life, and I'm so glad we had time together at the end." She chuckled, but her voice was filled with emotion. "Grandmere loved shoes. We did go shoe shopping."

"I'm a sanctimonious pig," he said.

She tipped her head all the way back and kissed him upside down. "And that's one of your finer attributes."

They talked a little more about family, and the people at work, and he suspected she was trying as hard as he was to ignore hunger pangs. He glanced at his watch. After midnight. They'd been here almost six hours. A few emergency generators had kicked in, so there were lights in some of the buildings, including, ironically, the one they were on top of, but the generators obviously didn't power the doors to the roof.

Well, the situation wasn't one he'd wish himself in, but it could be a lot worse. "We'll be fairly comfortable even if the fire dies in the night," he said, vowing silently to keep her warm no matter what.

While she snuggled against him, he looked past the smoking can outside where the flakes fell thick and white and there was nothing but snow. "It's so quiet here, just us and the elements. It's beautiful. It's like settling down for the night after a good climb in the mountains." He kissed the top of her head. "Without the tired muscles. It's really pretty special."

They wouldn't freeze to death out here, thanks to the shelter, but it would be uncomfortably cold once the fire died.

She chuckled. "I can't believe you did that."

"Did what?"

"You tried to cheer me up. You were perky."

Damn, so she'd seen right through his lame attempt at false optimism. "I've never been perky in my life."

"Yes, you were." She insisted. "You were perky." She looked up, her eyes twinkling up at him, her teeth white as the falling snow as she grinned. "And I appreciate it."

He wrapped his arms tighter around Marisa, and within

minutes, he realized with a rush of tenderness that she'd fallen asleep in his arms.

He kissed the top of her head gently, so as not to wake her. "Sleep well."

Rob didn't realize he'd fallen asleep until he was woken. "Rob, Marisa, are you all right?"

Rob woke to a crick in his neck, a dead weight in his lap, and an even deader, heavy feeling in his legs that told him they'd gone to sleep, as well.

In that blinking moment of disorientation before where he was and why came rushing back, he heard his name called again.

"Rob! Marisa! You're all right?"

"Mmm. Yeah. Fine," Rob managed. He opened his eyes and then stuck a hand in front of his face. "Get the light out of my face."

Marisa's head rose from his chest, and he felt her relaxed body stiffen as she glanced up at the station manager, Lenny Krajik, who was standing there with a maintenance guy shuffling from foot to foot holding an industrial flashlight.

She scrambled off Rob's lap, looking flustered.

"I'm so glad you made it," she said.

"It's colder than a witch's tit out here," Lenny said. "Are you sure you're all right?" he asked again.

"Yes," Marisa answered. "We're fine. Rob built a fire, and we stayed in here. Apart from missing dinner, the night was fairly uneventful."

Uneventful? Rob wanted to shake the woman. What was uneventful about sharing his deepest feelings?

Then she sent him a look of intimacy and promise. "So far," she murmured, so only he could hear.

"Well, let's get you off this roof. In all the panic after the lights went out, and everybody wanting to get home before the storm worsened, I guess . . . I can't believe we forgot about you up here."

"It's all right. Really." She was back to being miss perkiness and sunshine. So they might lose a couple of limbs to frostbite; she wouldn't want Lenny feeling bad.

"Well, the storm's still raging, and we could lose the power again, so I'd feel happier if we all got off this roof."

Rob struggled to his feet, trying to be manly and ignore the pain coursing through his legs as the feeling came back. He almost wished it wouldn't.

As he stumbled out of the shelter, he felt like a space traveler returning to earth. For the last few hours there had been only him and Marisa in all the silent, dark world. Now the lights were back on. From the rooftop, even through the fat snowflakes waltzing around him, he could see the lights below, the billboards, the ads. Traffic lights were back. Traffic was back. Not much of course, and what was down there crawled along, but he was definitely back in the world.

Already, he was beginning to miss the not-real world he'd lived in for the past few hours, legs going to sleep and all. He wondered if he'd forever ruined his work relationship with Marisa, now he'd babbled all that stuff he should have kept to himself.

"I'm going to stay and put some things together for the morning," the station manager said when they got back down to their floor.

"Do you want us to help?" Marisa asked.

Us? After the station had nearly suffered a double fatality in their weather team, he for one didn't feel much like giving up what was left of the night to pull together some perky bullshit that was bound to feature the words Winter Wonderland if Marisa had anything to do with it. He needed food, a shower, a toothbrush, and a real bed.

Fortunately, Lenny seemed to have the same idea. In fact, he was so nervous and agreeable, Rob wondered if he was afraid they'd sue the station. He stifled a tired grin. Marisa was probably planning to work extra hours to make up for the lost broadcast time. "No. No. You two go on home . . . unless you think you should go to the hospital and get checked out?" he asked uncertainly.

"We're fine," Rob said, before Marisa got her mouth open.

"Well, I insist you take a few days off. Tomorrow's Christmas. I know you're both scheduled to work, but I'm ordering you to stay home. No sense coming down with a cold at this time of year. Call me day after tomorrow and we'll see."

"But . . ." Marisa seemed about to argue.

Not Rob. He grabbed her arm and squeezed it in a message he hoped she correctly interpreted as *shut the hell up* before Lenny recanted his generosity.

"I've got snow tires on the van, and chains if we need them. Can I drive you both home?" Lenny asked so eagerly, Rob felt like mentioning the word lawyer just for the fun of it.

"Oh, well, my Ford's kind of—"

"I've got four wheel drive on my Jeep, thanks," Rob said. "I'll drive Marisa home."

The building seemed oddly alive after hours of darkness. There was almost no one within. Few souls had ventured back when the power came on. It was Christmas Day, after all. Under lights that suddenly seemed bright, they walked past offices that had been left in a hurry, computers that hadn't been shut down, desk lamps shining on papers in progress.

"Are you all right?" she asked as they got into the elevator. "You seem like you're limping."

"I'm fine," he said, "just stiff from the cold."

"I know. I feel like I'll never be completely warm again."

Given half an hour alone at either of their places, he thought, he'd like to give warming her up his best shot. At this point, he wasn't certain he'd get the chance, though. They'd fallen asleep with a certain intimacy promised, and woken with the awkwardness of strangers.

He swore silently as the elevator descended to the parking garage. If only he'd let her think he didn't like her.

Romantic fool.

Well, he wasn't going to shove himself at her any more tonight. He'd be cool. Let her send out some kind of subtle girl signals if she wanted to take this any farther.

His stomach growled audibly as the doors opened at the parking level. He'd been so busy suppressing his raging lust, he'd forgotten about his more obvious appetites.

"I'm starving," he said.

"Me, too."

"Do you want to get something to eat?" That wasn't throwing himself at her, exactly. There must be restaurants open again now that the power was back on. Even at this time of night. He knew a few places they could try.

She sent him a glance upward through her lashes that he'd seen on plenty of centerfolds, but never on her. Certainly never aimed his way. A dark cozy corner in a snug bar somewhere. That's where he'd take her.

"Sure I want something to eat. Do you have food at your place? It's a lot closer than mine."

He swallowed hard. She knew where he lived. That suggested she'd been checking up on him in the same juvenile way he'd checked up on her. "Yes."

"Good," she said, giving him the come-here smile that went with the glance up through the lashes. "We'll eat in bed."

He would have answered—he would have said something smooth and sophisticated—except that his tongue had lodged itself somewhere underneath his tonsils.

Chapter Five

Marisa wasn't normally the kind of woman to reduce a man to a speechless mass of quivering needs. Normally, her relationships progressed a little more slowly. But tonight was so far out of the realm of ordinary, she might never get back.

And she owed Rob some serious punishment for the way he'd treated her, as though being attracted to her was such a terrible thing. She decided reducing him to a speechless mass of quivering needs was a good start.

At least, temporarily.

It had been a no-brainer to choose his apartment, since he lived so much closer to work than she did, but she was also curious to see who he was when he wasn't working, and how he lived.

Her initial fear that he lived like a slob and slept on the floor in an old patched sleeping bag he'd worn out in the Himalayas was quickly put to rest when they entered his apartment.

He shut the door behind them, and she had a glimpse of large black-and-white photographs on white walls, furniture that was mostly beat-up oak, but beat up in a good way, as though families had lived with it for half a century or so, a hardwood floor that needed refinishing, and a rug that made her mouth water.

Maybe she didn't know much about the climbing peaks of Nepal, but she knew a great rug when she saw one.

Before she had a chance to really look around, he'd hung his jacket on a fifties-style coat rack, helped her out of her coat, then hung it on top of his own. Her coat ought to go on a hanger, especially now that it was wet, she thought vaguely, but with the heat churning inside her she couldn't bring herself to worry too much about her wardrobe. She pulled off her gloves and stuck them in her coat pocket.

They stood awkwardly for a moment in the tiny vestibule. She didn't like to go any farther without an invitation, and he seemed rooted to the deco tile.

She turned to him in a silent question, and he muttered, "I can't help myself," and pulled her to him.

He kissed her, and she felt that all those hours on the roof had been agonizing foreplay and that the real game was about to start. She pressed up close, loving the feel of the body that had carried this man up the highest mountains. It was tough, rangy, with long, lean muscles and light-footed agility. He'd be hell on a hiking trail, she figured.

More to the point, based on his kissing, she suspected he was going to be heaven in bed.

She shivered as the knowledge of what they were about to share skipped over her skin.

Rob pulled back slightly, and his eyes, which normally never even looked at her, now seemed to see right inside her to where all her secrets lurked. "You're cold," he said, misinterpreting her shiver—deliberately, she suspected. He put a hand to her brow like a doctor examining a patient. "I bet you've got hypothermia."

"Wrong," she said, pressing closer. "I'm something else that begins with the letter H."

His eyes glinted with amusement, but he kept up his charade. "Look, I've got a lot of experience in wilderness survival. You're probably feeling a little disoriented now, right?"

Well, sure. She was in the apartment of a man she believed

had despised her not eight hours ago, about to make love with him. "Yes," she realized. "I am a bit disoriented."

He nodded gravely, running his hands slowly down her arms and catching her wrists. He placed his thumbs over her pulse points, then shook his head. "Pulse is racing," he informed her.

And getting racier by the second as his thumbs caressed her.

"There's no time to lose. We'll have to try the emergency survival technique."

"And what does that involve?" she asked, having a hazy idea she knew.

"We have to get naked so I can share my body heat with you."

"Okay. Probably I have a really bad case of hypothermia. In fact, I think it's an emergency."

Her body was so warm right now she could melt the snow outside, but why spoil the fun? She shuddered artistically one more time, and was surprised and delighted when she felt herself scooped up and carried, Scarlett O'Hara style, to Rob's bedroom.

He bent, with her still in his arms, to flip on a lamp, and once more she had the impression of decent furniture that had been well lived in, and an iron bedstead that gave her ideas.

He twitched back the bedspread and laid her down, then rose and stood looking down at her. She shivered again, and this time no playacting was required.

"I can't believe you're here," he said in a low, husky voice.

"I can't believe I'm here, either," she said. He stood gazing at her, and she wondered if he was so used to staring at her through the camera lens while she did all the work that he couldn't adjust to a new role.

"I believe you said we had to get our clothes off," she reminded him, reaching for the top button on her sweater.

"I can't believe you're here."

"I think you said that already. Maybe *you've* got hypothermia." She got to her knees. "Let's see, do you feel disoriented?"

"Very."

She put her hand to his forehead. "Fever?"

"I'm burning up."

The light from the lamp was a warm circle of yellow against his bed. He'd kicked the door shut as they'd entered the room, so there was no other light. She felt a bit like a torch singer, lit up and displayed by the spotlight while Rob was a dark and shadowy figure outside the circle.

He took her hand from his forehead, brought it to his lips, and kissed her palm, and the pure romance of the gesture flooded her with sharp-sweet desire.

She tightened her grip and pulled, bringing him into the circle of lamplight with her.

She undid the first button of his shirt and leaned in close, kissing the underside of his jaw while she was there, inhaling him, loving the warm roughness of his he-man leathery mountain climbing skin.

While she was thus engaged he batted her hands out of the way and raced through the rest of the buttons. Oh, he was so right, she realized as she gazed at the warm brown skin and the play of muscles in his chest and abdomen. She needed to be naked very fast. It really was an emergency.

He yanked his shirt off all the way. She pulled off her sweater, T-shirt, and thermal underwear, while he watched so intently goose bumps danced over her flesh. Down to bra now, and he didn't move, still watched her, so she undid the thing herself and let it fall.

He smiled. Just the tiniest tilt of lips, crinkling around the eyes, and the intensity of his focus made her tingle. There was a sound of harsh breathing in the room, and she had no idea whose it was.

She reached for her pants. He reached for his. To avoid staring at his crotch while he undressed, she concentrated on getting herself out of pants, long johns, and panties before turning back.

It wasn't that she meant to stare straight at his penis; it sort of jumped into her line of sight, all jutting eagerness.

She glanced up quickly, found him watching her with an almost bemused expression. Their gazes connected, and suddenly they lunged for each other, kissing deep and fierce.

His tooth grazed her lip in their eagerness, and she didn't care. Her breasts pressed almost painfully against his chest, and she only pulled him against her harder, struggling to get closer. Between their bodies, his cock lodged against her belly, reminding her that there was another place it could be a whole lot more useful.

Their hands seemed to race over each other, trying to reach as much of the other's skin as possible in the shortest amount of time.

"I had no idea how much I wanted you," she mumbled against his lips, amazed that she hadn't known the truth earlier. Certain she'd never been this desperately hot for any man.

"I know exactly how long I've wanted you," he said, pulling back so he could reach her breasts. "I've wanted you three months and"—he stopped to think for a moment—"six days."

She sighed and tipped her head back, loving the feel of his hands on her. "That's exactly how long I've worked at WLPX."

"I know." He pushed her back onto the bed, and his mouth followed where his hands had been. He sucked a nipple gently into his mouth. "You don't know how many times I've watched you through the camera and I've imagined you like this."

Her wet nipple grew chilled in the air, but he was busy with the other one. "You imagined me naked? When we were working together? When you were barely speaking to me?"

"Not always."

"Well, that's good." She sighed again as he trailed his tongue down her belly, feeling the heat build.

"Sometimes I pictured you in a little black thong."

A burble of laughter made her belly dance against his tongue. "A thong?"

"Mmm." He lifted his mouth long enough to grin up at her. "A thin one, with tiny straps hooking over your hipbones." He trailed his fingers along her hips to show her where he meant.

"What else was I wearing in your little professional daydream?"

"Lots of things. I'm very creative." He circled her belly button and kept going south. "Maybe sometimes one of those corset things that lift your tits up."

"A bustier?"

"Yeah. I guess. And sometimes stockings with garters and high heels."

"Anything else?"

"Yeah. Red lipstick. I love that look."

She had a drawer full of fun stuff at home. She smiled to herself. He'd be amazed if he knew some of the underwear she did wear on camera. Underneath her clothes of course. She'd discovered they gave her hidden confidence. She didn't entirely understand why, but she wasn't going to knock it. She'd have worn something silky and risqué tonight if she hadn't remembered her own weather forecast and gone with the thermal underwear.

She had a feeling her weather reports were never going to be the same. She'd probably whisper in his ear just what she had on under her clothes and then watch the steam rise from behind the camera. At least the exercise would help her stay warm during the winter.

And speaking of steam rising, oh, she was starting to do some steaming of her own. While she'd been thinking about all the fancy underwear she was going to surprise him with— it wasn't only shoes she'd shopped for in Paris—he'd reached the hottest part of her.

He placed her knees over his shoulders and put his mouth on her.

Had she ever felt cold? She'd been freezing earlier, but all that was a distant memory now. Heat spiked through her, building so fast she could barely keep up. She was dimly aware that her head was tossing all over the place and she was making incoherent sounds, but she couldn't seem to control herself.

His tongue did this amazing thing. He concentrated only on her hot button, twirling his tongue around and gently pulling upward. It was the most extraordinary sensation. He went nowhere else; there was no straying from her clit. Just that one spot, and the same, relentless twirl, pull and slide, over and over, until she was following his mouth with her hips and realized she had to hang on to something if she was going to remain earthbound.

The bed had those great black iron railings, she remembered, when she reached behind her. Oh, she hung on tight and squeezed the bars, and having teased her to her limit, Rob gently pulled her right into his mouth. With a helpless cry, she felt the world slide out from under her.

Her head fell back, her body arched up, and with the gasps of pleasure still leaving her lips she felt him ready himself and then slide inside her body to share the tail end of her climax.

His hands skimmed up her arms, and when they reached her hands, clasped so tight to the metal rails, he wrapped his fingers over hers and held her there, bound to him, to his bed, to this moment.

He kissed her slowly, and she tasted herself, and their passion, and the heat of his own need, which flamed hers again. He stoked her up again with strong, easy thrusts until she exploded once again, and he followed right behind.

While they were still panting and coming slowly back to earth, his head lay heavy against her breast. With a smile of tenderness, she looked down at the brown tangle of his hair, thinking how much she liked his rugged, casual look, and how good he felt, even sprawled on top of her and panting like a guy who's won a major race.

She toyed with his hair idly, feeling the waft of his breath against her nipple.

She heard someone's stomach growl. Uncertain whether it came from her or her partner, she realized they'd never stopped to eat.

"We forgot to eat dinner," she said.

"Now you mention it." He raised his head and leaned toward her.

She kissed him. His lips were still soft and sweaty from their passion, so she kissed him again, knowing she was going to be pulled into round two if she didn't go get food. Now.

"Can I raid your fridge?"

"If you do it naked."

She chuckled. "Only because I am very hungry am I letting you blackmail me like this."

She got out of bed and padded to the kitchen, knowing his eyes were on her. She opened the fridge and imagined how she must look to him, suddenly bathed in the light from inside the refrigerator.

Before she'd finished thinking about it, or viewing her dining choices, she felt his warmth, and he wrapped one arm around her, giving her breast an absent squeeze while grabbing a block of cheese with the other.

Since he was as naked as she, she took a minute to enjoy watching a gorgeous nude man moving very efficiently in his own kitchen. It was a sight she could get used to.

He pulled a loaf of crusty-looking rye bread out of a drawer, grabbed a knife. "Mustard?"

"Never eat it."

"Pickles?"

"Why not."

"In the fridge."

She grabbed the jar of deli pickles, found cutlery and plates, while he grabbed a bottle of red wine and two glasses.

There was a wooden bowl on the counter with one apple, one orange, and a banana that was going spotted.

She grabbed the apple and bit into it. She felt the spurt of sweet-tart juice in her mouth, heard the crunch, was aware of the texture of apple on her tongue. Her senses seemed super heightened.

She passed the apple over, and he took a bite before hefting the stuff into his bedroom where they climbed in and she treated the bedspread like a picnic blanket.

While she cut cheese and stacked it on bread with pickles, he opened and poured the wine.

"Here," he said, handing her a glass.

She sat back against the stacked pillows and raised her glass. "To the weather," she said.

"To us," he replied.

She never remembered wine tasting better. Nor had she ever noticed the simple pleasure of food. The bread was hearty and a deep, rich brown. The cheese was plain old cheddar, but it tasted sharp and tangy. The pickles were salt-sour and crunchy, and the wine was the color of garnets and tasted a little smoky.

"This is the best meal I've ever eaten," she said.

"Good. Keep eating. You'll need your strength."

At those words everything inside her went still and heavy. She raised her gaze to his and found it slumberous and glowing with fresh desire.

He stuck his index finger into his wine and dabbed the liquid onto her nipples, painting them dark cherry. Then he leaned over and licked them clean.

She decided it looked like fun, so she did the same thing back to him, liking the extra warmth his body heat added to the wine and the way its flavor brought out the taste of his skin.

Then they used the wine like finger paint on each other. Touching here and licking, dabbing there and sucking, until they'd teased each other back to fever pitch and she needed him inside her so badly she pushed the food aside, climbed on top of him, and impaled herself.

With the first intense need out of the way, she took her time and enjoyed the feel of him inside her, the sounds he made as he approached his limit, the way his eyes went glassy and vague and the skin crinkled around the edges as though he were concentrating very hard on something important.

While she was watching his pleasure mount, he snuck a hand between them and toyed with her until she was pretty sure her eyes were just as glassy and vague, her breathing as noisy.

Once again her climax triggered his, and she pulled him into bliss along with her.

Once she collapsed back onto the bed, she made an unpleasant discovery. "There are crumbs in this bed," she complained. She looked down at her wine-stained nipples. "And I feel like the inside of a wine barrel."

"Shower."

"Right."

She got the shower just the way she liked it and climbed in, only to find her new lover climbing in behind her. Her eyes squinted against the steam. "There's something you should know about me. I hate sex in showers. I think it's totally overrated, usually uncomfortable, and I always end up with soap in my eye."

He gazed down at her with mock seriousness, and she wondered if she might make an exception.

"I see. Well, since I'm already here, is there anything I *can* do for you?"

She thought about it. "Yes. You can wash my hair."

So he did. And then he washed all of her. And then she washed all of him. They didn't have sex, but she was sure humming when she got out. He even found her an extra toothbrush.

He found clean sheets, and that impressed the hell out of her. She hadn't had to ask; he'd gone ahead and changed them. And the fact that he could, meant he owned two pairs. She liked men who didn't feel the need to live like pigs to prove their masculinity.

She crawled in beside him, her body clean, the sheets clean, and the world outside blanketed in new, white snow.

As she gazed out the window she watched the fall of flakes looking like wavy white lace curtains.

Probably she should have made noises about going home to her place, but she didn't feel like being coy. No one should drive in this weather if they didn't have to.

And she really wanted to stay the night as much as she was certain he wanted her to.

The last time they made love was slow and sleepy, with lots of kissing and the kind of touching that's more about the pleasure of intimacy than arousal. When she came she felt an emotion so intense she wanted to weep.

She fell asleep with his hand stroking her hair.

When Marisa woke up it was Christmas morning.

She stretched against Rob's warm, relaxed body and sighed. "Good morning," he said.

She kissed him and snuggled against his chest. "I wish I had a gift for you," she said.

"At the risk of sounding obnoxiously corny, waking up with you is the best Christmas present I ever had."

"Oh, that is so sweet that I am going to make you breakfast."

Everything seemed brighter and special and different today. Soon, she'd call her parents and do the long-distance thing, but she wanted to spend this special day with a very special man.

While she threw together an omelet, Rob made coffee with the same efficiency he seemed to bring to everything. A woman could get used to having a man like him around the house, she thought, and was amazed at how quickly this affair seemed to be moving. Except it wasn't all that fast. It was just that they'd been toying with each other for three months.

Rob watched her, beautiful and sexy with her rumpled hair and passion-sated eyes, wearing one of his T-shirts which hung to mid-thigh.

As he noticed the way she fit into his kitchen, into his bed, and into his life, he realized how stupid and blind he'd been not to realize she wasn't exactly wrong for him. She was exactly right.

Some part of him had known from the first second.

While they sat at his breakfast counter and shared breakfast he knew he had to tell her.

"So," he said, deciding this was the day everything changed. No more hiding his feelings, or trying to protect his optimist's heart in a pessimist's body. "Do you believe in love at first sight?"

"No," she answered calmly, looking at him over her coffee cup.

His heart sank. Of course she didn't. No one believed in love at first sight who hadn't experienced it. Like him. Obviously, what he'd experienced was unrequited love at first sight. And he had an awful feeling it couldn't be excised as quickly as it struck.

She leaned closer, and through his misery, he saw the way her eyes were shining, almost as though she felt an emotion so intense there wasn't room for it all inside.

She put her mug down with a tiny click. "In my experience," she said, wrapping her arms around his neck, "falling in love takes at least one full, and very snowy, night."

His heart started to hammer, and he knew he'd remember this moment forever. "You mean?"

She leaned forward, and her lips parted. Just before they kissed, she said, "Merry Christmas, darling."

YOU,
ACTUALLY

Erin McCarthy

Chapter One

Josh Black was about to tell Cassidy St. George that he was in love with her when he was attacked by a reindeer.

Trying to tuck the cartoon he'd drawn into her plaid Christmas stocking, the silver reindeer holding it in place suddenly toppled off the mantel. Josh caught the stocking with one hand in what could have been a great save, except there was no reason to save a fur-trimmed stocking from hitting the carpet. Meanwhile, the reindeer connected with his knee.

Hard. Josh swore out loud and clutched the fireplace in agony, eyes closed, knee throbbing.

"Josh?" Cassidy called in concern from her kitchen, the oven door slamming shut. "Are you okay?"

"Fine," he managed to lie, thinking that this was his punishment for not being upfront with Cassidy and just telling her how he felt. He got beaten by a five-pound Christmas decoration.

But as he tried again to shove the drawing down into the stocking gripped in his sweaty palm, he rationalized with himself. He hadn't wanted to risk a long-term friendship if Cassidy didn't feel the same way he did, that's all.

Or maybe he was just a huge pansy-ass wimp, terrified Cassidy would gag at the idea of him being in love with her. So instead of telling her face-to-face like a normal guy would, for weeks he had been hinting in his cartoon strip that his alter ego, Jack Block, was in love with his friend Kristen.

The first time the strip had hit the papers, with Jack mooning over Kristen, he'd about had a coronary, but if Cassidy had figured out she was Kristen, she hadn't said a word to Josh. With each subsequent cartoon, he'd gotten bolder, with Jack pursuing Kristen and her reciprocating his feelings.

Hey, Josh figured it was his cartoon. He was entitled to draw his love life any way he wanted, even if it didn't reflect reality. Because in the real world, Cassidy still treated him like a neutered basset hound.

Josh couldn't take the strain anymore. Christmas morning was a perfect time for confessions of the chicken-hearted. Cassidy would read the stocking-stuffed cartoon, where Jack announced to Kristen that he loved her, and of course she'd realize that it was really Josh confessing he loved Cassidy. He was hoping the whole Christmas spirit thing would create enough holiday guilt that Cassidy would at least refrain from screaming in horror at the moment of truth.

He'd take whatever he could get. There was no room for a desperate man to have pride, and he'd been desperate when it came to Cassidy for about half his life.

To the strains of the chipper "Feliz Navidad" playing on Cassidy's stereo, he rummaged in the depths of her stocking, hoping she'd find the cartoon drawing last, after pulling out the peppermints and hazelnut coffee beans. That way if she did shoot him down, they would have opened the other gifts first, and he could have a nice CD or whatever she'd bought him, as a consolation prize and parting gift.

You don't get the girl, but here's a Borders gift certificate. Go buy yourself a clue. Josh could just picture the bubble over poor Jack Block's brokenhearted head in next week's strip.

There was already a piece of paper in the stocking toe, right where Josh was trying to shove his drawing. He pulled it out, then rehung the stocking on the volatile reindeer. It never occurred to him not to read it. He just glanced down at it without thinking, relieved Cassidy hadn't strolled into the room and caught him with his hand invading her stocking.

The words on that paper jumped out at him and grabbed him in the heart, the nuts, and everything in between, squeezing like a thread wound around a finger too tight.

My Christmas wish is for Josh to fall in love with me.

That was convenient. He'd already fallen in love with Cassidy in about nineteen eighty-nine. He had just been minding his own business, riding his skateboard, when the old lady next door had brought her granddaughter home to live with her. Cassidy's parents had died in a car accident, and when she'd stepped out of Mrs. St. George's ancient Oldsmobile, Josh had taken one look at that sad brown-haired beauty in denim overalls, and he'd fallen off his board and landed in a bush.

She'd been having the same effect on him ever since.

He had the swollen knee and lovesick heart to prove it.

But if Cassidy felt the same way—and from the looks of her note, she did—he couldn't ask for a better Christmas gift.

Cassidy stuck more cookies on her grandmother's silver serving tray and wiped crumbs off her fingers onto her jeans. The snowman smiles looked lopsided again. She loved baking cookies, a tradition her grandmother had passed on to her before she died. But her grandma had always turned out stunning artistic creations that almost looked too pretty to eat. Cassidy labored intensively over the sprinkle jars, trying to make happy faces on the snowmen, but never got the same result.

It should be of little importance that Frosty looked like he needed orthodontic work, but she had wanted tonight to be perfect, for one simple but serious reason.

Cassidy was completely in love with Josh. He was in love with a mystery woman named Kristen. And this could very well be their last Christmas together.

But imperfect baked goods or not, Cassidy didn't want to waste a single minute of the dwindling time she had, so she took the tray and went into the living room. Josh was leaning over the fireplace, filling her feminine and cozy apartment with his blatant masculinity. He was fiddling with her faded stocking, caressing the fur trim on top, and Cassidy almost wished he would just turn and see her, really see her as a woman, one who wanted him.

She wanted with a deep possessive violence that startled her in its intensity. Wanting Josh was not new—wanting him to read the lust plastered all over her face was. But seeing his profile, the windows on either side of the fireplace framing him and casting a white glow from the falling snow over him, she didn't want to give him up.

He turned before she was ready, while she was still gawking like an undersexed pervert, and he cocked his head, studied her, like he'd noticed something different. Cassidy nearly dropped the cookies on the floor and ran. But then he grinned, and she stood rooted to the floor like she'd stepped in superglue.

Josh was so damn cute it wasn't fair. He was tall and worked hard at the gym to avoid sliding back into the lanky boy he'd been as a teenager. The result was that he was drool inspiring, from head to toe, jeans hugging all the right places, forest green sweatshirt not completely hiding a well-defined chest.

Josh moved with confidence, but not arrogance, and he wore an expression of puzzled amusement a lot of times, watching the world through his satirical cartoonist's eyes. Josh embraced life, was quick with a grin and a joke, and was forever doodling on a piece of paper or napkin. He had gained more control over his hair in the last few years, but it still tended to fall in his eyes like a chocolate waterfall.

And given the love story unfolding in his cartoon strip over the last two months, he had fallen for some unknown woman named Kristen. Cassidy wanted to cut her eyes out with nail scissors and pitch them in the recycling bin.

"Do you want a cookie?" she asked, stifling her mutilation thoughts, and smothering visions of spontaneously stripping for him to see what he would do.

Josh nodded, still watching her carefully, his eyes warm and . . . hidden. "Do you even have to ask? I never turn down one of your cookies." He took a step forward and winced, pain twisting his mouth.

"Why are you limping?" He was favoring his left knee, something she hadn't noticed when he'd arrived twenty minutes earlier.

He waved off her question. "I'm not limping. Just a little stiff, that's all." Before she could question him further, he took a pinwheel cookie off her tray and bit it, running his tongue over his lip to catch the stray bits, in a way that had her wishing more than anything she were a crumb.

Something was different. Josh almost seemed as aware of what he was doing with his tongue as she did. He seemed *flirtatious*. "I just love your cookies, Cass."

Or maybe she was seeing what she wanted to see, and which only existed in her very hot and graphic sex dreams. Cassidy took a self-conscious step backward, hitting the corner of the coffee tray. The movement unbalanced the tray, and three varieties of cookies rained down on the beige carpet.

She dropped down to pick them up, unnerved by her own reaction. He was going to notice her tension if she didn't get a grip, and the last thing in the world she wanted was to be the blubbering best friend, embarrassing them both, when he finally told her.

Because she knew that's why he was with her for one last Christmas Eve instead of with Kristen the cartoon character, who had a nonexistent waist, big breasts, and a tousled hairstyle that suggested she'd just tumbled out of bed. A man's bed. Not that Cassidy had noticed or given much thought to that Sunday comic strip slut. And not that anyone couldn't look good when drawn into a cartoon by a love-blind artist.

But Josh was there to tell her he was getting married, she just knew it, and while the words had to be spoken sooner or later, she didn't want to hear them tonight, when her apartment was crowded with presents and Josh, and saturated with rich baking smells.

Her jeans protested when she sank to her knees. In some kind of futile effort to show Josh his colossal mistake in choosing Kristen when Cassidy was right in front of his cute face, she had put on sexy low-rise jeans that emphasized her curves. Meaning they were too darn small. Oxygen seriously depleted, she started throwing cookies on the tray in a pile, hoping to get them all before Josh tried to help.

Too late. His legs bent, and his crotch was suddenly right in direct view as he helped the cookie clean-up. Cassidy swallowed hard. He had a really nice crotch, hard thighs covered by soft denim, and the squat was pulling the fabric tight across a bump that was not his cell phone or a sock.

Cassidy felt light-headed, and it wasn't from her tight jeans. "I've got it, Josh, don't worry about it."

But his fingers kept tossing cookies, occasionally brushing against her hand, until there was only one snowman left, his muddy brown hat cracked from the fall. Josh picked it up, blew on it, and bit the cookie in half, giving her a big smile.

"Good as new," he said.

Which was all fine and dandy until he took the second half of the snowman and placed it in her open mouth. Cassidy almost choked in surprise when the dry sugary cookie hit her tongue. The drool pooling in her cheeks from the crotch shot of Josh was the only thing that saved her from needing the Heimlich.

"What's the difference between snow men and snow women?" he asked her.

She shrugged, chewing hard, stealing a forbidden whiff of Josh's soapy clean scent as he leaned over her.

"Snow balls."

The snort happened before she could stop it, and wet half-chewed cookie bits burst out of her mouth and sprayed the front of Josh's sweatshirt.

And she wondered why he had fallen in love with someone else.

Chapter Two

Josh sat on the couch with Cassidy in a blind panic. He had proof crumpled up in his pocket that Cassidy wanted some kind of action from him, and yet the best he was capable of was telling juvenile snowmen jokes.

It was a wonder he wasn't a twenty-nine-year-old virgin.

Yet he'd never lacked confidence with other women, just Cassidy. Because it mattered. It had always mattered. He'd made it his life's work to make her laugh, both after she'd lost her parents, and then her grandmother five years ago.

Cassidy had always been quiet and solemn, and he had worked hard to put smiles on her face. Now he wanted to put unmitigated lust on her face and peel her out of those jeans that looked like she'd shrunk them.

As a grade school teacher Cassidy was partial to loose skirts and high-neck sweaters, and yet she was sitting next to him wearing jeans that made J Lo look modest, and a plunging top. It was rerouting the vast majority of his blood away from his brain down to his cock, which was now hard enough to cut glass. Just call him Diamond Dick.

Cassidy gave a sweet sigh as Jimmy Stewart tossed his movie child into the air. "How many times do you think we've watched *It's A Wonderful Life?*"

Josh shifted closer to her, smelling the clinging remnants of freshly baked cookies on her. Cassidy's cookies always looked misshapen and slightly demonic with their leering sprinkle smiles, but they usually tasted good. Even if they didn't, he'd still eat them. Hell, he'd swallow raw eggs if she asked him to.

"We watch it every Christmas Eve we've spent together."

"How many has that been?" Cassidy tossed back her shoulder-length brown hair, only to have it slide right back forward again.

"Every year you haven't had a loser boyfriend." Josh picked up Cassidy's legs and stretched them over his thighs. He had meant for it to force her closer to him, but somehow she wound up lying on her back with her feet in his lap.

"Hey! I don't date losers."

Taking what he was given, and just wanting to touch her, Josh started kneading her feet, running his thumbs over the red socks with Christmas trees on them. "What about Alex, who ran up your credit card bill, then left?"

Cassidy's nose wrinkled up. "Okay, so he was a loser. But we're all entitled to one mistake."

"Or Sean, who forgot to mention he was dating half of New York in addition to you."

"So that's only two." Her eyes fluttered shut, and her words were relaxed. "Mmm, that feels good."

Yes, it did, and he had the hard-on to prove it. Josh rubbed her toes, her ankle, then switched to the other foot. "And there was Stan and Mike and Chris and a few others I'm missing. Don't worry, Cass, it's not your fault. You're just too nice, and guys take advantage of you."

Despite all her losses and tough knocks, Cassidy had never gotten hard. If anything, she was the opposite. She cared to a fault and it was part of why he loved her.

"You never take advantage of me."

Her hand was behind her head, propping it up. The already tight top had shifted, showing a sliver of her stomach, and slipping down farther on top so he had a clear view of her breasts threatening to burst from her bra if she hiccupped.

He wanted to take advantage of her. He wanted to just lean over and suck that creamy rounded swell until she whimpered. Then he wanted to nudge around with his lips until the bra gave up trying to contain her and he could suckle her nipple, tasting her over and over.

It was time to tell her, before he felt her up without warning.

"Cass, I'd never take advantage of you. You're a great friend, and I care about you. A lot." Josh started to sweat as he built up to the crescendo, the part where he spilled his guts all over her ivory couch. He could do this, just as soon as his tongue detached from the roof of his mouth.

Cassidy sat up abruptly, eyes wary. "I care about you, too," she offered.

"Right." He rubbed his damp hands on his jeans. "But sometimes friendships change . . . things are different . . . people's lives change."

Where the hell was he going with this? He clamped his mouth shut before he told another testicle joke.

Cassidy jumped off the couch and bounded across the room faster than he would have thought those jeans could allow. "Let's play a board game. We haven't done that in a while."

She rummaged through her bookcase, which was overflowing with romance novels, mysteries, textbooks on the theories of teaching, and board games with nineteen-eighties families on the boxes. Cassidy didn't throw anything away and still had all of her parents' and her grandmother's possessions as well. Some were in storage on Long Island, but a lot were stuffed into her crowded third-floor apartment.

He didn't want to play a board game.

Especially not when she tugged out the one on top, spun around, and gave him a bright smile. "Look, it's Twister. We used to play that all the time in high school. Remember?"

Of course he remembered. After having her various body

parts dangled in his face, he'd usually gone home and locked himself in his bedroom with a clean-up towel.

It wasn't a good idea to play Twister now.

Then he pictured her ass in those jeans bent in front of him.

"Great idea, Cass, let's play Twister. It'll be fun."

Cassidy turned back to the bookcase so Josh wouldn't see her face turning red. Twister? Twister, for goodness sake? What on earth had possessed her to pull *that* box out? Risk would have been better. They could be studious at the table across from each other.

But she'd been desperate to keep him from telling her about Kristen and had pulled the first box out and run with it. Now she wanted to fling it out the window into the snow, especially since Josh was pushing his gym shoes off.

But she could endure snaking herself between Josh's legs if that meant she didn't have to hear him tell her the horrid rotten truth. That he was madly in love with the mystery woman, was getting married, moving to the New Jersey suburbs, and starting a family. All of which would mean there wouldn't be much time left for old friends like Cassidy. Etcetera, etcetera, and next Christmas Eve she would be alone.

Josh moved the coffee table to the hallway while she spread out the Twister mat and checked their spacing. "I won't put it too close to the tree. I don't think a five-foot pine with glass ornaments would feel very good crashing down on our heads."

"What makes you think it would fall?" Josh cracked his knuckles and pretended to stretch and shake his legs out.

Cassidy snickered. "Maybe I'm underestimating your Twister prowess."

"Hey, I'm a pro." Josh flicked the spinner. "Left hand red, baby, here we go."

It all started out innocently enough, each on opposite sides of the mat.

But by the time her CD changer flipped from Christmas

classics to Mariah Carey's *All I Want For Christmas Is You,*
Cassidy felt in kin with the singer. If she had the breath, she'd
sing it to Josh, but all her concentration was taken up maintaining the legs-entwined, arms-splayed position that had to
be thrusting her butt right into Josh's face.

Which was bad enough. Even worse was the realization
that she was aroused. As in hot under the collar, raring to go,
ready or not here she might come. And every time he brushed
his hand or leg or foot or head against her, the problem grew.
Until she was starting to worry about the integrity of her
jeans, given how tight they were.

With a little luck, if he noticed a damp spot, he'd think she
suffered from incontinence. Mortifying, but better than the alternative, which was that she was wet from playing Twister
with him.

"Right foot blue," she managed, wishing she could give the
game up, but frightened that if they did, he'd want to talk
again. Which would be worse than climaxing over a yellow
plastic dot.

Cassidy managed to right herself in a deformed squat. Josh's
arm spread forward, his wrist propped on her breast, mouth
hovering over hers, like Godiva chocolate just out of reach.
Cassidy closed her eyes for a split second. His sweatshirt hood
string brushed over her cheek, his breath tickling her chin.
Josh smelled so incredible, and when he was over her like this,
she could almost imagine what it would feel like to have him
deep inside her body, rocking them both in pleasure.

This was all her fault, for not telling him years ago how she
felt about him. But admitting that she was in love with him
had seemed like the fastest way to lose his friendship, and after
losing her parents, then her grandmother, Cassidy hadn't been
able to bear the thought of losing Josh. So she'd dated men
she'd known would never work out and had lusted after Josh
in private, knowing sooner or later he would get married.

Since they were almost thirty, technically she'd had a pretty
good run at being the most important woman in his life.

But she still wasn't ready to give that up.

"I can't reach the spinner, Cass." Josh's hair fell in his eyes, and he jerked his head to move it, unsuccessfully. He wasn't smiling.

Overwhelmed by her wrenching physical and emotional need for him, Cassidy turned her head and stretched for the spinner. "Right hand green."

Josh lifted away from her, restoring her sanity, and Cassidy went into a gymnastics bridge that she saw her second grade girls do all the time at recess.

Josh groaned.

"Did you pull a muscle?" she asked, hair falling in her face so she couldn't see Josh. The position was murder on the fore-arms, and she couldn't twist to check on him for fear of col-lapsing and breaking her back.

"No," Josh said, wondering if Cassidy realized that there was something really wrong with what they were doing. Grown men and women who were not having sex didn't play Twister together.

He would never play Twister with any of his male friends under any circumstances, and doing so with Cassidy was not helping his rapidly enlarging problem. He wanted to talk to her, explain that he was in love with her.

But he had lost the ability to speak coherently when con-fronted with the sight of Cassidy's inner thighs thrust up into his face. The fabric was molding her, the seam of the jeans nudging in between her soft folds, outlining her sex for him all too clearly.

If he reached out a couple of inches, he could grip her ass in his hands and bury his face right in that hot spot between her wide open legs. He would blow on her, kiss and nip, until she begged him to take her jeans off . . .

"Josh, I'm going to fall!"

He stuck his arm under her back and pulled her up so she could rest on her knees in front of him. But the momentum sent her sprawling into his chest, and they both went down on the mat like a quarterback being sacked.

Only Josh wasn't wearing any padding, and despite the pain from Cassidy's elbow jabbing his gut, the more immediate concern was the gigantic hard-on wedged right between her thighs. Damn, it felt good there, and his hips moved without instruction from him, rising just a little and bumping the denim of her jeans. Josh closed his eyes and silently recited every swear word he knew.

He got to six before he gave up, distracted beyond hope.

Cassidy drew in a sharp breath, but didn't move. Her head lifted, and he felt her warm breasts press deeper into his chest, her thighs molded to his. He was afraid to open his eyes, afraid to see fear or disgust in hers, but Cassidy spoke in what was simple concern.

"Are you okay, Josh? Your eyes are closed."

Sometimes she had the cutest way of stating the obvious. Josh pried his eyes open and studied her watching him, teeth chewing her bottom lip.

While she didn't look ready to tear off her clothes, she didn't look disgusted to be lying on him either.

"Just got the wind knocked out of me."

Warm fingers brushed the hair out of his eyes. Josh was painfully aware that only a couple of layers of clothes were between him and her hot, hot opening. Their heat was mixing together, reacting, until Josh burned and ached and lost all sense of the rational.

He put his hand on her ass.

There wasn't even time to appreciate it before Cassidy pushed on his chest and spiraled away across the carpet like an enthusiastic firefighter demonstration. Stop. Drop. Roll.

Only he was the one with the clothes on fire.

Chapter Three

Cassidy was so embarrassed she knew her face must be blending in with her cherry red shirt. Josh had given her a friendly butt tap, and she had almost revealed all by letting rip with a first-rate orgasmic moan.

"Do you mind if I change my clothes? I think these jeans are too small, they're bugging me." Plead innocence and get them the hell off, that was the plan. Maybe sloppy clothes would keep her arousal level down to a low simmer.

"No, go ahead. I'll pour some wine." He got up off the floor and spread the miniblinds on one of the two floor-to-ceiling windows she had in her living room. "It's snowing again. I'm glad I didn't go to my parents'. It's only a thirty-minute drive, but it's nasty out there."

"I bet they miss you, though." Cassidy always felt guilty that Josh neglected his family to spend time with her, the charity orphan.

"Nah. My sister and the new baby are the star this year. They'll all be cooing over Katie like she's the only five-month-old ever to exist." He smiled over his shoulder. "Go ahead and change, Cass. I'll be right here when you get back."

Cassidy's heart dropped to the floor like her cookies, but this time the carpet didn't break the fall. Tears pooled in her eyes as she moved blindly down the hall to her bedroom. Josh was always there, had always been, and he wouldn't be there anymore. That made her deeply and painfully sad.

After dragging gigantic fleece pajama pants with snowflakes out of her drawer, Cassidy wiggled out of the jeans, almost reaching for the scissors at one point. Removal was difficult, involving a lot of pulling and pushing and swearing. It wouldn't be any loss if she cut them. All the pants had proved was that she was insane since Josh had never even noticed what she was wearing.

The jeans finally gave way without resorting to slicing them off. Cool air swirled over her bare legs as she moved toward the window, embracing the crisp draft. Shivering, she bent over the sill and stared out into the crowded parking lot behind her apartment building. The lamplight beam illuminated fat snowflakes flying furiously, the cars below covered in a white layer of snow.

Tomorrow she needed to face the rest of her life. She needed to accept once and for all that she was alone, that she had no family. Cassidy St. George wasn't the most important person in anyone's life, and she needed to come to terms with that. It wasn't her fault, or anyone else's. It was just the way it was.

Cassidy rested her elbows on the smooth wood windowsill and pressed her nose to the frosty glass. She should put her pj pants on, she should go back to Josh, but she wanted just one more minute to believe in Christmas miracles and the magic of fresh-fallen snow.

"Cass, you okay?" Josh's voice came from her half-open doorway.

Cassidy froze, her bikini panties the only thing covering her backside, stuck in the air as she bent over. Josh had never, ever followed her down to her room before. He didn't even have to pass her bedroom to get to the bathroom, so why had he managed to walk in the one time she was half dressed?

With damp panties.

She stood up slowly, so as not to draw unnecessary attention to her butt. "I was just watching the snow."

The clingy top was no help in preserving her modesty so Cassidy turned and reached for her pj pants. A quick glance showed Josh was not looking at her face, and his eyes were abnormally large, like he was witnessing a six-car pile-up on the highway.

Damn. In fifteen years of friendship she didn't think he'd ever seen her in her underwear. It would probably create one more wedge between them, as if Kristen the cartoon wasn't enough. Cassidy stuck her left leg in the pants, then the other, and quickly covered her red panties with the jingle bell below the waistband.

"Did you just jingle?" Josh asked.

"Maybe. My underwear has a little bell on the front." Cassidy pushed past him into the hall. "Did you get the wine?"

God knew she needed it.

"It's on the coffee table."

He followed closely behind her as Cassidy padded in her socks, tying the drawstring on her pants.

"So a little bell, huh?" Josh was looking puzzled. "I don't think I've ever seen that on underwear before."

"They're Christmas panties," she said, biting her tongue so she didn't ask what kind of underwear Kristen wore. Probably none, since she had no waist to hold them up.

"You learn something new every day," Josh said, and stripped his sweatshirt off over his head.

Cassidy made a gurgling sound. "What are you doing?"

"What?" Josh straightened his white T-shirt on his shoulders, tossing the sweatshirt over the coffee table. "It's hot in here from the oven baking all those cookies."

Trying to smooth away the horror on her face, Cassidy grabbed one of the full glasses of Zinfandel. She tried to cover up her gaffe. "Oh, I didn't think it was hot in here."

"That's why you were hanging out in your underwear then?"

It just got more and more horrifying. This wasn't like a run in her pantyhose. This was like walking out of the restroom with her skirt tucked *into* her pantyhose. She was ruining her last Christmas with Josh by acting like a complete and utter idiot.

Josh was ruining Christmas Eve by acting like an idiot. Clearly Cassidy wasn't interested in discussing her panties with him, but he couldn't seem to drop the subject. Every fantasy he'd ever had about her had been proven accurate.

Cassidy had an ass worth killing over.

When they were teenagers, she had worn those goofy overalls everywhere, and as a woman, she wore loose skirts and shapeless khaki pants. But he'd always known she'd been hiding a hell of a package, and the jeans and panties had proven it.

He'd almost choked on his own drool when he'd walked in on her bent over in tiny red panties.

He hadn't recovered yet.

Even though Cassidy kept skirting the issue, he had to tell her how he felt before he had an accident that could not be written into a PG cartoon.

Maybe she didn't want to talk because she was nervous. This was uncharted territory for them. He could sympathize. Fear had kept him quiet for years.

No more. Josh took the other glass of wine and pointed toward the Christmas tree, a half a dozen gifts underneath it. He hadn't had a chance to shake the ones tagged for him. "So what did you get me?"

She smiled. "Like I'd tell you. You ask me every year on Christmas Eve, and have I ever even hinted to you?"

"No, you cruel wench."

Cassidy laughed. "And they're not even all for you, so don't get your hopes up. One's for your mom, and there's one for your niece."

"What does she need a present for? She's a baby. She can't even give gifts back."

Cassidy set down her wine on the end table, pushing aside

a basket filled with Christmas cards. She fingered a glass snowflake dangling from a tree branch, one of about a hundred ornaments he'd helped her hang on that tree two weeks earlier.

"Don't tell me you didn't get the baby a gift on her very first Christmas, Josh."

He'd gotten the baby eight gifts, but Cassidy didn't need to know that. "Alright, I got her a gift."

"I knew you would. You're really a softie, you know, no matter how much weight you bench press."

A softie wasn't the adjective he was looking for. "What can I say? I'm a sucker for brunettes."

Even in profile, he could see Cassidy's smile. She bent over and adjusted another ornament. "Does Katie even have enough hair yet to tell she's a brunette? When I saw her she only had about three hairs."

"And all three are brown." But his niece wasn't the only brunette he was a sucker for.

Cassidy laughed, tucking her own light brown hair behind her ear. She had hair that fascinated him with the way it slid and moved all about her. It seemed to be a variety of different lengths, but at the same time blended all together in one straight cascade of softness.

He couldn't resist touching it. Sticking his wineglass next to hers, Josh moved in right behind Cassidy and rested his hand on her shoulder, smoothing the closest strands between his thumb and index finger. Her glossy hair was the shade of a rich dark beer, like Guinness on draft, changing when the light shined through it.

"Blondes may have more fun, but brunettes are the kind of women a man can fall in love with. The kind *I* could fall in love with."

She stiffened, her shoulder rigid beneath his light caress. Josh moved in even closer, caging her hips with his thighs. The timing was right. His gut said *now,* and his body ached to own her. Dropping a slow kiss on the top of her head, he smelled her floral shampoo. With a sigh of pleasure, he rested his chin on that soft blanket of hair.

"Cass, have you read my strip lately?"

Josh had to tell Cassidy he loved her out loud, face to face. Or face to back, technically, before he exploded with keeping the emotion inside any longer. Which would really be a mess to clean up.

So he was absolutely going to tell her now.

Then he was going to make love to her, explore all the interesting contours of her gorgeous body, push his cock inside her body, and watch Cassidy's eyes roll back in her head, all because of him.

Her breath caught at his words. "Maybe. I mean, I try and always read it, but sometimes I don't get around to the Sunday paper until Monday, and then there's no time to read the comics. But I'm sure I've read some of them. Why do you ask?"

Josh's heart and a few other parts jumped for joy at her nervous answer. She knew. But she hadn't said anything to him, probably just as frightened as he was of jeopardizing their friendship.

"Because for the last few months, Jack Block has been falling in love, and now it's time for me to tell you that I'm—"

Cassidy turned so fast her head whacked his chin. Josh bit his tongue, but couldn't even swear at the pain before her hand clamped over his mouth.

"Josh, please, don't say it."

"We need to talk about it sooner or later," he said, his words muffled through her cold fingers.

What was she so afraid of? Fear was reflected in her green eyes—eyes that studied him anxiously. He didn't want Cassidy afraid, never that.

Josh put his arms around her and settled her in against his chest. Her hand squeezed harder over his lips.

"Cass, I can't breathe," he mumbled.

"Do you promise not to talk if I let go?"

Ever? He didn't think he could live up to that request. But he wanted to calm her down. "What should I do if I don't talk?"

Cassidy's chest heaved, those soft, enticing breasts rising and falling rapidly, and her round eyes looked a little wild. "Maybe . . . maybe you could kiss me?"

Chapter Four

Oh, hell's bells, now she'd done it.

Cassidy had said stupid things before, but this was the mother-load of stupid things. This was turning out to be her Big Fat Stupid Christmas.

She closed her eyes and waited for Josh to recoil.

Poor Josh didn't even know she was pining for him. He was off enjoying his newfound love, Kristen the cartoon, and had no idea that Cassidy thought of him as anything other than a friend.

He did now, poor guy.

"I think I see where you're coming from."

Yeah. La-la land. "What do you mean?"

"Are we standing under mistletoe or something?"

"No." Though that would have been a brilliant idea if she had thought of it.

"Cass, you've got to let go of my face."

"No." Neither was she ever going to open her eyes again. Not until he left tomorrow morning after unwrapping gifts. It would be tricky to cook breakfast with her eyes closed, but that would be better than the alternative, which was dying of mortification.

Josh's tongue licked her middle finger. Cassidy yelped and

broke her sightless vow. Josh was staring down at her as his
teeth lightly tugged the finger into his moist mouth.

He sucked her.

He pulled the whole length of that finger down into his
mouth, then out again, pausing to nip the tip.

"Oh, God," she said before she could catch herself. Her
knees buckled a little, and Josh's grip on her back tightened.
"What are you doing?"

Josh's head moved back a little until the fleshy pad of her
finger was resting on his bottom lip. "I can't kiss you, Cass, if
you don't free up my mouth."

Her skin was wet where he'd licked it. Her nipples were
pressing painfully against his chest. His thighs were entrapping
her. She dropped her hand down to his T-shirt and couldn't
prevent it from spreading over his pectoral muscle, squeezing
a little.

"Good point."

Josh tilted his head, a little smirk playing over his lips.
"You mean a little friendly peck, barely touching, don't you?"

She shook her head violently. In for a penny, in for a pound.
Which meant she'd gone this far, she might as well be aggressive and get what she really wanted.

"A real kiss? With tongue?"

He was torturing her with that seductive tone, one she
could honestly say she'd never heard from him in the fifteen
years she'd known him.

She liked it, and so did her inner thighs.

Cassidy nodded.

Josh smiled seductively, like he'd known where they were
heading the whole time. "You want to tell me what exactly is
going on here, Cass?"

She swallowed. "No, not really."

He gave a low sexy chuckle. "I'm going to kiss you,
Cassidy, but only because—"

Cassidy squeezed his lips shut, with more force than was

strictly necessary. "No! Shhh, don't say it." She could not stand to hear that it was a goodbye kiss before it even happened.

His eyebrow rose up under his hair. "I don't understand."

Going up on tiptoes to reach him, Cassidy moved her fingers and replaced them with her lips. Josh froze for a microsecond, than he crushed her body up against him and kissed her back.

He opened his mouth.

And Cassidy snuck her tongue in before he could change his mind.

This was not his good friend Cassidy St. George grinding up against him and giving him a hot mouthful of tongue. Cassidy was shy, vulnerable, good with children. Cassidy was generous and sweet and thought of him like a goofy brother.

Cassidy was . . . holy shit, grabbing his *ass*.

Which had to mean he was entitled to do the same.

Josh groaned, breaking the kiss to snag some oxygen, then closed his mouth over hers again and again. Cassidy tasted wonderful, like hot eager sex and sugar, and her tongue was stroking over his with a desperate sort of plea that robbed him of any rational thoughts that might remain in his testosterone-flooded brain.

Wanting to feel the curves that had been teasing him since he'd walked in the door, Josh slid his hands over the swell of her backside and cupped her sweet little ass in his hands.

Damn. It was better than he ever could have imagined, having Cass in his arms kissing the crap out of him. Her bulky pj pants masked the real feel of her, and before he could think or pause or click the stop button, he was wiggling under the waistband.

Cassidy moaned against his lips when his thumbs stroked over the back of her form-fitting panties.

"Oh, yes," she whispered, shooting a heady thrill through him.

She ripped his T-shirt out of his jeans, shocking him with

the voracious look on her face. In a good way, though, he decided as his balls tightened, and his gut clenched as her nails scratched across his bare chest.

"You have the sexiest chest," she said, pushing his shirt up farther. "Just let me look at it."

It got better and better. With Cassidy saying things like that, there was no doubt in Josh's mind where this kiss was leading. He was going to lay her down on the carpet next to the overornamented tree Cass enjoyed so much, and with the tiny white lights glowing on her skin, he was going to unwrap every inch of her.

It meant abandoning his position in her pants, but Josh crossed his arms and dragged off his shirt like she asked, letting it fall to the floor. Cassidy's eyes looked slumberous with desire, her lips wide and ripe, moist and swollen. Her delicate fingers traveled all over his chest, outlining every muscle, swirling around his nipples, even pausing to tangle in the dark cluster of hair.

Her look of awe humbled him, encouraged him, and made the love he had for her burn even brighter.

Josh appreciated that she'd never bothered to change out of the clingy top. It was still plastered to her, and he could see her pert nipples straining forward. He leaned over and sucked one through the cotton of her shirt, drawing it into his mouth like a juicy grape.

Cassidy figured she had the market cornered on moaning when she let out another lengthy blast of approval. She should be embarrassed. She should be worrying about the effect of what they were doing on tomorrow.

She didn't care one measly minute about tomorrow.

But she should be concerned that Josh appeared to be cheating on his girlfriend.

It was that thought that had her giving a pathetically inadequate push at his head. "Josh, is there any reason we shouldn't do this?"

Wow, that sounded firm and moral.

"None that I can think of."

Cassidy bit her lip when he returned to his previous occupation of driving her wild by sucking her nipple. It wasn't like Josh to cheat. He was the kindest, most thoughtful man she knew, and he didn't have a dishonest bone in his body.

Maybe Kristen was really just a cartoon, not a real person. She could only hope.

"So there's not like another person who could be affected by this if we . . . do this, whatever this might wind up being."

He paused, mouth hovering over her now damp shirt. "Are you dating someone, Cass?"

"No!" As if. She hadn't dated since Chris had shown up at her apartment drunk, suggesting she might look good in leather. And she certainly wouldn't be letting Josh kiss her nipple if she was dating someone.

"I'm not either, so I think that means we can do whatever we want." He glanced up at her. "I want to make love to you. I want to touch you all over your body, and I want to stroke inside you until you come in my arms. Can I do that, Cass?"

Yes, please.

Cassidy just about squirmed in anticipation. She'd known Josh wouldn't be the kind to cheat. She'd known Josh all these years and had trusted deep down in her heart that he was the best man she'd ever come across.

If he was in love with a woman named Kristen and hadn't told that woman, well, that still left him free for Cassidy to convince him she was the better choice anyway. And if Kristen really was just a cartoon, then the future had as many possibilities as New York had people.

Starting now.

"Yes, Josh." Cassidy ran her fingers through his unruly hair and wet her lips. "I really want you to make love to me."

Josh's eyes darkened. But he smiled, a wicked, tempting smile. "Good. Then lie down because I'm getting a cramp in my neck from bending over like this."

Cassidy laughed as Josh stood up and rolled his neck back

and forth. "Oh, poor baby. What can I do to make you feel better?"

"Take your shirt off. Then lie down like I asked you to."

A sharp bite of desire slammed into her belly. "Okay."

Cassidy pulled the tight top off, getting annoyed when it stuck on both her head and her arms. She yanked harder and finally dropped it, breathless, hair crinkling with static.

"Now lie down."

She hesitated, fiddling with her bra straps. It wasn't even a sexy bra, damn it. Maybe it would be better to just take it off.

But Josh shook his head. "No, I want to take it off you. Just lie down for me, Cass."

He tossed her faux fur chocolate-colored throw from her couch onto the floor. Spreading the edges out a little, Cassidy settled down on it, shivering at the soft caress of the thick fabric on her bare skin.

"You are beautiful, you know that?"

His expression had softened, a look of something warm and intimate that made her feel very sexy and very hopeful.

"I don't think you've ever told me that before."

"I thought it."

Josh dropped to his knees and winced.

"What's the matter?" Cassidy started to sit back up, but he pushed her down on the throw.

"Nothing, my knee is just a little bruised."

She was about to ask how when he kissed her. This kiss was slower than before, relaxed, open, exploratory. Cassidy caressed his hard back, laughed when he kissed each corner of her mouth.

"The good thing about these pajama pants . . . ," Josh said, "is that they come off really easily."

One tug and the voluminous fleece pants were at her ankles. He gave another jerk and they were gone. Cassidy arched her back, closed her eyes.

Josh groaned. "Holy shit, look at this underwear."

Cassidy almost wanted to laugh. She hadn't bought the red

panties to be sexy. It had been an impulse standing in a boutique at the mall to buy the cotton panties, because she'd thought they would put her in a Christmas mood. She'd thought the little green Christmas tree on the front with a jingle bell for a star was cute, festive.

She was feeling very festive right now.

"I thought they were cute."

Josh's finger flicked over the bell, making it jingle. "Hell, yeah."

Then his finger marched higher and higher until he was at the waistband. He played with it, rolling the panties back just a smidge, making her tight with anticipation. He shot her a hot, naughty smile. "What do you have under the tree for Josh this year?"

As he peeled back the panties and slipped his hand inside to cup her, Cassidy spread her legs. "This year you get something extra special."

"I can see that." Then he dipped his finger between her folds, stroking through the moist heat, and they both groaned. "Oh, Cass, you're really wet."

And it was all his fault.

"Tell me about it," she panted.

Josh felt Cassidy's body close around his finger, and he shuddered. She felt incredible, looked amazing, smelled like the most delectable mix of domesticity and wet and willing woman.

With every stroke, every plunge of his finger into her, every press of his thumb against her clitoris, she gave raw cries of approval while the bell on her panties jingled. He could take the things off, but he didn't want to waste time, not when Cassidy's back was arching, her hips thrusting, her breasts spilling out of the top of her bra. Not when her breath grew stilted, her nails clawed the blanket, her heels dug in for leverage.

When she came, turning her face and muffling her cries in the fur, the bell shook vigorously, and Josh almost came with her. He stroked until she settled down, then wiggled the panties past her thighs and knees.

"I'll never be able to walk into a store with a bell over the door ever again."

She pushed hair out of her eyes. "Why not?"

Josh popped the snap on his jeans. "It will be like a Pavlovian thing, you know. Because every time a bell rings . . . well, let's just say I won't be thinking about angels getting wings."

Her cheeks went pink.

"You're amazingly cute when you blush."

Then he reached for her bra to unwrap the last bits of the best Christmas present he'd ever had.

Chapter Five

That orgasm had been waiting in the wings a good five years, so Cassidy wasn't too surprised he'd barely breathed on her and she'd gone off like a bottle rocket. What she wanted now was a chance to touch him, make him a little crazy with want in return.

Except it was hard to move when he was doing interesting little things with his tongue across her stomach and up to her breasts. It was hard to stay focused on anything other than not going cross-eyed when he rounded the curve of her breast and flicked his tongue across her tight, aching nipple.

"Take your pants off," she managed to say, before she lost the thread of her thought again. Josh was licking in earnest now, and Cassidy squirmed on the throw, the fur on her bare bottom feeling decadent and ticklish.

Josh hesitated at her words. "Before I do that, I need to check and see if I have a condom in my bag. Wait here."

He moved with gratifying speed, his long legs eating up the space between them and her front door. Josh had dropped his overnight bag there, like he always did when he stayed over with her. Only this time, Cassidy didn't think he'd be crashing on the couch.

But she'd never anticipated this would be the outcome of what she'd thought would be their last Christmas Eve together, and she didn't happen to have protection lying around. She hoped Josh's sex life was more promising than hers, and that he had a jumbo box hanging around in his sports bag.

"Yes!" Josh threw his arms up like a referee signaling a touchdown. "We're good to go."

"Then take your pants off and get over here." Cassidy shivered. "I'm getting cold."

"I don't see why," Josh said as he unzipped his pants. "You have socks on."

Oh, God, she did. Cassidy looked down the length of her very much naked body and spotted her red socks. "Oh, boy, that's real sexy. Why didn't you say something?"

"You look cute." Josh bent over her, hair brushing her thigh. "And the socks so clearly match the panties, I didn't want to mess up the outfit." He peeled her socks off, tickling her arch. "But now that the panties are history, I guess these can go, too."

He added, "And so can my own socks while we're at it." He tugged them off, stretching one to nearly a foot in length before it gave at the heel and flew off his foot. "And my jeans."

This was the part she'd been waiting for. Cassidy propped her head up with her hand and watched him. She'd seen those legs in shorts, in swim trunks, and in a wide variety of pants, but never combined with an erection. She knew he wore boxers—she'd seen the waistbands when he'd bent over, and had seen his laundry lying around at various points in their friendship.

But imagining something was never as good as experiencing it. When Josh stepped out of his pants, she coached herself to breathe. "Impressive," she murmured, though she wanted to put her fingers between her lips and give a leering whistle.

"You haven't seen anything yet." He winked, making her laugh.

"Why boxers, Josh? Why not briefs?"

"Because briefs make my legs look skinny." He sent his

boxers to the floor and stood there with his hands on his hips, legs spread.

There wasn't a skinny thing about him. Everything was thick and well-muscled. She took in his penis. Yep. Everything.

"That's ridiculous. You're not a teenager anymore. You're totally hot, Josh."

Cassidy was amused by the discomfort on his face. He almost looked like he was blushing, but she couldn't tell with only the Christmas tree lights to go by. She was going to tease him, when he bent to lie next to her and she caught sight of his knee.

"What happened?" Running her fingers over the swollen kneecap, Cassidy felt him flinch. The skin was mottled and bruised deep purple just above the knee.

"Something fell on me. No big deal." He wasn't looking at her as he rolled on the condom.

Cassidy put her hand on her forehead, chagrined. "And here I had you playing Twister! Why didn't you say something?" Which was a stupid question, she realized immediately. Josh could be bleeding out his eyes and wouldn't admit it.

He shook his head, scoffing as he looked up and met her gaze, protection in place. "Are you crazy?"

His body lowered down over hers, his hot skin colliding with her from shoulder to toes, hard muscle covering her, strong fingers digging into her hair. His mouth hovered over hers. "And miss the chance to have you go into a bridge in tight jeans right in front of my face?"

His warmth seeped into her, that full erection pressed against her, and Cassidy instinctively tried to widen her thighs to accommodate him. His weight held her still. "So you did notice my tight jeans?"

"I notice everything about you. Everything." Josh pulled his hips back a little, hands on either side of her head.

"I love you, Cassidy St. George."

His words were so unexpected Cassidy actually forgot to

moan when he nudged forward again, pressing a little deeper this time. A face that she knew as well as her own stared down at her, all hard lines, rough skin, and serious deep brown eyes. She had no idea what the morning would bring, but for that moment, as he poised over her, and love was on his lips, he was hers.

"Oh, Josh." Cassidy traced the smooth underside of his mouth, his jaw.

"I wanted you to know that I love you before I do this."

Without warning he was deep inside her, stretching her, filling a very real need in both her body and her heart. A shudder wracked her. Goose bumps rose on damp flesh.

Their bodies pulsed and throbbed together, fitted so intimately that Cassidy arched up, snaking her hands around that muscled back, to hold him there, with her, against her. Forever.

Some of his heavy weight lifted. Josh's voice was rough and urgent, but still controlled. "Just a minute, sweetheart." Heavy lidded, he watched her carefully as he pulled all the way out of her, leaving her wiggling and unsatisfied and bereft.

She hadn't been that let down since *90210* had been canceled. "Josh! Where are you going?" Cassidy half sat up and mustered her most evil glare.

Didn't he know it was dangerous to tease a woman like that? Brimming with anguished frustration, it was not mollifying to hear him chuckle like this was a really clever move on his part.

"I just want you to spread your legs, that's all." A callused thumb dragged across her thigh. "I wasn't deep enough inside you for my taste."

A jolt of desire stabbed through her lower half, and since her shaky arms wouldn't hold her up anymore, she collapsed back on the throw. If he wanted to play, she supposed she could humor him. "How deep do you want to be?"

"So deep that I make it all the way to your heart, and once I'm there, nothing you do can kick me out. So deep that you never want another man again."

Hope mixed with love, which mixed with lust, and made Cassidy's mouth dry as dust. "You want me to be celibate after tonight?"

"No. I want you to fall as deep in love with me as I am with you. I want you to spread your legs for me again and again, whenever the urge strikes you or me."

Under that friendly exterior, Josh had a sexy, seductive streak longer than a strand of Christmas lights. And he was suggesting everything she had ever wanted.

"In case you haven't noticed, Joshua Black, I've been in love with you for at least a decade." She stroked her hand over his swollen penis, closing a fist over the head, enjoying his muttered curse. "Now I'm going to spread my legs, and you can go as deep as you want, as often as you'd like."

Guiding him to her, Cassidy smiled at Josh in pure joy. "I really, hopelessly love you."

"Oh, Cass." Josh covered her mouth in a hot kiss, while he slowly, wonderfully, sank back inside her.

There was no pausing, no teasing this time. He just moved in and out with a slow and steady, full and complete rhythm that had her mindlessly reaching for him, with him, climbing up a spiral of pleasure that dampened her skin and tingled her mouth.

Their breathing blended together, their hearts beat against each other, and Josh rested his forehead on hers, the pressure sweaty and sweet and rough. Cassidy felt the orgasm rip through her, and she didn't hold back, just clamped her legs around Josh's thighs and let it take her.

When Cassidy's body stiffened, her breath sucking in on an elegant pause, then flowing past his ear in a blissful moan, Josh knew that nothing could make him give up Cassidy now.

She was his, totally and completely, body, mind, and heart, and he was going to love her and cherish her for the rest of his life.

He whispered in her ear, "I love you," then let his body join hers in pounding ecstasy.

Chapter Six

Cassidy lay wrapped up in faux fur and Josh, as he drank from one of the forgotten wineglasses he'd retrieved. Exhausted and satisfied, she was lying on her back, but Josh was half up, leaning over her, his foot and leg entwined with hers.

"I like your tree, Cass. It's just as traditional and beautiful as you are."

"I like tradition," she whispered, happiness spreading through her veins like an addictive drug.

A drop of wine hit her chest, startling her, and ran between her breasts. The quick glance up revealed it wasn't an accident. Josh's finger was still dangling, a red droplet hovering on the tip.

"Sorry. Let me clean that up for you."

Cassidy had thought after an hour and three orgasms, she wouldn't have the ambition to get aroused, but when Josh's tongue followed the sticky red stream from her neck, down between her breasts, making a lengthy detour by her nipple, she acknowledged she was wrong.

But while she could get aroused, she truly didn't have the muscle endurance to actually do anything about it. "Josh," she moaned with deep, profound regret, "I can't. I'm too tired."

A steady stream of kisses rained over the swell of her

breast, her shoulder, her neck. "Don't worry, I'm just playing. I love the way you taste."

She loved the way he felt, caressing her, his long, hard limbs wrapped around her protectively. She loved the musky male smell of him and the way he couldn't keep his hair out of his eyes. Cassidy sighed with a blissful, bone-deep contentment she wasn't sure she had known since her parents had died.

"Do you really love me, Cass? As more than a friend or a surrogate brother?"

Josh sounded so unsure, so amazed, Cassidy laughed. "I most certainly do not think of you as a brother." She nudged her slightly sore inner thighs against his half-hard penis. "And way more than a friend." She kissed his chin. "I love you as a man, and have since, oh, about the first day I met you."

"I fell off my skateboard," he said ruefully, still pissed by that embarrassing truth.

"I remember. I thought it was cute, and it was the first thing that pulled a laugh out of me after my parents died."

Great, he was laughable. Cute and hilarious, very flattering. "Nice first impression, apparently, if you still remember fifteen years later."

"It was." Cassidy twisted to meet his gaze. "I realized right away what a wonderful guy you were. You knew I was upset, hurting, and you used to do all kinds of crazy things to make me laugh. It was sweet."

So she'd thought he tumbled into the bush like an ass on purpose? Cool. Josh was astounded at how perfect everything was turning out.

"I think I started to fall in love with you right away, that first day, at fourteen years old."

"Then why haven't we done anything about it before now?"

"I was busy dating losers, and you were busy dating blondes like Kristen." An edge came into her voice.

Josh lay back down and went to pull Cassidy farther into his arms. She resisted a little, and he was puzzled. "Who's Kristen?"

"The woman in your cartoon strip! The woman you've been falling in love with, or so I thought." Cassidy glared at him. "Tell me who she is so I can have her killed."

It honestly took him a full thirty seconds to figure out what she was trying to tell him. Then he groaned. So much for his subtle and witty courtship. "You thought I was dating someone named Kristen? Falling in love with her?"

"Yes. Weren't you? Please tell me she isn't real, that it was just a marketing ploy to entertain your readers."

Putting his nuts on the line had not been a marketing gimmick. "Not even close. Kristen is you, Cassidy." He kissed the tip of her little button nose.

Cassidy blinked. "Come again?"

"Kristen is you. I was trying to finally tell you how I feel about you." It had seemed so neon-light-in-a-dark-room obvious to him that he almost doubted her. "You really didn't think it was you?"

"No! How was I supposed to know? Kristen doesn't sound anything like Cassidy."

"Why does that matter?"

"Because your name is Josh Black and your cartoon character is Jack Block, so if you were going to write me into your cartoon it would make sense if you named me Cody, maybe, but not Kristen."

"I thought Cody was a boy's name."

Cassidy thumped him in the chest. "Melody, then, because it ends in the 'e' sound, or Chastity. But Kristen is not even remotely similar. Totally out of the ballpark, Josh."

"Okay." He still didn't get it, but he was smart enough to keep his jaw shut.

"And you made her blond. I'm not blond." An indignant finger pointed at her hair.

That he had to protest. "I made her hair amber, just like yours."

The response to that was an eye roll. "And don't even get me started on those breasts, they look like water balloons."

Josh couldn't help but glide his hand over and cup Cassidy's full, rounded breast. "It's a cartoon, Cass. I exaggerate reality to make it more interesting and amusing." Not that Cassidy was lacking volume, which she had to have noticed when bra shopping.

"I've always hated that you draw Jack Block so skinny he's almost a stick figure. That's not what you look like." Now Cassidy's fingers were wandering, too, playing with the hairs on his thighs. "But you made Kristen sexy, so I had no idea you were talking about me."

She still sounded indignant, so Josh didn't let loose the laugh that was threatening. "I'm sorry, Cass. I was afraid to tell you how I felt, so I was trying to be clever and romantic, hoping for some kind of signal from you in return that you wouldn't mind a change in our relationship. I never dreamed that you thought I was falling for someone else."

"Well . . . the end result is all that matters." Her eyes were suspiciously moist. "But I thought I was losing you. I couldn't bear that."

Her soft body gave against his as he pulled her to him, tight, fierce. "You've got me as long as you want me."

The question hovered there between them, shining like that star on top of her tree. All he needed to do was ask. Brushing a tender kiss across her open lips, he eased back. "Let me show you something."

Injured knee creaking, he pushed himself up and approached her fireplace and that damn reindeer with caution. "I put something in your stocking when you were getting the cookies." It occurred to him now how completely sideswiped Cassidy would have been by his little drawing, since she had thought Kristen was another woman. Thank God he'd found her note, and the courage to open his trap and tell her he loved her before Christmas morning.

"Just keep in mind that you are Kristen."

He handed her the piece of paper, then dropped to one knee, aware this was slightly ridiculous given that he was naked, but also aware that he spent too much time hiding behind his cartoon persona.

Time to put it all out there as Josh Black.

Cassidy's eyes stung with tears, and she blinked fast and violently to focus on the drawing Josh had given her. Hell's bells, Jack Block was on his knees proposing to Kristen, with a fireplace and a Christmas tree that looked a heck of a lot like hers in the background. It even had her grandmother's glass ornaments hung on it, little lines winking around each one to show the light reflecting.

Kristen had improved in this strip, or maybe Cassidy was just seeing her through new eyes. She was also wearing a long floral skirt and turtleneck sweater that matched in color and style about a half dozen outfits hanging in Cassidy's own closet.

Kristen's eyes were perfectly round, looking innocent and unaware of the power she wielded. Poor Jack had beads of sweat trickling down his face and flying off the sides, and his hands and legs were drawn with squiggly lines to indicate they were wobbling. In the air above his head he chanted, *Please, please, please, toss the dog a bone and say something!*

Cassidy swallowed hard, glancing up as Josh dropped to one knee in front of her. "Oh, Josh. Damn, I'm going to cry."

Buff and naked, he knelt, back straight, tenderness in his touch when he lifted her hand into his. "Cassidy, I love you with all my heart. I want to build traditions and a family with you. I would be truly honored if you would be my wife."

Sucking in a shaky breath, Cassidy clamped down on the urge to sob like a bottleless baby and nodded. "Yes, Josh, I will marry you."

Then Cassidy launched herself against him so hard he lost his balance and went down on the carpet. Which wasn't a bad thing since he had warm and naked woman draped all over him. And after pelting him with kisses, she was licking along his pectoral muscle, tracing an interesting pattern that seemed to be leading her rapidly south.

"I'm so glad you wrote that note," he said, while he collapsed back and mentally begged her to keep going until her mouth landed on his cock.

"What note?"

She was down to his abs now, and man, oh man, Cassidy knew how to use that tongue. "The note I found in your stocking."

Damn it, she stopped. Just stopped, hovering right over him. "I didn't write any note."

"Sure you did. It said you're in love with me." *Now forget the damn note and get back to work.*

"Where is it?" Her voice warbled, startling his eyes open.

"In the pocket of my jeans."

Cassidy crawled across the floor, nearly causing him blindness. She had no idea the power of her wiggling backside. He moved toward her, thinking to keep her just like that, on all fours.

But great big noisy tears burst out of Cassidy, scaring the crap out of him and sending him into a rapid knee crawl to get to her. "What's the matter?"

"Oh, Josh." She turned and fell into his arms. "I didn't just write this note. I wrote this when I was fourteen and put it in my stocking. I was so lonely that year and you were so sweet that I had the worst crush on you. You took me sled riding, remember?"

He remembered. He remembered her pink cheeks and the solemn darkness in her green eyes. He remembered her reticence, her shrugs and shyness, her unfashionable orange-and-purple-striped scarf, and the deep breaths she'd taken as she had leaned against him on the sled, closing her eyes.

"I remember, babe. I told you, I noticed everything about you, and I remember everything about you."

"I guess I forgot it was in my stocking." She quieted down, sighing on his chest, the rush of air from her nose tickling his skin.

"I'm glad you forgot about it. It spurred me into action.

Though I have to tell you that your stocking holder attacked me."

"What?"

"That damn reindeer is dangerous. It jumped off the mantel and smashed me in the knee. It practically wrestled me to the ground."

Cassidy gave an incredulous laugh. "Is that how you got that bruise on your knee?"

"Yes. See what I'll suffer in the name of love?"

"You poor baby." Now it was Cassidy who dropped to her knees. "Let me kiss it and make it better."

A feather-light touch landed on his skin.

"Thanks, it feels better."

But Cassidy hadn't pulled back. She was making her way north this time, and her searing wet mouth closed over his aching flesh.

"That feels even better."

That throaty chuckle she gave as she took him deeper had him digging into her shoulders. Oh, yeah, she knew how to make him crazy.

"You know how we talked about starting traditions, Cass? I'm thinking we should make what you're doing right now our Christmas Eve one."

Shiny lips pulled back, her cheeks flushed. "Great idea. Just don't write it into your cartoon."

Josh laughed. "I won't." He finger combed her satin-smooth hair.

Cassidy's tongue swirled over the tip of his erection, before she pulled him back deep inside her moist cheeks, in and out. Josh could picture the cartoon square—Jack Block twitching, his brain whipped up like scrambled eggs, incoherent babblings spilling out of his mouth.

"Cass, I'm really close . . ." The suck and pull of her lips and tongue had him on the ragged edge, and he wanted to pull back but didn't have the willpower.

Cassidy gripped his thighs and kept stroking, giving him

permission to keep going, and he rode the orgasm hard, moving his hips in sync with her.

Shuddering at the power, the pleasure, Josh collapsed down on the carpet, pulling Cass with him. Through the thin slats of the miniblinds, he could see the snow continued to fall, the night bright and luminous. Surprised he could even form words again after that out-of-body experience, he spoke. "I should call Santa on his cell phone and tell him to skip your apartment this year. I have everything I ever wanted right here."

"So do I."

Holding her tight against him, her skin dewy and soft, her hair covering his shoulder, Josh sighed. "You've made me happy, Cass."

"We make each other happy," she said, pressing her hand to his heart to feel the steady rhythm. "We always have, you know."

UNDERCOVER CLAUS

MaryJanice Davidson

For my parents and my in-laws, who went out of their way to make every Christmas fabulous.

"A lovely thing about Christmas is that it's compulsory, like a thunderstorm, and we all go through it together."
—Garrison Keillor

Chapter One

Corinne Bullwinkle rang her bell, and trolled for snatchers. Snow spat down from the sky, and it was, by her estimation, about a hundred degrees below zero. Just another morning on the corner of Seventh and Washington. Yippee freakin' skippee.

When her lieutenant told her about the job, it didn't sound so bad. With a hot cup of coffee in her hands and the smell of wet wool in her nose, with the radiator gurgling heat in the corner and her sergeant trying to get the new guy to bet about her tongue, it didn't sound bad at all.

Now, it was an even race: who would she strangle given the chance? Lieutenant Kruchev, or the purse snatcher?

"Merry Christmas," a passerby said, tucking a dollar into her bucket.

Aw, shut the hell up.

"Merry Christmas," she burbled back.

Actually, this bah-humbug stuff wasn't like her at all. She loved this time of year. Correction: when she was warm. People were actually *nice* to each other, and major crime was down across the board.

The snatcher, however, seemed intent on ruining everyone's holidays. Nobody had run across a serial purse snatcher before: he actually had a type. Well-dressed women in their forties, beautifully groomed, carrying nice bags. There had been over thirty complaints, which meant he'd probably stolen about a hundred purses. In a month!

Thus, she was out here freezing her ass off. And what would you bet Kruchev was sitting in his toasty office, laughing his head off at the thought of her fingers freezing to her bell.

She was so busy feeling sorry for herself she almost missed the teens scoping her bucket. And then, in a cascade of events worthy of a Michael Creichton novel, everything went haywire.

A middle-aged mom with two small blond kids marched up. "Put the quarters in Santa's bucket," the mom ordered, determined to Show Her Kids How To Do The Right Thing During The Holidays.

Corinne rang her bell. Ding DING ding DING ding DING ding DING . . .

The tall, dark-haired man with the briefcase glanced at her, then looked away, then glanced back. She'd seen him come by this way every morning. He always looked, and never spoke.

Ding DING ding DING ding DING . . .

The owner of the Spaghetti Factory passed her on the left—also a daily occurrence—and said, "Morning, sunshine—come in later for a hot lunch, willya?"

" 'Kay," she replied, watching the street. Ding DING ding DING ding DING . . .

The teens made their move, one ready to flank, one ready to snatch and grab.

The man with the briefcase slipped and clutched at her. It was pure instinct—he didn't want to go down—and unfortunately her reaction was instinctual as well: she clocked him with her bell.

DING ding DING ding BRONK!

"Ow!" the man with the briefcase said, just before he went down. And he pulled her right down with him, so they were sprawled side-by-side on the snowy walk. Her bucket went flying, and the crappy, fifty-cent lock broke. Change and dollar bills spilled into the snow.

"Santa!" the two kids cried in unison, then leapt on the man and began pummeling him with tiny fists. "Stop it! Leave Santa alone!"

At the sight of such unimaginable violence and chaos, the would-be bucket-stealing teens freaked out and vacated.

"Jenny! Sara!" The mom tried to pry her offspring off the tall dark-haired man with the briefcase, who was fending them off with his elbows. "Quit that!"

"Goddammit," Corinne cursed, then remembered there were children in the vicinity. "Ho, ho, ho."

"That hurt like bloody hell," the man complained, rubbing his forehead, which was turning red. He'd have a gorgeous bruise.

"Aw, shut up. And help me up."

With a groan, he climbed to his feet. He extended a hand, which she grabbed and used to pull herself up. The mom had successfully pulled her kids off and was now comforting them.

"See? Santa's okay, Santa's just fine, it's okay, you guys, don't cry."

"Ho, ho, ho," Corinne said sourly, scanning for the teens—long gone, of course. Not that she could charge them with anything. Intent to be jerkoffs? But still. Would have been nice to know where they were.

"I say, I'm terribly sorry," dark-haired guy with briefcase said. "I didn't mean to pull you down."

"The important thing is, you held on to your briefcase," Corinne observed, straightening her beard. "What a relief for us all."

"Hey!" One of the kids—Jenny? Sara?—pointed. "You're a girl!" She stamped her small foot. "Santa's not a girl!"

"I'm just helping him out this week," she explained. "He's so busy this time of year. With toys, and, um, placating the elf unions. You know."

Briefcase coughed into his gloved hand as the mom glared, then yanked her kids away.

Corinne bent and righted her bucket, saw a few dimes rattling around inside, then sighed and started groping in the snow for the spilled change.

After a moment, she noticed Briefcase was down on his knees, helping.

"You don't have to do that," she said nervously. He was gorgeous, to be sure, and worse, she was a sucker for an English accent. Why else would she have stuck with "Buffy the Vampire Slayer" for more than two years? Spike and Giles, yum. "Seriously, I got it. You don't have to."

"I think so," he said. "You wouldn't have fallen if I hadn't tried to break my own fall. I'm terribly sorry."

"That's okay," she said. "Talk more."

"Really, I feel bad." Snowflakes were spinning down from the sky and landing in his dark hair, on his dark greatcoat, and some even caught in his long, long eyelashes. God! What eyelashes. Men had all the luck. "Are you finished here soon? May I take you out for a hot drink?"

"Sorry, blue eyes," she said. "My shift just started."

"It's Grant, actually. Grant Daniels."

"Okey-dokey," she replied.

"And you're Kris Kringle, I take it?"

"Sure I am." She grinned, and he smiled back. Sigh. Great smile, naturally. He was probably married to some frigid cow in the London suburbs and had a bunch of blue-eyed, dark-haired spoiled kids on the other side of the ocean.

They both stood, painfully. Corinne flexed her knees a bit to make sure they weren't cracking in the cold. "Well, I apologize again," he said, making "again" rhyme with "brain." Oofta. English accents! "It looks like we probably got it all, don't you think?"

She looked around at the messy sidewalk, the snow everywhere, pedestrians streaming by. They probably hadn't gotten it all, as a matter of fact, but it was the thought that counted.

Briefcase was pulling out his wallet, digging, and handing her three—four!—twenties. "I do hope this makes up for anything that might have—ah—walked off on its own," he said with another smile.

"Oh—really—you don't—I mean, I'm not—I mean—"

He waved her off and stuffed the twenties into her bucket. "See you tomorrow, then?"

"Yeah, okay."

He touched his first two fingers to the edge of his left eyebrow, a kind of salute which actually made her weak in the knees, kind of like his fingers were somewhere else, and walked past her, swinging his briefcase and whistling.

"Yeah, okay," she muttered. *Oh, very nice! Soooo sophisticated. You dumbass!* "Yeah, okay? Yeah . . . okay!" *Argh.*

She swung her bell so hard, the racket actually scared people away from her bucket.

Chapter Two

"You got over a hundred bucks yesterday?" her buddy, Barb Ristau, asked her. They were both descending the steps of the precinct into the street. Barb was going to try to buy drugs again—bitch, she never shared, even when she did score—and Corinne was back on bell duty. "Seriously? Jeez, imagine if you were doing it for real."

"What can I say?" she said. "It's the season of giving."

"My ass," Barb observed. "Did you keep any of it?"

"For heaven's sake, use your head. Your tiny little head. I dumped it all in a real Salvation Army bucket."

"Shame," Barb said. She was dressed like a well-to-do college student in wool tights, a gorgeous A-line black skirt, and a fuzzy pink sweater. Her chocolate brown hair was pulled back into a headband, and her freshly scrubbed face was free of makeup.

Barb had had a hard time on the streets in uniform—the bad guys never took her seriously—until they pulled her inside and had her try to buy drugs. Now she was the top narc in the state.

It was the face, Corinne decided, studying her friend. That freckly, fresh, pleasantly cute face. Even her lips were naturally pastel pink!

"Well, I'd trade with you in a minute," Barb grumbled, plucking at her tights. "These things itch."

"Don't even tell me. You're in a nice warm dorm room or bar trying to buy drugs and drowning your sorrows over hot coffee. Try shaking your belly like a bowl full of jelly all damn day. Outside! Fucking bell gives me a headache."

"I don't think Santa should say fucking," Barb said soberly, then cracked up and wandered off.

"Yeah, well, fuck you!" Corinne called after her, and got the one-finger salute in return.

She was at her spot again in no time, and to her amazement, Briefcase was waiting for her!

"Good morning, then," he said, and held out a cup of coffee to her.

"You're married, aren't you?" she said by way of greeting. "It's okay, I don't mind. But I think you should tell me, you know, up front. I mean, I have rules. A few rules. Okay, one rule."

He blinked at her, then pulled off his left glove and showed her his hand. "No. Not married."

"Oh. Then what are you doing here?"

He blinked again. Nervous tic? "Well, I felt badly about knocking you down, and you looked cold yesterday, so I thought I'd bring you something hot—"

Oh, you have, big boy!

Stop that, she admonished herself.

"—and apologize again."

"Oh. Well, thanks. A-GAIN." She smiled at her own attempt at his accent. "But don't worry. Don't you have to be somewhere?"

"Actually, yes. But I'm afraid to go."

"Oh, yeah? You sure you're not married?"

"I'm quite certain I don't have a misplaced spouse somewhere," he said dryly. "Oh . . . before I forget . . . I'll start your day off." He tucked another twenty into her bucket.

"Thanks." She started ringing her bell, and immediately, the headache sank into her temples. "Ohhhhh . . . well, you got better things to do than hang out here, freezing your ass off, right?"

"You'd think," he said, and smiled at her.

"I'm confused," she admitted, "because we've both agreed you've got other stuff to do, and yet, I can't help but notice you're still here."

"It's a long story," he said. "Tell you over tea?"

"How about lunch?" She glanced at her watch. "I get a break in three hours." Courtesy of Lynn Carlson, the poor bitch. She *hated* the cold. Not that anybody really enjoyed it, but Lynn had, like, a thing about it. She spent every evening after shift immersed in her bathtub. The next morning her skin was still pink from the hot water. Sad. "We could get something up the street." She pointed with her bell at The Old Spaghetti Factory. "If, y'know, you want to."

"Delighted." He gave her that odd two-fingered salute again, then put his glove back on. "I'll see you then."

"Yeah, okay." Well, lunch it was. And if he thought oozing on the charm and hitting her between the thighs with that accent was gonna get him somewhere . . .

. . . he was right.

Chapter Three

"So, Cool Brit Guy," she said, looking at the menu. Noodles, noodles, and for a change, noodles. "What brings you to balmy Minneapolis?"

"It's Grant," he reminded her, like she hadn't memorized it. "And it's the season, actually, that brings me here."

"Uh huh." She pulled off her beard and moustache, took off her Santa hat, and shook her head. "Sounds mysterious. Hot chocolate," she told the waitress, "and keep it coming." She looked at Grant, who was staring. "What?"

"My God."

"What? Did I miss some fake hair? What?" She covertly felt for stray moustache hairs.

"You're—you're really quite lovely. I knew you had big dark eyes, but I couldn't see your hair, or really much of your face—"

"Yeah, well, surprise. My mom was from China, and my dad was from the Bronx. They live in Missouri now."

"Why in the world are you working for charity? You could be a model anywhere in the world."

She rolled her eyes. "Right. Because standing and posing for fourteen hours a day is soooo interesting." *Also, I'm a cop. But never you mind.*

"Sorry. Of course, you're right."

"Ah. I never get tired of hearing that. Hi," she said to the waitress. "I'll have a plate of spaghetti, extra meatballs, extra sauce."

"That sounds delicious," Grant said. "I'll have the same."

"Two stomach staples," the waitress said, scribbling, "coming up."

"Errr . . . what?"

"Never mind," Corinne told him as the waitress hurried away. "So, you were telling me why you were afraid to go to work."

"Actually, I wasn't. You're very persistent, do you know?"

"It's been mentioned from time to time," she admitted. "So: spill."

"Well." He sighed. "Friday is Christmas, as you know."

"So my calendar says."

"And I'm the head of a company that makes mantelpieces."

"You sell chatchkas," she said. "Got it."

"Well . . . as you can imagine . . . this being the season and whatnot . . ."

"You're busier than shit."

"Quite. So in order to keep up with demand, my staff has to work long hours. And, naturally—"

"They resent the bejeezus out of it. And you."

"Right."

"So?"

"Well . . . my vice president's name is Bob."

"Oh. Oh!" She giggled. "Don't even tell me. Don't *even* tell me! He's got a son—"

"Timothy."

"Tiny Tim!" she crowed. "And you're cracking the whip over everyone at—"

"A subsidiary of Kratchet Enterprises." As she snickered, he added, "Only to make our quotas. If we don't, the parent company is prepared to make massive layoffs. I find I'm—"

"Scrooge!" she finished, and went into gales of laughter.

"I had hoped," he said stiffly, while she snorted into her napkin, "for some feminine sympathy."

"Sorry, Ebenezer, guess the moment sort of got away with me."

"I'm a damned cliché," he snapped, showing the first bit of temper she'd seen.

"Boo hoo. You're telling this to someone named Bullwinkle."

He blinked again. "Truly?"

"And my boss is Russian."

The corner of his mouth twitched. "Oh, dear."

"So pardon me if I don't cry you a river."

"Oh, I don't expect a river," he assured her. "But it's nice to discuss my problem with someone."

"I bet."

"Does your boss call you Moose?"

"Let's not go there. So, what's your plan?"

He stared at her. "Plan?"

"Yeah, what are you going to do about being a Christmas cliché?"

"Ah . . . make our quotas."

"Oh. So, *no* plan."

"I'm only here for two more weeks anyway," he explained. "Then I must return to London."

"Oh." Annoyingly, this hurt her. Right in the midsection— and she hadn't even eaten her spaghetti yet. "So, you're, like, slumming here?"

He looked puzzled. "I was sent here to fix the production problem."

"And then you're out of here."

"Yes."

"Well," she said with a gaiety she didn't feel, "lots of luck with that!"

"Errr . . . thank you. But I would like to see you again. Before I go."

"I'm pretty busy," she hedged. He was yummy, no doubt,

and she was single, *sadly* no doubt, but there was no way. *No* way she was going to waste her time on somebody who wanted a nine- or ten-night stand, then hightailed it back to Jolly Old England.

She was disappointed, which made her mad, which embarrassed her, which made her madder.

"—time for a proper dinner?"

"Huh?"

"I said, surely you've time for a proper dinner."

"Like I said," she said shortly as the waitress brought steaming piles of pasta, "I'm pretty busy."

"Working your corner."

"What's *that* supposed to mean?"

"Nothing," he muttered, and fell to his lunch. She gobbled hers down in record time, ignored his occasional lame question, finally tossed down a twenty over his protests, grabbed her hat and beard, and bolted.

Chapter Four

"You're incredibly dumb," Barb pointed out. "Not just a little bit dumb. Like, 'let's do experiments on her' dumb."

"Oh, go home and soak in your tub," she snapped.

"That's Lynn, not me. I just drink myself into oblivion. Tough to feel the cold when you're drunk off your ass." She raised a finger at Ted, who nodded back and, after a minute, set another cosmopolitan in front of her. They were at their favorite bar, which was to say, the only one that believed Barb's I.D. was real. "Ahhh. Sweet nectar of life."

"Cosmos," Corinne sneered. "That is *so* 2002."

"Hey, I was drinking these way before those sluts on HBO made them cool. So, what's the trouble? Cool Brit Guy seemed to like you. He didn't run screaming when you took off your facial hair. A first, I might add."

"No," she said gloomily, poking at the ice in her Coke. "He said I was quite lovely."

"Oooh, in that velvety voice of his, I bet. And in return, you sulked and then ran off. My, it's a pure miracle that you're single, a sweetheart like you." Barb took a gulp of her drink. "None of us at the shop can figure it out."

"Shut up. And the worst part of it is—"

"You don't even know why you did it." Barb yawned. "Thus, my comment on your mental faculties."

"I mean, what kinds of guys do we meet on the job, any-way?"

"Cops, drunks, drug dealers, wife beaters, thieves, killers, prostitutes, crooked politicians, and worst of all, straight politicians."

"Exactly. And it never works out when I date a cop. Or a drug dealer. Don't even get me started on the crooked politicians. Jesus, I haven't had a date in . . ." She started counting on her fingers.

"Yeah, but you said yourself, Cool Brit Guy isn't here for long. So he probably just wants to get into your pants."

"Prob'ly."

"So what's wrong with that?" Barb smoothed a wrinkle in her college girl skirt. "You get laid, there's a smile on your otherwise dour face, and you can shake it on the corner with a little more enthusiasm until you catch the snatcher. We all win."

"The thing is," Corinne said almost apologetically, "I'm not that kind of girl."

Barb made a rude noise and finished her cosmo.

"Anymore," Corinne clarified.

"One bad experience . . ."

"Try twelve. One-night stands suck."

"So I hear," Barb leered.

"Seriously. I'm not a kid anymore, Barb," she explained patiently. *The party girl might have trouble getting this,* she knew. There was also the five-year age difference. "I don't want to be on the streets when I'm forty, and I don't want a desk job, either. I want—"

"The kids and the hubby and the picket fence?"

"I'll settle for a boyfriend and a dog and a condo in Woodbury."

"Hmm." Barb picked up Corinne's Coke and drained it. "Then I guess you were right not to get sweaty with Cool Brit Guy."

"Exactly," Corinne said miserably, trying to forget about long lashes and broad shoulders and the smell of wool and snow and aftershave.

"Dumbass," Barb said kindly.

Chapter Five

Entirely against his will, Grant found himself at the ATM, getting twenties for Corinne's bucket.

Bloody ridiculous, was what it was. She'd made it clear she wanted nothing to do with him. Which was just fine. Yes, indeed. He certainly had no urge to get involved with anyone right now. What did he want with a Yank who had a dazzling smile and fathomless tip-tilted brown eyes and a glorious cap of blond curls? Nothing, that's what.

So, he got ten twenties out of the machine and went looking for the shapely Santa with the great dark eyes.

It was for charity, anyway. Yes. Charity.

As he neared Seventh Street, he heard a cry—a scream, really—and quickened his pace. Corinne? Was one of those pimply dolts after her bucket again? Why, he'd wrap his fingers around their cowardly throats and squeeze until their eyeballs—

No, it was someone else, a woman clutching her purse with all her might, skidding on her heels, while a scruffy individual in a Vikings jacket pulled on the strap, pulled and yelled and basically made an absolute ass of himself.

But what's this? Corinne was—why, she was going after the wretch! The brave, foolhardy, silly thing! He would—

He would save the purse, protect Corinne from getting in

over her curly head, be the man of the hour! Then have tea! With Corinne!

He reached the cowardly cretin, his fists clenched, already bracing himself—he'd have skinned knuckles for the better part of a fortnight—then walloped the would-be thief in the face. It was almost—satisfying? Embarrassing, but there it was. He hadn't been in a fight since he was at Oxford.

There was a familiar-sounding crunch as the wretch's nose broke, a deadening pain in Grant's hand, and then Corinne kicked the snatcher's feet out from under him.

She stomped on the thief's throat with her black Santa boot. Ah, efficient *and* beautiful . . . good to know. Grant bent to help her, and she backed him up with her gun.

Er.

Her gun?

"Great," she snapped, gesturing to the bleeding, shrieking would-be purse snatcher. "Now I have to arrest *both* your asses."

"Oh, dear," was all Grant could think to say. Followed by, "I have some money for your bucket."

"Save it, pal."

"And you don't have to arrest *me.*"

"By dose, he broge my fuggin' dose. I'be gudda fuggin' sue you, you modderfugger!"

"Shut the fuck up," Corinne barked.

"Rather," Grant said. Then he added, "Nice gun, darling."

Chapter Six

"You are *so* lucky you're not under arrest for assault."

"The mayor's wife," Grant said dryly, "was happy to be able to hang on to her purse."

"*So* lucky."

"And I doubt it's your habit to arrest helpful citizens."

"Hmph."

It would have been worth it, he thought, to be arrested by Corinne. He could have looked into her dark eyes and listened to her read him his rights forever.

"—think you were doing, numbnuts?"

"Pardon?"

"Wading in there with fists flying like some fucked-up cowboy. You could have gotten your ass shot. Or knifed. Or punched."

"Are you angry with me?" he asked, delighted.

"I'm just saying," she said, sounding—could it be?—upset, "you should've stayed out of it. I mean, what if he'd pulled a knife on you?"

"Then I would have made him eat it," Grant said matter-of-factly.

"Sure you would have."

"Don't let the accent and the clothes fool you. I grew up on the streets of London, which are not known for their kindness and ability to nurture."

"I know all about you," she sneered. "Orphaned, bounced around as a kid, adopted by some tycoon when you were sixteen—a regular Oliver Twist. Or Richie Rich. I always get those two mixed up. Prob'ly because I never read *Oliver Twist*. How come you talk all snooty like, then?"

"Pardon?"

"You know, like, the upper-class accent? How come you're not all, 'Shine yer shoes fer a tuppence, Guvna?' "

He shuddered. "Please don't ever attempt a Cockney accent again." Then he realized what she'd said. "You checked up on me?"

She shrugged.

"How? Minneapolis police don't keep records on English citizens."

"No, but your cops cooperate with our cops. It's like, a hands-across-the-world kind of thing."

"I'm touched," he said sincerely, "if mildly frightened." She'd been angry he'd risked himself, she had cared enough to check up on him . . . she . . . really, she was a delight.

"I still should have arrested your big British butt," she grumped, slumping back in her chair and crossing her arms across her chest. "Still might."

"That's very touching," he said. "Would you like another hot chocolate?"

"That'll be six for me."

"Yes, I know."

"That's kind of a lot."

"Yes."

"And I don't need to be running off for a piss while I'm trying to catch bad guys," she confided. "That's not, y'know, convenient."

"I thought your Russian gave you the rest of the day off?"

"He's not *my* Russian. And yeah," she added thoughtfully. "He did."

"I think you should risk it."

"Okay, I will." No sooner were the words out of her mouth than the waiter reappeared, bearing a new drink brimming with whipped cream and chocolate sprinkles. "Oooh, thank you!"

"Is there cocoa in there?" Grant asked, peering at her drink. "Somewhere?"

"Back off, man. You can't drink chocolate without lots of whipped cream. It's like a law."

"Federal or state?"

She laughed. "Moral."

"I asked for a coffee from a street vendor the other day," he said. "And I got a cup of whipped cream. Eventually I worked my way down to the coffee, but by then I wasn't thirsty anymore."

"My," Corinne said. "What an interesting story. And by interesting, I mean unbelievably boring and pointless."

"Pardon *me*."

"Okay." Corinne looked around appreciatively. "This place is awesome. Did you know it used to be a grain elevator? Before they converted it into a ridiculously expensive hotel?"

"Yes. The shape of the building is fairly unmistakable."

"These hot chocolates are probably eight bucks apiece."

"Don't worry about it."

"Can you imagine staying here? It's, like, three hundred bucks a night. To sleep in a grain elevator! And the whole top floor is, like, the penthouse. You know, I heard some rich asshole from London booked the whole top—aww, shit."

He just smiled at her.

"Not that you're an asshole," she added.

"But I *am* rich."

"Which brings me to the question, what the hell do you care if your company doesn't make quota? It's not like you need the job."

Though pleased she remembered his problem, he still frowned. "If we don't make quota, the company will lay off several of my employees. I do not wish for them to be jobless in this economy."

"Aww, that's sweet. In a brutal, Scroogelike sort of way."

"I had thought of giving them the rest of the week off and taking the blame from the senior partners, but then—"

"What?"

But then, jobless, he would be shipped immediately back to England. And he would likely never see Corinne again.

"Helloooo? Earth to Grant?"

He shook off the bad mood with an effort. "Would you like to see the penthouse?"

"Great line. Does it work on all the girls you bring here and woo with cocoa?"

"You have whipped cream under your left nostril. And you're the only girl I've brought here and wooed."

"Really?" She seemed pleased, if disbelieving. She stuck out her long pink tongue and licked the cream off her upper lip.

"Christ," he said, startled.

"Oh, sorry. What can I say, I'm a freak of nature. I make tons of money with this thing."

"*What?*"

"Cops always bet me I can't stick my tongue into one of my nostrils. And they always lose. One time I made over a hundred bucks! Now we can only get the new guys to bet. Want to see?"

"No."

"Sure?"

"Yes."

"Suit yourself. And yes."

"What?" He was losing track of the conversation.

"I'd love to see the penthouse. See, your great line worked."

"It isn't like that, Corinne."

"Actually," she said, "it's exactly like that, blue eyes. Let's get that hot chocolate to go."

Chapter Seven

"I'm really not this kind of girl," she gasped as they stumbled across the living room of the suite, past the baby grand piano, into the first bedroom. "Okay, I kind of am."

"Well," he said, pulling off her big black Santa belt, "I'm not that kind of boy, either. I can assure you I'm not in the habit of bringing police officers to my suite."

"You're gonna talk while we do it, right? Because I could listen to you talk all day."

"Corinne darling, you'll have to gag me to shut me up."

"Ooooh, maybe later." She was struggling out of her Santa pants, and he was trying not to laugh, watching her. "I love the way you say that. Like it's all one word: corINNdahling. Son of a bitching Santa suit!" She swore again and struggled to be free of it, and he lost it and fell on the bed, laughing.

"Oh, man, are you gonna get it," she vowed.

"Don't menace me with your preternaturally long tongue, or I'll call the police."

"The police are here. Oof!" The pants went flying. "*Boy*, are you gonna get it!"

"Excellent, Corinne darling. I confess it's all I've been thinking of since you struck me with your bell."

She laughed. "You're weird, Grant."

He sat up and beckoned. "Maybe so. Come here."

She did, and he saw she was wearing navy blue shorts and a white T-shirt beneath the suit. "That thing is hot," she confided as he slipped his arms around her waist and pressed his lips to her stomach. "I'm either freezing my ass off or boiling in it."

He raised her shirt and kissed her belly button. He was surprised to see she was small and delicately built. From the attitude—and foul language—he expected someone larger, bulkier, rougher. But her hands and feet were tiny, her limbs slender and short, and those attributes, coupled with her cap of blond curls, made her seem almost elfin.

"You're so small," he said, unable to keep the surprise out of his voice.

"Don't even start with me. We can't all be hulking six-footers."

"I resent 'hulking.' "

"Dude. Are we going to talk or fuck?"

"I thought we were going to do both," he said, and she chuckled.

He twisted and rolled with her onto the bed, assisting her out of her T-shirt on the way. He still couldn't get over the smallness of her, how delicate she was. It was so incongruous, especially since she was now digging into his shorts and pronouncing, "My, what a big dick you have, Grandma!" Disconcerting, to say the least.

"I've noticed," he said, nuzzling her nipples, "you have a certain vulnerability."

She stopped in midstroke and appeared to think it over. "Well," she said at last. "Cops aren't vulnerable, you know? Especially *short* female cops."

"Right."

"It'd be totally against the rules. How do you convince some punk to give it up if you're vulnerable?"

"Right."

"Right," she repeated, then slid her hand up and down with mind-boggling friction. "Umm . . . I sort of quit with the Pill after I quit with the blind dates."

"That's all right," he gasped. "I have some prophylactics in my top dresser drawer."

"Okay, I'll go get one, but you must promise never to call them that again."

While she was rooting around in his underwear drawer, he took the opportunity to divest himself of the rest of his clothes. So, he saw with delight when she bounced back toward the bed, had she.

He caught her around the waist as she grinned down at him. "Ribbed for my pleasure, huh?" she asked, shaking the box. "By the way, you're awfully confident . . . the receipt was dated yesterday."

"More like prayerfully hopeful," he said, reaching up to tickle the undersides of her breasts. "But I see I've overstepped myself. Never get nude with a trained investigator."

"Rule number one in the big city," she said, and bent to him, and kissed him.

"I'm gonna need an orange juice or something," she groaned, much later. "Possibly some crack."

"Oh, poor darling. Did I wear you out so completely?"

"Grant, if you'd been able to say that without gasping for breath, I *might* be impressed." She chuckled and reached between his legs. He was soft now, but still formidable. "I had no idea Brits were so good in the sack."

"Frankly, I had no idea Yanks—"

"Oh, never mind." She stretched, then nestled into his side. She was still having trouble following the sequence of events. One minute they were tickling and teasing and yakking away, and the next his head was bobbing between her thighs and she thought she was going to implode, right there on the bed.

His tongue was everywhere, his lips, his mouth, and when he wasn't sucking on—er—various parts of her, he was kissing her stomach and slipping his fingers into her, stroking softly, sweetly.

When he came up to her she was more than ready; she was, in fact, ready to climb the curtains and yowl like a cat. She'd urged him to her and felt the deepest satisfaction she'd ever known as he sank into her so deeply their stomachs slapped together.

She was happy enough to help him come—God knew he'd brought *her* over that edge about half a dozen times—but he wasn't finished with her, not even close, as it turned out. They'd pumped hips and plundered each other's mouths for another ten minutes until finally he was shuddering above her, and was he—he was! He was whispering, "Sorry," as he collapsed on one shoulder beside her.

"What?"

"I'll do better next time," he said, kissing the side of her neck.

"Then you'll *kill* me!" she groaned, and he laughed.

Chapter Eight

"So, is there, like, a Sex Olympics in England, or what? Because you're really really good at it. Really good. Humongously, tremendously good."

"Oh, stop," he said modestly. "You're starting to repeat yourself."

"Disgustingly, annoyingly good," she continued. "Thanks for ruining me to the rest of the world."

"All part of my sinister plan," he said, tucking the blankets around her chin. "Stay the night?"

"Um . . ." She had no clothes. Not even a toothbrush. Or a roommate or cat who would miss her. Pathetic. But tonight, freeing.

"It wasn't really a question," he said. "I had no intention of letting you out of the room."

"Not too creepy. Try to stop me from leaving, bud, you might get a surprise. But okay." She shrugged, silently pleased at his possessiveness. "But I'll shoot you in the head if you steal the covers."

"Duly noted." He paused, settling beside her in the gigantic bed. "You know, I've never—that is to say, it's not really my habit to—ah—"

"Well, it used to be mine. Not anymore, though. I think it's being a cop. I mostly meet creeps. Like an idiot, I used to mostly *date* creeps."

"Well, that's how we learn, I suppose."

"What, you dated jerks, too?"

"Not so much that, as I made most of my mistakes while I was growing up. I didn't exactly have a parental figure to emulate. In fact, I hate to ruin my newly forged reputation, but I haven't had that much experience with women."

"Suuuuuure you haven't. How come you're so good at it, then?"

"I read a lot," he said, completely straight faced.

"Oh, brother," she giggled. "I guess you could say I took the opposite, hands-on approach."

"It's difficult to meet people outside of work," he admitted. "For example, what were the chances of our meeting? If I hadn't slipped—"

"And grabbed me like a big lame drowning loser—"

"Right," he said dryly. "I confess I'm curious. If it's not Eyes Only, may I ask who you're looking for on your corner?"

Eyes *what?* Oh, who cared. "Yeah, I can tell you. It's not like a deep secret or anything. I'm trolling for a purse snatcher."

"Really? Another one?"

"Yeah, the one I got today didn't count. This one's kind of wrecking the holidays for everybody. The mayor, the chief, my boss, me . . . not to mention the poor slobs who lose their shoulder bags."

"Ah . . . forgive me, but I'd read . . . that is to say, the crime rate in the States . . ."

She nodded. "Right, how come we're going to all this trouble to catch a purse snatcher?"

"Well . . ."

"It's making us look *really* bad. I mean, you can't even go downtown for some Christmas shopping without some creep grabbing your purse? The mayor's super pissed. One of his nieces was one of the first victims . . . then another snatcher goes for his wife *today* . . . tell you, I wouldn't want to be the chief this month. I mean, it worked out kind of nice that you saved his wife's stuff and all, but that just made everything worse, because the guy we caught wasn't the guy we wanted. Now the mayor's, like, rabid on the subject. So there's always a Santa-cop on that corner now."

"How do you know I'm not the snatcher?"

"You mean how do I know you're not a rich foreign guy sticking it to us arrogant Americans by stealing purses?"

"Errr . . ."

"Believe me," she said with heartless cheer, "I already checked you out."

"How . . . flattering."

"Don't get grumpy. It's my job. Besides, even if you hadn't checked out, you're totally the wrong profile. We're looking for someone smaller, quicker, from that neighborhood, a blend-in-the-shadows type who likes the finer things."

"Oh?"

"Yeah, all the purses snatched have been Coach or Prada knockoffs. And your briefcase is an English brand, your shoes are Kenneth Cole, and your suits are Italian. Not a Coach in sight."

"*Really.*"

"Knock it off. And he's not big—the victim barely sees him and he's gone. And he's not going for anybody's beat-up denim shoulder bag, you know? In fact, half the purses turn up in a garbage can and get turned in to the Cop Shop. Whatever this guy wants, it's *not* the purses. Or at least, not the ones he's taking. I think he might be doing it to get off—the thrill of getting the woman upset, the screaming, the sprinting, everybody hollering, and then, finally, getting away. My partner thinks he might be gay," she added thoughtfully. "A closeted gay and this is how he gets his thrills."

"Luckily, you put me to the test and eliminated me as a suspect."

"There is that," she said, reaching over and giving him a playful tweak. "A grueling job, but one I attend to with a never-ending sense of duty, or whatever." She laughed.

"Corinne darling, do you like being a police officer?"

"Sometimes."

"Corinne . . ."

"Okay, hardly ever," she admitted. "But let me tell you . . . I've got the best bennies in the world."

"Bennies?"

"Benefits."

"Surely there's more to it than that. You could get bennies if you worked for 3M."

"I'll tell you what there *isn't*. The problem is, there's only so much I can do. It's not the job, it's—it's the limitations of the job. There's this woman, lives down on Fifth? I know her husband smacks her around. Either that or she falls down the same stairs every fucking *week*, right? But she chickens out whenever my partner and I show up. And the D.A. won't touch it because it's an election year next year and he doesn't want to screw up his conviction rates."

"That must be difficult."

"Here's what's difficult: restraining the urge to catch the wife-beating jackoff outside his office, whip out my stick, and break out all his teeth."

"Ah."

"And I can name, like, a million other cases just like that one. The problem is, I can help people, but some don't want to be helped." She sighed and kicked moodily at the bedcovers. "They really don't. I just don't get it."

"No, you wouldn't. I'm sorry."

"Thanks. But I'm not a victim or anything. I chose this life. Thought it'd be cool, you know? Get paid to help people out? Should have bought my own bar instead," she finished gloomily. "*Really* help people."

He stroked her curls and didn't comment.

Finally, she said, "I guess you could say I have kind of an

unglamorous view of police work. It's mostly paperwork and attitude and kissing the chief's ass. I'll tell you what I'd like to do. I'd like to open my own P.I. biz."

"Pee Eye?"

"Private Investigator. Help women nail their cheating husbands, look for lost kids, stuff like that. Set my own hours, my own rules. That would be really cool. And if some guy who wants me to work for him is an asshole, I can be all, 'fuck off, asshole,' and refuse to take the case."

"It sounds like a noble goal. Why don't you do it?"

"Oh, I will, someday," she said cheerfully. *Two words: student loans. It was a little early to be striking out on her own.* "Aren't you tired? It's late."

"I like listening to you."

"Really?" she said, astonished.

"Really."

"Well, go to sleep. I'll talk more tomorrow."

He laughed and snuggled her against him until they were like spoons in a drawer. "I'll hold you to that."

Whew, she thought as she felt him drift toward sleep. *We didn't get into the whole money thing. Specifically, he's rich and I'm not.*

Well, good. Because she really liked him. And even though he could solve all her problems, she'd die before letting him do it.

Besides, he was out of town in another week. She knew. She'd checked his itinerary.

She just did it with him to get him out of her system. And it totally, totally worked.

Yeah.

Chapter Nine

DING ding DING ding DING ding DINK!

"Ack!"

"Good morning to you, too."

"What are you doing here?"

"I woke up alone," Grant said through gritted teeth. "I detest that."

"Well, I had to get to work, ya big whiner," she pointed out. "Now get lost, I've got to catch bad guys. Go supervise someone designing a chatchka, or whatever it is you do."

"I gave them the rest of the week off."

"First of all, Grant, you can't be so obvious the way you look around. You're not taking pics of the Foshay Tower, for Christ's sake. Second, I thought they were going to get fired if they didn't make quota."

"Well," he said, still looking around like a dork, "they made quota. Or close enough to it. Tomorrow is Christmas, you know."

"Yeah, yeah. Waitaminute. Did they make quota, or didn't they?"

"I might have told the senior partners to sod off," he admitted, "and taken all the blame."

"Oh, great," she said, but couldn't quite keep the admiration out of her voice. "Bob and Tiny Tim will be thrilled." She almost asked him how long he could stay if he was jobless, but didn't want to hear the bad news. Last night had been magical enough, but it was over. Better get used to it. "Listen, will you blow?"

"Have dinner with me."

"Sure. Go away."

"Promise."

"I promise, all right? Now get lost."

He bent and kissed her cheek, and she managed to ignore the thrill that brought to her nether regions. Amazing. She'd thought she was too cold to feel a thing!

"Goodbye."

"Later, gator."

She watched him walk up the street, noticed he was sans briefcase, and put it out of her mind. It was really too bad. She could fall in love with someone like that. Which was stupid, because she barely knew him. Fabulous sheet skills did not a husband make. Or something like that. Sure, he was a good person, putting his job on the line to help out his team, but what did he care? He was rich. It wasn't the sacrifice for him it would have been for a regular joe. But . . .

He disappeared around the corner.

Ten bucks says he's circling around to keep an eye on you.

No way.

Ten bucks.

What, I'm betting with myself, here?

Okay, okay, she told herself, ringing her bell harder than ever. *Say he is. What does that mean?*

She made a deal with herself: if he was in fact circling back, she'd propose. Marriage to a U.S. citizen would let him stay as long as he wanted.

If he was diddy-bopping on his way, that was fine, too, but he could just toddle off back to London town when he—they—were done.

Stupid, she told herself. She didn't even know if he wanted to stay. He might be perfectly happy back home.

I grew up on the streets of London, which are not known for their kindness and ability to nurture.

Then again, maybe not.

She rang, and hoped, and even prayed a little.

Chapter Ten

Police interview of Wendy Abraham.
December 24, 2004
55012 @ 12:11:32–14:15:01
Filed by Officer Corinne Bullwinkle and Lieutenant Kruchev
Third Precinct, Minneapolis, Minnesota

Suspect was read her rights and waived a lawyer. Suspect requested a can of Coca-Cola and a sandwich, both of which were provided. Suspect waived the rest of her rights, stating, "I just want to get it off my chest."

LT. KRUCHEV: Miss Abraham, this is the statement Officer Bullwinkle typed up after your arrest. Would you read it and sign it here if it's accurate?

ABRAHAM: It's accurate.

LT. KRUCHEV: Then you understand, by signing this you are—

ABRAHAM: I just want to know why all those people jumped on me.

LT. KRUCHEV: Ah, well, we had an officer on the scene—

ABRAHAM: How many, for Christ's sake? My neck's still out of whack.

LT. KRUCHEV: You waived medical treatment. If you'll look at this part of your—

ABRAHAM: I *know*. I'm just asking how many cops you had on that corner. I mean, Jesus.

LT. KRUCHEV: Officer Bullwinkle has made, um, several friends in the neighborhood, and it seems a few of them felt she was in trouble and wished to come to her assistance.

ABRAHAM: Right. The Spaghetti guy, the British guy, three little kids, and the lady with the fat purse.

LT. KRUCHEV: Crime doesn't pay, Miss Abraham.

ABRAHAM: Oh, go fuck yourself, you fucking Commie bastard.

END INTERVIEW

"How many times are you going to read that police report? Come to bed."

"I can't help it," Corinne said, giggling. "The ending's the best part. 'Crime doesn't pay.' He actually said that! 'Fucking Commie bastard.' Poor Kruchev. His accent's hardly noticeable, you know."

She put her paperwork away and bounded toward the bed. "And you. I won a bet with myself today—but that doesn't change the fact that you were supposed to go away and let me work. I totally forgot I meant to kick your ass when we got back to your room."

"Indeed, no," he said coolly.

"Indeed, yes!" She pounced on him and nuzzled his crisp, dark chest hair. "What did you think you were doing, jumping on the bad guy? Bad girl, rather?"

"I was afraid she'd hurt you."

"The deadliest thing on her person was a tube of grape Chapstick, ya moron."

"I still don't understand why."

"I told you on the way to the Cop Shop. Actually, she told us, remember? She saved for sixteen months to buy the perfect Coach billfold, and rather than save up again for the perfect matching purse, she took a shortcut. That's why all the vics lost nice-looking bags. She wasn't even looking for the money—that's why the billfolds would show up at the station a week later. She wanted a matching accessory."

"As I recall," Grant said dryly, "she was appalled at the number of knockoffs masquerading as quality goods."

"Yeah, well, it's a tough old world. What's really sad is, if she'd kept the money she stole, she probably could have reached her goal a lot quicker. Bad guys are dumb."

"Spoken like a true champion of justice."

"When I think of all the man-hours we put in to catch this gal . . . then you come swinging down on your vine like an English Tarzan . . ."

"Tarzan *was* English."

"Oh, shut up. Bottom line, I was on the job and you totally interfered."

"If you're angry with me, why are you smiling?"

"Because I'm finally off corner duty!" She smacked his chest in celebration. "Waa-hoo! Oh, right, before I forget, will you marry me?"

"What?"

"Oh, your English isn't so good now?"

"Dammit, Corinne!" He gently pushed her aside and stood. "I can't believe this."

"What?" Feeling truly frightened for the first time since she'd met him, Corinne clutched the blanket to her breasts. "What's wrong?" *Stupid, pushy idiot! Nice going! I bet he breaks a speed record to the elevator. Three, two, one, zoom!*

"What's wrong is, I'd like to beat you to the punch, as you might say, in just one thing." He clicked open his briefcase, fumbled in it for a moment, then tossed her a small velvet box.

She plucked it out of the air. "Oh. Oh?" She opened it. "Oh."

"I was going to ask you tomorrow."

"Oh."

"But not because I want to stay in the country, although I do like it here."

"Oh."

"It's because I wish to stay with you. I know we don't know each other very well, but I've never met anyone like you. I don't dare go back home next week . . . who knows who will have scooped up the treasure that is Corinne Bullwinkle while I'm gone?"

"Oh."

"My, my," he teased. "Speechless?"

"It's just, I'm surprised," she admitted as he climbed back onto the bed beside her. "I thought I'd have to talk you into it. Possibly show you my gun. And it's not because you're rich."

"I know."

"It's *not.*"

"I know, Corinne darling."

"That's just, like, frosting on the cake, you know?"

"I know."

"Because I liked you when I thought you were just a regular chatchka-making drone. In fact, I liked you before I thought you were a regular chatchka-making drone."

"I know."

"All right."

"All right."

She slipped the diamond ring onto her finger, ignoring the tremors in her hands. It didn't seem real that everything she wanted was in this room. This grain elevator.

"Grant . . . I . . . these last few days . . . they've meant so much. I don't really have the . . . I mean, I'm not too good at this part . . ."

"I know."

"Insufferable Brit bastard."

"I know," he said smugly, and pulled her to him, and kissed her until her toes curled.

SILVER BELLA

Lucy Monroe

For Renee Hunsaker, a wonderful friend and very smart lady. Thank you for all of your help this past year. Love and blessings,
Lucy

Chapter One

Sexless mannequin.

The words reverberated through Bella Jackson's head as she stepped out onto the catwalk.

"A man could get frostbite touching you. You're all smoke and no fire, babe. If the world knew what a total fraud you are, you'd never get another modeling job again. Who wants the original ice queen modeling clothes for today's sensual woman?" Curt's vitriol echoed around her, drowning out the announcer's modulated voice, even though the confrontation had taken place miles away and days ago.

She couldn't forget.

Maybe because Curt had taken his story to the press, and her face and body were plastered all over the tabloids with headlines that made her cringe.

Bella Jackson, Ice Queen or Sexpot?
Model Freezes Boyfriend Out of Bed
Lexi's Creations Cover Model Fraud
Ex-boyfriend Says This Model's Bed Needs an Electric Blanket to Stay Warm

And the one that had given her mother heart palpitations: *Ex-boyfriend Speculates Bella Is Gay.*

She'd done hundreds of trunk shows in her ten-year modeling career, but never had she been so nervous stepping onto a stage.

Had everyone in the audience seen the stories? Were they laughing behind their hands as she modeled clothes that only a woman extremely in touch with her own sexuality would wear?

That woman was not Bella.

She didn't have hang-ups, no matter what that jerk Curt had said. It was just that she'd been so career minded since her teens the whole man-woman thing had pretty much passed her by. Not to mention the fact that she wasn't interested in getting intimate with a man who couldn't see beyond her body to the woman inside.

She'd had her bad experiences with idiots who thought her bra size was equivalent to her I.Q. and men who wanted a trophy on their arm, not a living, breathing woman in their life, so she'd pretty much stopped dating. Until Curt.

When he'd pressed for sex, she'd been unable to share her secret with him . . . or her body.

The truth was, she hadn't wanted to.

His kisses and what he'd wanted to do afterward had left her as cold as he'd accused her of being.

She was a twenty-six-year-old virgin with a reputation for extravagant sex and a supposed list of lovers the length of the Miami yellow pages. It wasn't her fault that the press speculated, or that men who hadn't made it to first base had bragged about their homeruns, but neither had she denied the rumors. Lexi said her reputation was good for the line, and Bella had considered it another cost of her career.

Her bad-girl reputation had done its own job keeping her insulated from the type of men she could actually want. The men attracted to the persona she presented to the world were very rarely the type of men she could be honestly attracted to.

Curt had been different, or so she'd thought.

She'd found out too late that the conservative accountant

had only wanted the bad girl, not the real Bella. He'd wanted to take a walk on the wild side with *her* as his tour guide.

The last day wear model was returning up the catwalk when the announcer introduced Lexi's evening wear, and Bella began her signature glide down the Plexiglas stage, her hands damp and her heart beating too fast.

Subdued lighting made it possible for her to make eye contact with the audience, but that was the last thing she wanted. Still, she couldn't help subtly scanning the patrons seated in the ultra classy Dallas hotel, looking for signs that the tabloid stories had done their damage.

But this audience seemed just like all the others, their gazes fixed on her shocking white silk dress.

She was halfway down the catwalk when her gaze snagged on a pair of green eyes. The color of new grass, they were set in a face as hard as granite and as sexy as sin.

The look in those eyes caught her as effectively as if the man's hands had closed over her shoulders and halted her midstep. She did in fact stop, her body freezing with a blast of sensations totally alien to her. Sensations that belied every one of the nasty headlines.

Her pause lasted only a second, but she felt the first blush she'd had in years crawling hotly up her skin.

The man's thin lips quirked in a knowing smile.

Obviously aware that he was the cause of her hesitation, his expression reflected a mixture of mocking humor and blatant male approval.

She'd spent years learning to ignore the masculine admiration her body elicited. For her, the perfectly proportioned curves were a tool of her trade, nothing more, but this man's look went zinging to the very heart of her.

Frissons of awareness skittered along her nerve endings, leaving goose bumps of sensation in unlikely places.

She stopped at the end of the stage, which happened to be right in front of his table, while two other models wearing evening wear came down the catwalk to flank her.

His eyes flared with pleasure as she stood in a mannequin-still pose before him, and his dark blond head tilted slightly, as if he was adjusting his angle to look at her better.

An electric current vibrated across the space between them, inexorably connecting them. Unbelievably, her nipples grew hard, and her breasts felt tight while her thighs trembled with the effort it took to maintain her pose.

She'd never reacted during a show this way. Not ever.

Only years of practice and discipline made it possible for her to move through her choreographed routine with the other two models. However, no matter which direction she turned, she felt that amazing connection.

It was scary.

Relief mixed with disappointment when the announcer cued her to return up the catwalk. She walked away from the green-eyed man, supremely aware of the almost nonexistent nature of the back of her gown.

It dipped to a V that ended right above her bottom, the white silk semitransparent. She wore minimal undergarments, and if he was looking closely enough, he would see the shadow of her cheeks and the outline of her legs beneath the fabric. Shards of excitement speared her inner thighs at the thought.

For the first time in her modeling career, she felt *exposed,* as if her body was more than a living mannequin used to show off a designer's creations.

That the dress was in fact showing her off.

She could not help wondering what *he* thought of an outfit that left so little of her body's secrets to the imagination.

Jake Barton watched the beautiful brunette retreat up the catwalk with the biggest, most painful hard-on he'd had in years . . . maybe ever.

It was such an unexpected turn-on that he wanted to howl at the moon. "Damn it, Lise, you didn't tell me this was going to be a lingerie show."

"Shh," his sister hissed from her seat beside him, not turning to look at him. "Haute couture tends to be more revealing. The lingerie comes later."

"You're kidding."

"No, I'm not. It's on the program if you'd bothered to look at it."

He looked at it now, and sure enough, there was a finale of night wear by Lexi.

He didn't know how he was going to stand seeing the model who had been introduced as Bella in anything sexier without coming in his pants.

That little lady was a walking work of art. A perfect pocket Venus. She definitely didn't fit the current trend of boy-thin, Amazon-tall models that graced most magazine covers.

The other models in the show for Lexi's Creations designed especially for petite women were small in stature, too, but none of them had this model's voluptuous curves or the air of sensual promise her pouting lips gave her. Despite those sensual lips, her brown eyes had reflected an unconscious vulnerability that he found every bit as enticing as her sexy body.

For the first time since his sister had talked him into attending a series of trunk shows with her while she researched the professional world of fashion for her latest book, he thought he just might enjoy himself.

The program said the sexy beauty was the official cover model for Lexi Creations, which meant she would no doubt feature in *all* of the shows. Considering the number of them he'd promised Lise he would attend, he would have ample opportunity to meet Bella. He smiled, the prospect affecting his mood and his libido in a very definite way.

His dick was already making emphatic statements about what it wanted to do when they met, and it wasn't to engage in polite conversation.

For the first time in the hour since the after-show schmoozing began, Bella found herself alone. On a normal night, she would disappear about now, going back to her hotel to enjoy some solitude, but she was hoping to see him, the man with the green eyes and the smile that made her insides shake.

A hand materialized in front of her holding a flute of champagne. "Drink?"

Bella turned and looked up, knowing before she did who the deep drawl would belong to.

Towering above her own petite five feet, four inches, he exuded palpable sexual heat, and she felt burned simply standing so close. This man would not need a tour guide for an extended trip on the wild side.

She took the glass of champagne. "Thank you."

"My pleasure." He lifted his glass.

She automatically clinked hers against it. *"Salud."*

"To new friendships." The slow Texas drawl went through her like the vibrations from a bass guitar, making her shiver.

His brow rose.

"It's a little cold." Not. But no way was she going to admit the real reason for her body's betraying quiver.

"It feels pretty hot in here to me." He slipped off his suit jacket and slid it around her shoulders, engulfing her as effectively as if he'd put an overcoat on her. The man was big. "There, now, we'll both feel better."

Her usual flirtatious façade abandoned her, and she nodded dumbly.

His scent surrounded her, expensive and masculine, making her ultra aware of the intimacy of wearing his jacket.

"Better?" he asked.

"Yes." What else could she say?

That the way he was looking at her made her much warmer than the extra layer of clothing and she hadn't been cold to begin with?

She took a gulping sip of the bubbly wine.

His lips twitched. "You must be thirsty."

"I am."

"Maybe I should have gotten you a glass of water instead."

"Actually that wouldn't be a bad idea." For more reasons

than that she normally stuck to fruit juice or other equally innocuous beverages at the after-show soirees. She had a feeling she needed all her wits about her because this man could turn her brain to mush with a look. "It's hard to stay hydrated during a trunk show."

"You look hydrated to me." His green gaze slid down her body with tactile pleasure, and the tone of his voice was enough to make her insides liquefy.

"It's the clothes," she said automatically. "Lexi's Creations always make me look my best."

He pulled one side of his jacket away from her body to reveal the clothes beneath it and took his time looking them over. "I don't remember that outfit from the show," he said finally, releasing his suit coat.

"It's from the day wear line."

The short skirt and button-up man-style shirt worn loose with a hip chain belt was a lot less revealing than the evening wear or lingerie she'd modeled during the show, but it was still signature sexy.

"That explains it."

"What?"

"You weren't wearing it."

"You mean you weren't watching the other models?"

He shook his head. "There was only one who could hold my interest."

"The *clothes* are supposed to hold your interest."

"They did. When you were wearing them." He reached out to touch her cheek. "Feels real enough to me."

"What do you mean?" She'd lost the thread of the conversation somewhere along the way.

"You said it was the clothes and I don't agree. No outfit, no matter how appealing, can give a woman such a flawless complexion or petal-soft skin."

She couldn't believe the urge she had to turn her face into his big hand, to inhale his scent from *his* skin, to taste him.

"The right food and exercise," she choked out.

His hand dropped away, and he smiled. "Maybe, but I think you were probably born with some of it."

"I guess." She shrugged, trying for an air of nonchalance she did not begin to feel. "Did you see anything you liked in the show?"

It was a stock question she'd asked on numerous occasions after a show, but this time she felt her cheeks heat with embarrassment at the possible double entendre.

He moved closer, hemming her in until the rest of the patrons and models ceased to exist. "Oh, I'd say so."

His eyes left no doubt that he wasn't talking about one of Lexi's creations, the dark blond hair on his head cut in a conservative, modern style at odds with the primitive and almost wild cast to his features.

She laughed nervously. "There's nothing subtle about you, is there?"

"I don't play games."

"That's nice to know." But she couldn't say the same.

Her whole approach to the male species was based on a game of pretend that had come crashing down around her ears when Curt walked away from her and sold his story as her ex-boyfriend to the tabloids.

And when this man saw the headlines and heard the new rumors about her, the burning look of passion in his eyes would grow as cold as she was purported to be in bed.

"Darling, you'll have to introduce me to your delicious escort." Lexi's accented voice shattered the sense of intimacy surrounding Bella and the man.

She turned to face the flamboyant designer. "He's not my escort. He attended the trunk show."

Lexi's mouth pursed, and her brows rose suggestively. "But that suit coat, it is not one of my creations and much too large for you, darling."

The man put his hand out. "Jake Barton. I was just complimenting Ms. Jackson on how well she shows your styles."

"Ah, it is a match made in heaven, no? *Magnifique!*" Lexi

kissed the tips of her fingers in an Old World gesture of approval. "She is perfect for my clothes, and they are perfect for her."

"You won't get any arguments from me, ma'am."

Lexi smiled. "Ah, the Texas drawl. It is so charming. I look forward to the time we will spend here."

His eyes narrowed on something over Lexi's shoulder, and then he looked at Bella. "I've got to go. It's been a pleasure meeting you."

She shrugged his jacket off and handed it to him, feeling bereft and disbelieving all at once.

He was going to leave? Just like that?

Apparently he was, because he took the coat, put it back on, and turned to go.

"Goodbye."

He stopped and looked back at her. "I'm sure we'll be seeing each other again."

She didn't see how, but she merely inclined her head.

He'd said he didn't play games, but he'd implied interest in her and then walked away without following up on it.

And she didn't know just how she felt about that.

"If you had dated such a man, not this boring accountant with an unknown penchant for sensationalism, your name would not now be synonymous with goodie-two-shoes in the gossip press. *Monsieur* Barton would not have gone to the media with stories of your supposed lack of sexual warmth."

Bella shrugged. There wasn't a lot she could do about it now, but she hated knowing she'd made such a drastic mistake in trusting Curt.

Lexi's eyes narrowed, though her smile did not falter. "This is a problem for Lexi's Creations, you realize?"

"In what way?"

Had Curt been right? Could the fact she'd been labeled an ice queen hurt her career? She supposed it made sense. If one false reputation could aid it, an equally false one in the opposite direction could do some serious damage.

"My designs, they are known for their sensuality, yes?"

"Undeniably."

"Yet my cover model has now been labeled a sexless mannequin by her most recent lover. This is not good." Lexi's matter-of-fact voice held no anger, but her words cut through Bella like a knife.

"Are you *firing* me?"

"Not yet, but something must be done."

Bella didn't know what, and while she hadn't minded paying the price of having a certain reputation in order to further her career, Lexi's implication the reputation was as important as the model didn't sit well.

"What do you expect me to do? I'm not about to have sex on a tabletop in a semipublic place to assuage your or anyone else's view of my image."

"Ah, is this what the stupid accountant wanted you to do?" Lexi clicked her tongue and shook her head. "That one, he has no imagination."

For the second time that night, Bella felt her cheeks heat. "That's not the issue."

"No, it is not," her boss agreed. "Your image and therefore the image of the line you represent is in question, and I am not happy about this."

Bella's patience was wearing thin. If Lexi really thought she was any more displeased about the tabloid stories than Bella, she was off her rocker. "I repeat, what do you want me to do about it?"

It was Lexi's turn to shrug. "Perhaps you should cultivate a friendship with a man like *Monsieur* Barton."

And maybe she could rack up frequent flyer miles on a pig. The man had walked away without a backward glance.

Chapter Two

Bella peeked out from behind the stage curtain, obsessively preoccupied with the need to know if Jake Barton had shown up again.

The last two weeks had been the most frustrating of her life. Between Lexi's heavy hints laced with subtle pressure that Bella needed to do something to shore up her sexy bad-girl image and Jake Barton's inexplicable behavior, she was ready to quit her modeling career and take up Christmas tree farming.

And she was allergic to pine needles.

Oh, yes, he was there again, sitting in the front row.

Her entire body tightened in anticipation, and her nipples went hard in a Pavlovian response to his presence they'd learned at that very first show.

She gritted her teeth and tried to ignore the ache, all the while drinking in his appearance with the enthusiasm of a woman lost in the desert who happened upon an oasis. Which was all out of proportion because the man deserved to be ignored, or maybe pummeled, but definitely not lusted over.

He was driving her stark, staring crazy.

At the last show, he'd been near the back, behind a woman whose hair had looked as though it was competing to play in the Cotton Bowl. It didn't matter how far from the stage he sat, Bella became aware of him on a wholly primal level from the moment she stepped onto the stage.

She could *feel* him.

And it frustrated her.

Because although they'd spoken twice more and he'd flirted with her in a possessive, primitive manner that implied an interest as deep as her own, Mr. I-don't-play-games hadn't made a single move to ask her out.

He remained infuriatingly out of reach, there in the audience, sometimes coming to the after-show parties, more often disappearing as if he were a phantom of her imagination.

Why did he come? And what was she going to do about it?

He'd never bought anything. Sometimes he didn't even stay for the whole presentation, and he didn't know anyone else in the show personally. She'd asked around.

Yet, today was the fifth Lexi's Creations trunk show he'd attended in two weeks. He'd been at the two events in Houston, and the one following in Austin, but he hadn't made the one in San Antonio. She'd been depressed for two days after.

They'd returned north to Forth Worth, and here he was again.

One of the other models, a former West Texan, had told her that Jake Barton wasn't married, owned a huge ranch about an hour from Austin, and was well known for his extensive oil holdings as well.

None of which explained the fascination he held for her or the feeling of connection she experienced when their eyes met, nor did anything in his background account for his attendance at one fashion show after another.

Which was the tiny kernel of hope in her burnt popcorn existence at the moment.

Maybe, an insidious little voice inside her insisted, *he came to see me and is working up to asking me out.*

Only he didn't seem like the type of man to be hindered by reticence when it came to going after something he wanted.

SILVER BELLA / 225

Which was one of the reasons she hadn't made the first move. She didn't want to approach him only to be rejected.

On the other hand, the faint heart never won the fair maiden, or something like that. He wasn't a maiden, but she'd like very much to win him. She was seriously considering showing up on his ranch during her Christmas hiatus and going for what *she* wanted.

Jake waited for Bella to come out onto the stage, allowing the anticipation to zing through him.

He had the whole program memorized, and it was time for her to wear the black dress again.

The first time he'd seen it, he'd thought it was more modest than the other designs by Lexi, but as Bella got closer, he'd realized that she wasn't wearing anything under the lace bodice and her nipples were only partially hidden behind the scrolling roses.

As she walked down the stage, his blood heated with satisfaction as he got his first glimpse of the sweet valley between her luscious curves.

Captivated, he watched as she met his gaze like she had every single time she'd walked out onto the stage since the first time. It was as if she had a radar to pick him out in the audience. He liked that.

She tried unsuccessfully to look away. He could feel her effort, and her eyes begged him to release hers.

He was more than willing to show her mercy and let his own gaze wander.

Down her body.

The dress moved flirtatiously around her legs with each step, and she picked up one side and fanned it out to show the audience the fullness of the skirt. His gaze slid up to her bodice, and he sucked in air at the sight of her hardened nipples behind the revealing lace.

A corresponding reaction occurred below his waist. Was she growing wet as well? He'd bet his prize bull she was.

Amazing that he could affect her like this, just by watching her do her job. Even more incredible was that kind of stimulation could have such a powerful effect on him. It was the most exciting foreplay he'd ever indulged in.

When they finally got into bed together, they were going to set the sheets on fire.

He wondered if she was getting as much of a kick out of prolonging the anticipation as he was. He'd been tempted more than once to put them both out of their misery, but he wanted more than a quick roll in the hay with her, and until the trunk show was over, she wouldn't be able to indulge in anything like what it would take to sate his senses.

Or hers either if he was reading her right.

His sister had told him that the models got a month of vacation after the last show before choreography would start for the next season's designs. Several of them filled their time with freelance work, but he was going to convince Bella to spend some time on his ranch. Maybe she would even stay around for Christmas.

He'd like to wake up and unwrap her on Christmas morning.

His gaze slid back up to catch hers.

Her mouth opened slightly, and he would swear he could hear her gasp.

There was an invitation in her doe eyes the primal man in him wanted to answer. And he would.

Tonight.

It was the last show, and he planned to make his move on Bella Jackson.

Bella rushed to finish dressing in street clothes. Jake Barton wasn't leaving this time without talking to her. She'd gotten another model to cover her final lingerie promenade so she could track him down in the audience before the end of the show.

Lexi was going to have apoplexy, but Bella was past caring.

She had to do this. Her career had been her entire life for too many years. Maybe it was time to start rethinking her priorities.

She checked her image out in the full-length mirror in front of her.

Her low-rider burgundy pants and body-snug sweater in the same color showed off her curves to their best advantage. She'd put a pair of huge, thin gold hoops in her ears and swept her hair into a casual up-do that looked as though she'd just gotten out of bed. The macramé kerchief belt around her hips emphasized the snug fit of the pants. Good.

She was going for sexy, and she thought she'd definitely hit the right note.

"Go get 'em, Tiger."

She grinned at her friend who had agreed to cover her final promenade so she could track the man down. "I plan to."

But when she reached his seat in the auditorium, Jake Barton was gone.

Bella wanted to scream, stomp her feet, and throw things . . . preferably oversized Texans. However, she merely smiled at the people around her, excused the interruption of her presence, and walked back out. She was muttering to herself about inconsiderate, game-playing, men who were too sexy for her own good when a large hand landed on her shoulder.

"Looking for someone?"

She squeaked, her hand landing against her heart. "You scared me," she accused. Then, *"You left."*

"I had a call I had to take. I was going back in. No way did I want to miss the lingerie finale."

Bella glared. "You have before."

"Couldn't be helped. You can believe I didn't want to, darlin'."

"Well, you'd better get back inside if you want to see it," she said contrarily, knowing he wasn't interested in watching the other models promenade.

"I'd rather stay out here."

"Would you?"

He'd been steadily backing her against the wall, and now he laid his hand on the wall beside her head. "Oh, definitely."

She swallowed in a suddenly dry throat. "I'm glad," she said inanely.

"Me, too, but why are you out here?"

"I didn't want to miss you tonight."

"Not much chance of that happening."

"Right." She drawled the word out in true Texas fashion. His dark blond brows quirked.

She couldn't believe she had to explain it. "You've left before," she reminded him.

"But this is the last show before you leave Texas, and I've got a vested interest in you sticking around for a while."

"Oh, really?" She tried to sound cool and questioning, but her voice came out all breathy and teasing.

He smiled. "Really. Don't tell me you aren't aware of what is going on between us."

"*Nothing* has happened between us." Not yet anyway.

He stood back, his expression going grim. "I told you, I don't play games."

Oh, that was rich. "Then what have the last two weeks been about?"

"Foreplay."

"*What?*"

He looked serious, but her brain couldn't take that in.

His eyes smoldered, and she was glad for the wall behind her. "We've been building up the anticipation."

For two weeks? "*We* haven't been doing anything."

This time both hands landed on the wall beside her, completely hemming her in and filling her senses with his nearness. "We've been engaged in the sexiest form of foreplay, honey, and you can't tell me you don't know it."

She hadn't, but that was beside the point. "*For two weeks?*"

"I know. It was hard for me to wait, too, but it was necessary."

"Why?"

"I didn't want a bite of the apple; I wanted the whole thing. Now that the show is over, we can spend real time together."

"Time together?" she parroted, feeling like she'd missed a vital element of the conversation.

His big body leaned infinitesimally closer to hers. "Yeah, time."

"When?"

"I'd like to start now, if you're willing."

"You want to *go to bed?*"

His smile sent her nerves jangling.

"Now?" she squeaked.

"Hell yes, but I figure I've waited this long, I can wait at least until after dinner. I've got reservations at my hotel at eight."

He could wait until after dinner. He made it sound like a huge concession while she was hyperventilating on the inside at the whole prospect. "You already have reservations?"

"Sure."

"You were that confident I'd agree to go out with you?" This man was not short on moxy.

"I was that positive the attraction was *mutual.*"

Considering the way her body was humming from his nearness, she knew he was right, but she didn't say anything, unwilling to make it that easy for him.

His expression got serious again. "I don't like lies, even flirting ones. Don't pretend with me, Bella. I want you and you want me. Admit it."

"You're pretty arrogant."

"And I don't have cause? You skipped the last part of the show to make sure you didn't miss me." He smiled then. "As if I would walk away. I liked that, honey, I really did."

"But you *did* plan to stay after the show and ask me out this time?"

"How can you doubt it?"

She rolled her eyes, her humor returning even if the ability to breathe normally hadn't. "Because you never have before."

"I told you . . . I knew once I asked you out we'd end up in bed together, and I didn't want a couple of short hours between shows and rehearsals. The kind of pleasure I want to give you takes all night, sometimes longer."

Oh, man. She was going under, and there was no life ring in sight. "I don't make a habit of having sex with men on the first date," she said, rallying.

"So your ex-boyfriend the tell-all accountant said."

She felt the blood recede from her face. "Do you believe everything you read?" she asked with more pain than sarcasm.

"If I did, I'd have to believe you've had more ex-lovers than my prize bull."

He'd read the other gossip, too. "The tabloids rarely get it right."

"I believe it."

"You do?"

"Yes." He shook his head. "Bella, you're sensual as hell, and I can't wait to get my hands on your body, but I've watched how you respond to other men at the after-show parties. You react to me with your whole body, but you keep other men at bay. And sometimes you look so vulnerable, I feel guilty for the things I want to do with you. I'd have to be an idiot to believe the speculation of pseudo-journalists over what my eyes tell me is true."

"And what do your eyes tell you is true?"

"Come to dinner with me and you'll find out."

In the end, she had no choice.

He was right. She wanted him, and dinner was the first step.

The restaurant in the ground floor of Jake's hotel wasn't so swank that Bella had needed to change clothes, but it was nice, and she enjoyed the way candlelight softened the bold lines of his features.

The waiter took their order, and Jake relaxed back in his chair. "Why did you start modeling so young?"

"It was all I ever wanted to do. My mother helped me find out how to do it. Neither of us thought I could make international status because of my height and figure, but then Lexi found me."

"And you became her cover model."

"Eventually. I started with just the trunk shows and then doing a few feature layouts. I became the cover model about five years ago."

"You do a damn fine job of showing off her designs."

"It's been good so far, but I'm getting older. Pretty soon I'm going to have to decide if I want to retire or be relegated to second string."

"You're kidding. You can't be thirty yet."

"Twenty-six, and yes, I've got a couple of years yet." If she wanted them. Her dream had started to pall as she realized what she had sacrificed to achieve it and would have to continue to sacrifice to maintain it. Things like a home, family, and hot fudge sundaes. "But the modeling world is like the sports world. You're pretty much used up by the time you're thirty."

"So, are you going home to Massachusetts?"

"What did you do, research me?"

He didn't even look disconcerted when he said, "Yes."

"Don't you think that's a little excessive?" But she was flattered.

She was also nervous. Being in the public eye like she was, there was a lot of information out there for him to find. He'd already said he didn't believe gossip, but there was so much of it.

He looked at her with a wry expression. "Are you saying you didn't try to find out anything about me?"

"Maybe a little." She licked lips that felt all too dry despite her moisturizing lipstick and a sip of water. "One of the other models is from West Texas."

"What did she say?"

"That you're a rancher and have a lot of oil holdings."

"I'm rich."

"I'm beautiful." She threw it out just as he had, as if it were a gauntlet, and waited to see if he would pick it up.

"There's more to you than beauty."

"There's more to you than money." And Lord help her, she meant it. She sensed a depth in him that pulled at much more than the hormone-driven impulses of her body.

"I'm glad we established that."

"Me, too."

Chapter Three

Frustration gnawed at Jake.

He wanted to touch Bella.

Badly.

They'd spent over an hour sharing a leisurely dinner, and he'd enjoyed talking to her, getting to know the reticent woman behind the man-killer façade. Bella Jackson was a lot more innocent than she'd ever admit to being, he'd bet.

She was also sexy.

And if he didn't get her in his arms soon, he was going to start hallucinating from the strain.

A live band played near an empty dance floor in the center of the restaurant.

He stood up and put his hand out. "Dance with me."

She took his hand, but she didn't get up. She looked past him, a slight frown marring her features. "But no one else is."

"So?"

"I . . ." Her gaze lifted to his, and she bit her lip.

"Don't tell me you'd be embarrassed?" Being a public spectacle was life as she knew it for this woman. "You parade down a stage in front of hundreds of people with less covering than a lot of women wear to bed."

"That's different." She tugged at her hand, looking put out with him. "It's my job."

He tightened his grip and pulled her from the chair, loving the way her eyes flared and her pretty pink lips parted on a soft little, "Oh," as he pulled her close to him.

"I want to hold you, and unless you want to go up to my room, this is the only way I can do it without being arrested for performing lewd acts in a public place."

"Dancing sounds good." Her smile was both a little nervous and flirtatious at the same time.

A woman filled with contradictions, she fascinated him more than anyone had since reaching puberty and discovering Suzy Miller would let him touch her budding breasts behind the school cafeteria during recess.

He pulled Bella toward the softly lit dance floor. Then tucking her up against his body, he began a slow sway to the forties-style music. Holding a woman had never felt so good. She fit perfectly against him, despite the disparity in their heights.

Laying her head against his chest, she let him press her as close as two bodies could get without clothes.

He felt an immediate and powerful reaction below his belt. He'd been semiaroused all evening, but now he was so hard, he was like to bust through his zipper.

He sucked in air like a man who'd been kicked by a bull.

She went stiff and stopped moving. "Jake?"

"What?" He sounded surly, and he hadn't meant to, but it was taking all he had not to do something about the hard-on in his pants.

"Maybe this isn't such a good idea."

"Why not?"

"You're, um . . . excited."

And that surprised her? "If I didn't react to the feel of you this close, I'd be dead from the neck down."

She choked on a laugh. "You're definitely not dead."

"No. Neither are you." Her nipples were pressing against his chest in a way designed to drive a sane man loony.

"When I'm with you, I feel more alive than I did promenading in my first trunk show." The breathless pleasure in her voice finished the job her body had started.

"Good," he managed to get out, though his mind was turning off and instinct was taking over.

Maybe she'd been right and this *wasn't* such a good idea.

He let one hand drift down to settle against the top curve of her bottom and used the other to press against her back. He wanted to be naked with her, but he had to dance right now.

She wiggled against him, and it excited him no end, but he got the impression she was trying to find a less intimate position. "You're acting like you've never danced with an aroused man before."

"I haven't."

He'd have to travel halfway around the world to believe that one. "Right." What other condition could a man be in dancing with her?

Bella's small hands slid up his chest, leaving a burning trail of sensation in their wake, and locked around his neck. "I don't let my dates hold me this close, and to tell the truth, I don't dance much either."

"Too busy flirting?"

"Too busy working. I can count the number of men I've dated in the last year on one hand, Jake, and it wouldn't even use all my fingers."

She sounded like she was trying to tell him something.

"Were you coming off a bad relationship?" Something worse than having her private life splashed all over the gossip papers?

"I've *never* had a serious relationship."

It was his turn to stop and stare down at her. The top of her head gave nothing away. "Never?"

"I told you, I was too busy working."

"So, what are you saying? You're a virgin?" He asked it jokingly as he started moving again and about fell over when he felt her head nodding against his chest.

She pulled back a little so he could see her face. "My parents raised me to see sex as a commitment, and I've never been that committed."

"You didn't even experiment?" She was too beautiful to be that innocent. It simply wasn't possible.

"I didn't have time." The clarity in her velvet brown eyes compelled him to believe her. "My job required all the hours of my day not dedicated to going to school and sleeping. If I wasn't modeling, I was exercising, or taking a class in nutrition, weight lifting, photography . . . If I thought it would help me do my job better than anyone else, I did it. I knew I had my size against me, so I was determined to make it up in other ways."

"But you're twenty-six."

"I know how old I am," she said, sounding a mite testy. "When I finished with school, I started working longer hours and traveling."

"Men must have wanted you."

"Maybe. Not the right kind. I didn't want them."

"You want me." But he wondered what she meant by the right kind.

"Yes, and to tell you the truth that scares me to death."

"Why?" Did she think he wouldn't take her inexperience into consideration when he made love to her?

"Because I was more devastated by the thought of never seeing you again than I was when my last boyfriend broke up with me, and *we'd been dating for weeks*. He'd even mentioned marriage."

She was saying that this thing between them was more than physical for her. He liked hearing that, because no woman, no matter how sexually tempting, would have gotten to him the way she did if there wasn't some primitive emotional link there.

"Don't let it scare you, honey. I'm not going to hurt you."

"Will you be able to help it? You said it. You want me, but it's physical for you."

"It couldn't be this strong and only be physical."

She didn't believe him. He could see it in her eyes, but he didn't know what to say to convince her. So, he pulled her against him again and danced some more. Words were his sister's stock in trade, not his.

But Bella's silence got to him.

It felt loaded, like the calm before an unbroken horse started bucking.

"I can't promise you forever." Not yet, maybe never. He didn't know what he wanted from her besides time to sate a desire that grew with each passing minute. "But I can promise you it will be worth it."

"That was never in question," she muttered against his chest.

He hoped it would be enough, because he had to have her. They danced in silence for several songs, his body slowly getting more and more aroused by the sensation of having her so close to him.

It was a really stupid thing to do.

How was he supposed to walk back to the table without letting the whole restaurant know what kind of condition he was in? Heck, he didn't know if he could walk period.

He set her about six inches away from him, his hands settled on her waist.

Her eyes opened, the dark brown irises hazy and unfocused. "What's the matter?"

"It's either carry you out of here over my shoulder and up to my room, or get myself back under control."

"I probably wouldn't fight you if you did the over-your-shoulder thing . . ." Her voice trailed off, her cheeks staining pink in an unexpected, but charming way.

He glared at her, though, his libido having gone into nuclear meltdown at her words. "Don't say things like that."

She jerked, her eyes going wide. "I'm sorry."

"You'd be sorrier if I took you up on it."

"Would I?" Her expression was back to hazy.

It was all he could do not to curse to hell and back out of

frustration because it was obvious she was turned on just as badly as he was. Only if he took her to bed tonight, there was no saying she wouldn't leave Texas in the morning.

He wanted more than a feverish night of coupling, and she deserved more. She was a virgin.

She'd also as good as admitted she had feelings growing for him besides passion.

She needed tender taking care of.

Not to be the recipient of the result of a build up of lust gone out of control.

"Come to my ranch with me."

"Christmas is in two weeks."

"So? Do you have a lot of Christmas shopping to do yet? I'll help you."

"Seriously?"

If it meant getting to spend the time with her, he'd go to the next town council meeting, and those were about the word in boring. "Yes."

"I'd really like that, but . . ."

"Are you worried about staying at my ranch with me all alone?"

"I don't know you well," she said, hedging.

"My sister lives with me. Her name is Lise."

"Lise *Barton,* the writer? I love her books!"

"Yep. Did that tip the invitation in my favor? Because if it did, I can even get you a whole collection of signed copies of her books."

"You make it sound tempting."

"It's a cruel blow to a man's ego for him to take second place as enticement behind a bunch of books."

Bella's expression turned all too serious and vulnerable. "You're not. You're too enticing, if you want the truth."

"Oh, yes. I always want the truth from you."

"Will your sister be there the whole time?"

"No. She's there for the next couple of days, and then she's going off on a research trip to Paris."

He waited to see if knowing they'd be alone for several days would turn Bella off the idea.

"I'd like to come."

The temptation to pick her up and carry her all the way to his ranch right that minute was so strong, he had to force himself to step away from her and let her go completely. "Can you travel early tomorrow morning?"

She nodded, her eyes mirroring doubts he had no trouble reading.

"It's going to be all right."

"Yes."

"We can't walk away from this."

"I don't want to."

Those four little words had him smiling off and on for the rest of the night.

The next morning, Bella climbed into Jake's big black Suburban. "This thing is huge."

"You should see my pickup truck."

"You have a truck, too?"

"Of course I do. I run a ranch, but I like this for town driving."

"Most people would not consider this a town vehicle."

"I'm not most people."

She looked at him dressed more casually than she'd seen him to date in a pair of jeans and tight-fitting, ribbed T-shirt under a black-and-navy-checked flannel shirt and had to agree. He was more man than any other male she'd ever known, except maybe her brother who was a mercenary . . . and then it was a tie.

It took a few hours to reach the ranch, and they talked the whole time. His father had died only a few years ago, and from all Jake said, Bella couldn't grieve the man's loss. He sounded like one of the coldest human beings she'd ever heard of. Way different from her own affectionate and caring father.

When she told Jake so, he nodded.

"The ranch was the only thing that ever really mattered to him. He would have had a heart attack if he'd lived long enough to see me signing drilling rights over, but it's made me enough money to keep the ranch a going concern despite the shaky beef market."

"You really like living on a ranch?" She couldn't imagine being raised in such isolation. Miles from the nearest neighbor.

"You'll love it, too."

Maybe. She'd had her fill of people, especially in the past weeks when the tabloids had done their best to assassinate her character along with the bad-girl reputation Lexi valued so highly.

"I'll only be there for a week, or so."

"We'll see."

She tried not to read too much into those two little words, but she liked the sound of them, and she smiled. "Yes, we will."

The ranch house was big, but not ostentatious. The wrap-around porch was painted white and so was the trim, but the rest of the house was a soft, buttery yellow.

Roses grew along the front of the porch, though they weren't in bloom. It wasn't snowy or anything, not like back home around Christmas, but it was winter . . . even in Texas.

Jake came around and opened her door, lifting her from the SUV with two hands around her waist. He didn't put her down, but held her up, her face inches from his, her feet dangling six inches off the ground.

"I have to kiss you." The stark need in his voice acted like an aphrodisiac on her senses, and she didn't even think about playing hard to get.

It had been there in the car, shimmering between them the whole way here. This wrenching hunger to connect on an intimate level.

"*Yes.*"

Jake bent his head, blocking out the winter sun and mesmerizing Bella as his lips came closer to hers, the sunlight creating a halolike glow around his head. His pale green eyes turned dark by the shadow stayed open, too, and they watched each other as their lips met for the first time.

His hard mouth pressed gently against hers, and passion flared in his eyes, while pleasure radiated from her lips outward in wave after wild wave of sensation. Her whole body shook even though he'd done nothing more than touch her lips with his. Oh, but how he used those lips.

He hadn't even trespassed the interior of her mouth with his tongue, but she felt her body changing and preparing for an intimacy she'd never known.

His hands were hot brands on her waist, and he tasted like every dream she'd ever had.

If she weren't experiencing it, she would have thought such a reaction from something as basic as a kiss was impossible.

Her nipples stung with needle-sharp prickles as they tightened into hard buds, and her breasts swelled against her bra, aching with an unfamiliar need to be touched. Her feminine core grew damp and needy, and she pressed her thighs together, but all that did was to increase the throbbing sense of emptiness.

He backed her up against the SUV, his big body pressing into hers with insistent demand.

He was aroused again. The evidence was hard against her stomach, and unlike the night before, she didn't attempt to pull back. The primitive woman inside of her was glad she could excite him like this. If she was going ballistic over a kiss, so was he.

In a wholly instinctive move, she reached down between them and rubbed the back of her fingers along the hard length of him.

He groaned like a man coming out of hell, or reaching for heaven.

So she did it again, this time lingering on the tip, rubbing her finger over the broad, blunt end of him.

His tongue made an abrupt and no-holds-barred assault on her mouth as his body moved against hers with unmistakable intent. She was trying to figure out a way to get her legs around him so she could get closer when his mouth tore from hers. In the next instant, he stepped back, letting her feet land abruptly on the ground.

He was breathing hard, his eyes a brilliant green and his skin flushed with excitement. Her own lungs felt as though there was a metal band constricting them, and heat radiated throughout her body with furnacelike intensity.

He leaned forward, his hands braced against his thighs like a man who'd been running hard and fast. "That damn near got out of hand."

She was going to explode now. "If that was only a near miss, what does really out of hand feel like?"

He did that groan thing again, and she sort of slid down the SUV until she was barely standing.

"Come inside and find out."

Chapter Four

"I can't."

"You're not ready?" He sounded incredulous, and after that kiss, he should be.

So she corrected him. "I can't walk."

He didn't laugh, even though it should have been funny. She should be joking, but she wasn't.

He silently stepped forward, then picked her up and swung her over one shoulder just like he'd said he wanted to do the night before. He'd gotten halfway to the house before she realized they had an audience, and it wasn't a silent one.

Cowboys stood around laughing like hyenas on speed.

One of them called out, "Hey, boss, you bringing home a woman or a sack of potatoes?"

"Do you feel like a sack of potatoes?" Jake demanded, actually sounding worried about the possibility.

She put her hands on his backside so she could lift her torso and look the cowboys over right side up. "No. I feel like a martini . . . but I'm both shaken and stirred."

Very, very stirred. The presence of an audience did not lower the level of pheromones rushing through her most sensitive places one tiny bit.

He laughed at that, his chuckle low and sexy, and she found herself grinning. She liked his laugh.

The cowboy who'd spoken tipped his hat at her. "Ma'am."

That got rid of her grin real fast. "The next one that calls me *ma'am* is going to learn all about what my brother taught me after assassin training in the Special Forces."

Joshua hadn't trained to be an assassin, but these grinning loons didn't need to know that.

Another cowboy laughed out loud. "She's all right, boss."

"I like a woman with spirit," another one said.

"Get your own," Jake growled before sweeping into the house and kicking the big door shut behind them.

"Señor Jake, what is this you are doing?"

The woman's voice reached Bella, and she wanted to shout out her frustration. Wasn't there privacy, even in the house? Then she remembered the sister and gritted her teeth. The last thing she wanted to do was meet her favorite author when all she could think about was getting the woman's brother into the nearest bed.

Jake said something in Spanish, and the woman clucked her tongue, then responded in the same language.

Bella made out the word for sister and bad, but the rest of it was incomprehensible. She'd only had one semester of Spanish in high school. She got a glimpse of a living room decorated with simplicity for comfort, lots of hardwood floors, and then some stairs. Jake's broad shoulder jolted her stomach as he took the stairs two at a time.

He carried her straight into a bedroom and shut the door.

She assumed it was his, but at that point, it could have been the housekeeper's and she would have offered to change the sheets afterward.

He dumped her on the bed, and she bounced. "Now I feel like a sack of potatoes," she teased.

He grimaced. "Sorry."

She sat up in the middle of the big mattress. "What happened to your sister?"

"Nothing."

"I heard the word bad."

"Eva thinks I'll come to a bad end if I go around carrying beautiful women over my shoulder."

"Oh."

"Lise flew out early for her research trip," he said with the air of a man admitting some deep, dark sin.

Which surprised her, so it took a second for the import of his words to fully register.

They were alone.

The hallelujah chorus was going off in her head while her body continued melting from the inside out, her desire not in the least abated by her tummy-jolting ride up the stairs.

"I didn't lie to you. I thought she was going to be here," he said, mistaking her silence for accusation.

"I didn't think you had."

"Oh." He unbuttoned his flannel shirt, skimming it off and tossing it on a nearby chair. "Good."

Her sweater came off in one swift move over her head, leaving her in a pair of tight jeans and a black lace bra.

His hands froze on the hem of his T-shirt, and he said a word that made her ears burn. "Honey, you are one gorgeous woman."

For no reason she could understand, his comment made her feel self-conscious and she didn't do anything about taking off her pants.

He wasn't so reticent. His black T-shirt went first, revealing a chest bronzed from working in the sun, with a light dusting of hair and rippling with muscle. Then he sat down on the chair he'd tossed his shirt onto so he could take off his boots.

She was digesting the fact that men could have sexy feet when his jeans went the way of his shirt, and her heart stopped beating. His legs were covered with hair, so different from her waxed smoothness that she could just imagine how they were going to feel against her own.

Him on top of her, their legs entwined.

Suddenly, her jeans were too constricting, but she still couldn't quite make herself take them off. So, she kicked off her platforms instead, and the tight denim of her jeans rubbed against highly sensitized flesh when she moved.

Then her breath suspended in her throat as he pulled off the nondescript black boxers.

Oh, wow.

She crossed herself. "You're awfully big, aren't you?"

Or was it just her perspective? After all, she'd only ever seen a naked and erect penis in an erotic woman's magazine a friend of hers had given her as a gag gift for her twenty-first birthday. Even the male strippers at the show she'd been taken to that night had kept their G-strings on. She'd seen lots of male ass, but this was way different.

His laugh sounded gargled.

"It moves when you laugh. That's cool."

He said that word again, the one that made her blush. "I thought virgins were supposed to be shy."

"I don't like being average."

For some reason, that cracked him up again, and he was still laughing when he pushed her back on the bed and his lips landed against hers.

It was just like it had been outside, only more.

His hot, excited body was covering hers, and the hair on his chest tickled her nipples through the black lace.

"I want you naked," he said against her lips and then tasted her with his tongue.

She didn't get a chance to answer before he was undoing her pants and pushing them down her thighs, all the while wreaking erotic havoc with his mouth on hers. The pants were tight, and her panties went with them. What should have made her feel vulnerable only succeeded in making her feel incredibly sexy. She'd never been naked with a man before, but she had the sneaking feeling that if she had had several lovers, being this way with Jake Barton would feel different.

His hands were busy at her back, unhooking her bra and then pulling it from her body. This time he stopped kissing her long enough to look.

And, man, did he make looking feel like another form of foreplay.

His eyes roamed over her, and everywhere they touched, goose bumps of desire formed on her skin. She was shivering uncontrollably by the time he reached out to gently ruffle the damp curls between her legs.

Hair was sensitive. She hadn't known that, but the light touch went all the way to her core.

She shuddered. "That feels good."

"It gets better."

She didn't doubt it.

He was leaning over her when he slipped his forefinger between the very slick lips of her outer vulva and pressed against her straining clitoris.

Bowing off the bed, she screamed as she had the first orgasm sparked by another person in her life. His hand rubbed, drawing out the pleasure until she grabbed his wrist and begged him to stop. He did, keeping his hand there, cupped protectively over her mound.

Her eyes had shut with the first convulsion, and now she opened them, wondering how he was going to react to a woman who came before they'd even gotten serious about foreplay.

He looked stunned and . . . very pleased.

"You're amazing, Bella."

She licked her lips. They were so dry. So was her throat.

"I'm thirsty," she croaked.

He reached out and brushed her cheek. "I'll get you something."

He came back seconds later with a glass of water, and she drank it down like a frat boy guzzling beer. She'd never been so thirsty. Some of the water spilled, and he leaned forward to lick it up, but once his tongue touched her chest, they both forgot the water.

The empty glass dropped from her hand as she fell back against the bed, unbelievably excited again by the rasping of his tongue against one turgid nipple.

"Jake, please . . ."

He lifted his head. "What do you want, baby?"

"I don't know." Yes, she did. "I want to touch you."

His eyes widened as though she'd surprised him, but he shook his head. "If I let you touch me now, I'm going to come before I ever get inside you."

"Oh, no!" she wailed, remembering something insurmountable. "You can't come inside me. I'm not on the pill."

She wanted to cry. She wanted to throw things.

She wanted—

"I've got condoms."

"You do?" Of course he did. He wasn't a twenty-six-year-old virgin and pathetically unprepared to change that status.

"Yeah." He smiled, looking smug again. "I'm even wearing one. Didn't you notice?"

She hadn't, but she looked now.

His big erection was covered in an almost transparent layer of protection. He must have put it on when he went into the bathroom to get her a glass of water.

She threw her arms around his neck and started kissing him, filled with gratitude for his forethought and a heady dose of excitement. He responded with all the enthusiasm she could want, his mouth opening, letting her tongue inside.

Oh, man, he tasted good. She'd French kissed men before. She'd even enjoyed it, but never like this.

He tasted like he belonged to her, and even if that was an illusion, she liked it.

She kept kissing him, running her hands up and down his body, touching him everywhere she could reach. He jumped when she touched the back of his scrotum between his legs. Then he thrust his body toward her, spreading his legs so she could touch him some more. She did, and it felt as if the hardness nestled against her was growing, but that could not be possible.

He pressed her thighs apart with one knee, and a second later she felt the blunt tip of his erection at her opening.

She tilted up toward him, but though his head slid inside her, that was all he would let her have.

She wanted all of him inside her.

Now.

She grabbed his butt and pulled, but he resisted.

"I want you," she practically shouted.

"Are you sure you're ready?" He touched her again, this time exploring all her secrets. "This is your first time, honey. We can't rush it."

Yes they could, but the words wouldn't come out. Her jaw was locked in indescribable pleasure as one of his fingers slipped inside.

She pressed against his hand.

He moved his hand, possessing her in a way she wanted his whole body to do, and she forced strained throat muscles to work. "That feels incredible. So intimate and wonderful, but I want it *all,* Jake."

"I don't want to hurt you." His voice sounded even more ragged than hers.

"You won't." How could anything hurt when it felt this good?

"But . . ."

"Jake, I'm twenty-six."

He shook his head, sweat beading on his forehead and upper lip while his fingers continued to make love to her and his body moved convulsively against her. "Age isn't a barrier to pain your first time."

"I don't care if it hurts."

And she didn't. She was too excited to feel pain.

He pressed a second finger inside with the first and pushed them both deep. It felt tight, and the barrier was there, but it broke with very little pressure. She managed a choked laugh at Jake's huge sigh of relief.

"I told you s—"

He stopped her words with a very insistent mouth, and this time when she felt him against her opening, she knew it was going to happen.

His fingers weren't nearly as thick as he was, and despite her slick wetness, he didn't just slide right in. Jake didn't seem bothered by that, but rocked against her, gaining centimeter by centimeter in an agonizing torture of pleasure. She locked her legs around his thighs and strained up against him, but all she did was gain maybe one more inch. She could have screamed her frustration.

It wasn't going to work.

When she said as much, he only laughed. "You can take me, Bella. Trust me."

Maybe he was used to it taking this much effort to achieve total penetration, but this was her first time, and she couldn't stand the prospect that it might not work. "The problem is that you don't seem to be able to take me," she accused.

His chest rumbled with humor against her heated and swollen breasts. "Honey, I've never laughed so hard when I was making love to a woman before."

She hadn't meant to make him laugh, but she found herself smiling at him anyway and giving him one of those goofy looks women gave the men they cared about. "I'm glad."

Then neither of them could talk because he pulled her hips toward him with his strong hands. Her body absorbed him, and his hard penis completed its penetration, pushing sensitive and swollen tissues to their max.

She felt unbearably stretched, but filled so beautifully that tears spilled over from her eyes.

"Damn it, I knew it would hurt." He started to pull out, but she wouldn't let him go.

She locked her legs around him with all the strength of her well-toned thigh muscles. "Don't you dare. *It doesn't hurt.*"

"You're crying."

She nodded. "I can't help myself. It's so beautiful. I didn't know it could be this beautiful."

A profound expression crossed his features, and then he started moving inside her with a purpose and rhythm that soon had her tears drying and her hips thrusting her upward to meet every plunge. This time the pleasure built and built and built, but she didn't go over.

"What's wrong?" she demanded in a tortured cry.

"Nothing's wrong, sweetheart."

"But I'm not coming!" Maybe he didn't think that mattered. After all, she'd already climaxed once.

"You will." His voice was filled with promise.

And she believed him.

He reached down between them and spread her wet and swollen lips so that her clitoris got stronger, direct stimulation with every powerful thrust of his body.

Fireworks exploded in her head, and she screamed her throat raw with the power of it.

His shout was deafening, and his entire body went rigid above hers as they climaxed together with mind-altering pleasure.

Jake came back from the bathroom and couldn't believe how right it felt to see Bella Jackson lying in his bed as if she belonged there. She was curled up on her side, watching him with dark, bedroom eyes that still glowed from their mutual pleasure.

He'd gotten rid of the condom, but was hoping he could convince her to share his shower.

She rolled on her back and stretched, her generous curves slipping from beneath the loose sheet over her, and his mouth went dry. Her rosy nipples were soft, but he knew that one brush of his finger and they would grow hard and swell with excitement.

She was that responsive.

"How the hell did you stay a virgin for so long?"

Her head turned, and her gaze locked with his. "I explained that."

"This wasn't exactly committed sex." It was the truth, but

he didn't have to be so blunt, and he could have kicked himself into next Tuesday when her face paled and she turned her head away.

"I know."

He crossed the room and sat next to her on the bed, his hand going out to touch the soft skin of her cheek so he could gently tip her head back toward him. "I didn't mean that the way it sounded."

"Don't apologize. I knew what I was doing when I agreed to come to your ranch, and you're right. We had sex, but we didn't make any promises."

"That wasn't just sex." What they had shared in his bed had been life altering, and that was more than physical lust. "I was your first man; that carries a promise all on its own."

"Does it? I didn't think men saw things that way anymore." Her tone was light, teasing, but her eyes were dark with vulnerability.

"Maybe I'm a throwback, but the thought of you doing what you just did with me with anyone else makes my gut twist in knots strong enough to hobble a raging bull."

"Don't worry. I'm not going to go out and start propositioning your cowboys."

"Good. I'd hate to have to fire anybody. My winter crew is made up of men that have been with me for a long time." He was only half kidding.

She grabbed his hand and pressed it against her creamy smooth breast, her mouth all pouty and soft. "That does not mean I won't proposition you, however."

"You're bold for a virgin."

"I'm not a blushing teenager anymore. I know what I want." And she wanted him.

He gently molded her breast, arousing her peak with the palm of his hand. Sure enough, as he'd thought earlier, her nipple hardened and her breathing quickened just that fast. "You still blush, but I won't deny you know what you want."

"You."

He leaned down and kissed her. "Me. And I want you."

They didn't get into the shower until the sun had started to sink in the horizon and its golden glow turned the off-white curtains on his window a soft orange.

She showed as much aptitude for water games as she had for bed gymnastics, and he could barely stand in order to dry off.

A towel draped toga style around her, she looked in the mirror above his sink and brushed her hair. "You ready to do some Christmas shopping?"

"You've got enough energy to walk?" he asked half humorously and half incredulously.

She looked at him over her shoulder. "If I want to indulge in any more intimacy, I need to stretch my muscles. I'm not used to this particular form of exercise."

He couldn't resist pulling her into his arms. "Then that means we're going shopping, I guess."

She let her head fall back against his shoulder. "We can't spend all of our time in bed."

"Sure we can."

They didn't, but they came close. The next few days flew by as they made love and his sexy little ex-virgin taught him things he didn't know about his own body's responses. They also went Christmas shopping, and he liked the way she asked for his opinion on the gifts she bought her family.

He asked her to help him find something for his sister, and she took him to the office supply store where they bought a small laser printer that printed an obscene number of pages per minute. It had to be ordered, along with an extra input tray.

Christmas was four days away when they went into town to pick up the printer.

Bella hadn't said anything, but he knew she planned to spend the holiday with her family. He hated the thought of her leaving and did his best to ignore her imminent departure.

* * *

Bella picked up the engraved money clip she'd ordered for Jake while he was busy at the office supply store getting his sister's printer.

The last week had been the happiest of her life.

They had talked about everything from family to dreams for the future.

They had played.

He'd taken her riding and introduced her to his motley crew of cowboys, men with a wicked sense of humor.

They made love often.

He'd cajoled Eva into teaching her how to make empanadas after dinner one night when she'd said she wanted to learn. She'd worried the housekeeper would think she was easy, coming home with Jake and making love with him all morning and afternoon that first day, but Eva had been nothing but sweet to Bella. She wanted her boss to get married and made no bones about the fact.

Jake didn't say anything about marriage, or even seeing her again after she left, but Bella could not believe he was ready to dismiss her out of his life after the things they'd shared in and out of bed over the last week.

She thanked the jeweler and turned to go and ran head-on into Jake's big, powerful body.

She bounced backward, her air expelling in a rush.

He grabbed her arms to steady her, but let her go as soon as she showed signs of being stable on her feet.

"Hi." She smiled up at him, expecting the usual kiss of greeting he gave her when they'd been apart longer than five minutes.

She didn't get it.

What she got was a frown.

"What's the matter? Wasn't the printer in?"

"It's in the truck."

"So, why the cranky face?"

And he did look cranky. His green eyes were narrowed dangerously, and his jaw was set in rocklike lines.

"What the hell does this mean?" He brandished a newspaper in front of her.

She took the paper, looking to see what had him so upset, and felt her stomach fall right into her Prada shoes. It was a scandal rag, the type that had so plagued her after her last break-up. Only this one had a big picture of her and Jake on the front cover. They were kissing, and his hand was on her bottom.

She remembered the occasion. They'd been in a mall parking lot, and she'd wanted to do more shopping, but he'd wanted to go home. He'd been convincing her.

It had worked.

So well apparently, neither of them had noticed their picture being taken.

The headline read, "Bad Girl Bella Jackson Spends Week on Rich Lover's Ranch."

She flipped open the tabloid and read the lurid details of her supposed ongoing affair with Jake Barton. The fact that he'd faithfully attended five of her trunk shows was used as proof that there was something between the two of them well before her week on his ranch.

Lexi was quoted as saying she didn't think the relationship would last because Bella was too much of a bad girl to settle down, but she was no doubt enjoying her rich lover's hospitality. The article went on to postulate that her ex-boyfriend, the accountant, had been dining on sour grapes when he wrote his exposé of her supposed frigidity.

People around the small town near Jake's ranch had been interviewed to add speculation and details to the article. From the pictures inside the tabloid, it was obvious a photographer had followed them pretty much everywhere but to the ranch.

The article ended with the announcement that Lexi's Creations would be signing bad girl Bella Jackson to represent them as cover model for another year.

She looked up from the weekly, and met the hostile expression in Jake's eyes.

"I'm sorry," she said.

There wasn't much else she could say. He wasn't used to this sort of publicity, and she hated it. Nevertheless, it was her fault. If she hadn't allowed the whole bad-girl persona to be created, she wouldn't be so newsworthy now.

"Did you tip them off when I invited you to the ranch?"

She shook her head, trying to clear it. He couldn't have meant what it sounded like, but the question had been pretty straightforward.

"You think I alerted the press that I was going to your ranch?" she asked just to be sure.

"How else would they have found out?"

She crossed her arms over her chest, her small shopping bag dangling from her fingers. "Oh, I don't know, Jake. Maybe the reporter followed me? Or maybe Lexi tipped them off." She hated the very idea her employer had betrayed her like that, but Lexi had agreed to comment in the article, and that said something to Bella about the other woman's motives.

Jake's hostility immediately transformed to outrage. "She would do something like that to you?" he demanded.

"I don't know, but it's possible. She was worried about how the recent publicity would impact my reputation and therefore the sensual image of the line."

"How did she know I'd attended five of the shows?"

Bella wasn't answering any more questions until she knew exactly what his motive was for asking them. "Are you implying I told her in some attempt to drum up publicity?"

"No." He ran his fingers through his hair, his expression full of frustration. "Look, you're the one that told me your bad-girl reputation didn't bother you, but you hated being the butt of jokes because of that idiot ex-boyfriend's tell-all exclusives."

She had told him that, and so much more in the last week.

"And that equates to you a willingness on my part to cheapen our relationship by capitalizing on it with the press?"

"No." He glared. "Hell, no. I'm sorry, honey."

She relaxed a little. "Your attendance at the shows wasn't a big secret, Jake. I wasn't the only model that noticed the tall, sexy Texan that came to the shows, but never bought anything."

He sighed. "Of course. My sister could have said something, too."

"You told your sister you were going to the shows?"

"I came to the shows with my sister." He put his hand on her shoulder and started guiding her toward the mall's exit. "Come on, we can talk about this back at the ranch."

She followed, but she wasn't done asking questions. "You came to the shows with your sister?"

"Yes."

"I didn't see her."

"She was there, although after the first couple, she spent most of her time talking to the coordinators and buyers from different stores."

Jake was helping her into his truck.

She clipped her seat belt into place and waited for him to get inside the cab before continuing her questions. "Why was your sister at the shows?"

"She was researching certain aspects of the fashion industry for her next book. That's why she's gone now. She has interviews set up in Paris and New York before she comes home."

"I see." But she didn't. Not really. "You're saying you were only at the shows because of your sister?"

"She's shy. I agreed to escort her so she wouldn't feel so out of place."

"She went to Paris alone," Bella pointed out.

Jake shrugged. "I don't always understand how Lise's mind works."

Bella was starting to understand how Jake's worked, though.

She'd believed he'd come to the trunk shows to see her. Looking back, she realized it had been a ridiculous assumption to make, but she'd been so enthralled by him at first sight, she'd wanted to believe the impact had been mutual.

It hadn't.

Remembering how she'd practically thrown herself into his bed made her go hot with mortification.

She'd offered herself, and he'd taken her up on the offer, but no wonder he hadn't said anything about the future. He didn't see one for them. He'd made his lack of commitment clear from the very beginning.

She couldn't pretend otherwise.

How could she have been so stupid?

No wonder he had left the shows so many times without talking to her. The consuming interest had not gone both ways. He was a highly sexed man; he'd proven that to her in the last few days. He would hardly turn her down when she'd made it so obvious she wanted him.

But that said nothing about his feelings.

Men didn't have to feel anything emotional to enjoy sex. Didn't all the women's magazines say so?

She hadn't realized right up until that moment how much she had been counting on feelings that were strong enough to bring a man back to trunk show after trunk show to grow into something more. Something lasting.

"You've gotten quiet all of a sudden."

"It's probably time I went home. You don't need this type of publicity, and Christmas is almost here."

Jake drove toward the ranch in stunned silence. He shouldn't be surprised. Christmas was coming, and she'd made it clear from the beginning she planned to spend it with her family. And he had acted like an idiot when he first saw the story, but damn it, he hadn't meant he wanted her to leave.

"I don't care about the publicity."

The sound she made must be universal feminine for, "Yeah, right," because his sister did the same thing.

"I don't. I said I was sorry about the way I reacted at first, and I am."

"It's okay, Jake. I'm pretty upset, myself. I hate the fact that Lexi's more interested in my image in the tabloids than the way I represent her clothes on the cover of a magazine or on the catwalk."

"Her world is pretty superficial."

"You're right. It is, and I'm not sure how much longer I want to stay in it."

He about drove off the road, and Bella gasped.

"Jake!"

"Sorry."

He straightened the truck. "Are you serious about leaving modeling?"

"Yes, but I'm not sure where I want to go from here. My career has consumed my life for so long."

"You've been doing pretty good at the ranch, and we don't have a single catwalk."

That made her laugh, but she didn't reply. She just looked out the window, her face averted, so he couldn't read her expression, no matter how many sideways glances he slanted her way.

Every mile nearer the ranch came, the more he felt a sense of urgency to do or say something to cement his relationship with Bella. If she walked away now, would she ever come back?

He'd follow her if she didn't. He wasn't in the habit of giving up on something important to him, and that's just what she was. Important. Necessary.

Did she realize it?

Probably not . . . because until he faced the prospect of losing her, he hadn't allowed himself to accept how much that scenario bothered him.

When they got back to the ranch, he had to take a call from a beef buyer, and Bella wandered off.

He found her an hour later in his bedroom packing.

She looked up when he walked in. "I've got a flight out of Austin tomorrow afternoon. I thought maybe I should go to a hotel near the airport tonight."

Her eyes looked puffy, as though she'd been crying, but they were dry.

"Like hell."

Her doe eyes widened, her lip quivered, and his heart contracted in his chest.

"Why are you leaving?"

"I told you. It's almost Christmas."

"And spending it with me instead of your family would be some kind of nightmare?"

"You want to spend Christmas with me?" she asked, hope flickering in her eyes.

She didn't want to leave him any more than he wanted her to go. "Yes."

"But my family . . ."

"I'll have to meet them sometime."

"You want to meet them?" The flicker had turned into a positive glow, and he was going to make darn sure it stayed lit.

"Yes, do you think your mother would mind a couple of extra guests for Christmas dinner?"

"A couple?"

"I can't leave Lise alone for such an important holiday. She's too solitary as it is."

"I'd love for your sister to join us." Suddenly she was flying across the floor.

She landed against him with a thump, and he wrapped his arms around her good and tight.

"I didn't want to say goodbye."

"I don't either."

Then he kissed her, and they spent the rest of the night proving just how good they were at not saying goodbye.

* * *

Bella woke up Christmas morning snuggled into Jake's furry chest. They'd attended Christmas Eve services the night before with her family and his sister. Bella liked Lise Barton. She was quiet, but very sweet.

And she was a heck of a writer.

Bella's family liked Jake, too. Joshua hadn't been there, but she was sure her brother was going to get along just fine with the man she'd fallen in love with.

It had been love at first sight, and the feelings had only grown the more time they spent together.

She was almost positive he felt the same way, even if he hadn't attended the trunk shows just because of her. He was so affectionate, and seeing him around her family had shown her how totally different he was with her than other people. He'd been polite with her parents, but taciturn, and he hadn't smiled at her sister once. Daisy had told Bella it didn't bother her a bit because he did such a good job of smiling at Bella and making her happy.

She nuzzled into his chest, inhaling his unique, masculine scent. The fragrance of her lover.

She reveled in it.

Her hand brushed up the inside of his thigh, his warm skin making her fingers tingle.

"Here now, none of that just yet."

His deep voice rumbled in his chest, and she looked up to meet a smiling green gaze.

"Good morning."

"Merry Christmas, sweetheart." He reached behind himself and then dropped a red velvet stocking between the two of them. "Look at what Santa brought in the night."

She grinned and upended the stocking. Foil wrapped chocolates dropped out and then a small black velvet box. She stared at it, afraid to pick it up.

What if it wasn't what she thought it was?

What if it was?

"Aren't you going to open it?" he asked.

She licked her lips and nodded. She flipped open the box, and tears filled her eyes.

The ring was a dazzling cluster of diamonds and deep red rubies. "It's beautiful."

"But not nearly as beautiful as the woman I hope will wear it for the rest my life and hers." He sat up and took her with him. He pulled the ring from the box and then slid it onto the tip of her ring finger. "I love you. Will you marry me, Bella?"

She opened her mouth to say yes, but nothing would come out, so she nodded so hard her hair flew around her face.

He slid the ring onto her finger the rest of the way and started kissing and touching her. She told him she loved him as his body took possession of hers.

Afterward, they got ready to go to her family's for Christmas, but something was still niggling at her.

She sat down on the vanity chair to watch him pull on his boots. He was a very sexy man, and she liked his cowboy ways.

"Jake."

"Yeah?"

"I fell in love with you at first sight."

He straightened up and smiled, the expression in his eyes so warm she needed to fan herself. "I did, too."

"I mean the first time I saw you in the audience."

"I know. That's when I lost it over you, too."

"But you came to the shows because of Lise, not me."

"Honey, you said it yourself. Lise went to Paris alone. I knew she'd be okay after the first show and she got a lay of the land. I didn't think for a minute she'd hold me to my promise to attend five fashion shows with her."

"But you kept coming."

"You were there. The truth is, Lise missed one of the shows . . . but I didn't."

She went to him, and he pulled her into his body, right next to his heart.

"I didn't know it could happen like that," she whispered.

"Me either, but I'm glad it did, Bella. I'll love you for a lifetime and beyond."

She twined her arms around his neck and pulled his head down for a kiss. "I love you, too, cowboy. I always will."

Their kiss sealed more than that promise. It sealed their future.

SNOW DAY

Susanna Carr

Chapter One

Tyler Stevens scowled at the blinking Christmas tree lights as they twinkled mockingly in his face. He couldn't let it happen. He would not have Karen Price go to another man's bed. Not now, not ever.

And definitely not while he was under the same roof.

The wind rapped against the windowpanes. Tyler saw the snow blowing violently across the night sky. Damn inconvenient blizzard. If Karen wanted to solidify her relationship with Corey, tonight would be the night.

The only thing he could do to stop it was to speed up his plans. But not too fast or he'd risk pushing Karen right back into Corey's arms. Tyler's sigh shuddered through him. What was he thinking? It was never going to work.

And why couldn't he have been snowed in with only Karen? That would have worked perfectly. But no, Tyler reluctantly surveyed Zack's living room. He was stuck with ten of his childhood friends. As much as he appreciated them, they were the kind of guys you called when you needed help, not when you needed to set a seduction scene.

While most of the Christmas party guests were comparing tall tales of the last blizzard, others talked on cell phones, checking in with their families in the area. Karen was nowhere around.

But then, she had neither tales to swap nor family to call. He remembered when her family coasted into town, their ancient minivan billowing with smoke. People still talked about that day.

The Price family had no intentions to live in the area. They stayed for about a year, enough time to scrape money together to fix the van and leave an indelible impression on the town. By the time the Prices left in a cloud of dust, Karen had turned eighteen and refused to join her family on their next journey.

Tyler had never understood Karen's insistence to live in a place that was slowly dying into a ghost town. He had craved adventure, had been desperate for some excitement. The moment he'd graduated from high school he'd joined the army and never looked back. He'd sworn nothing would entice him to return home.

Funny how people change.

He smiled wryly and decided to look for Karen. He wouldn't have much time alone with her. If he was going to set his plan into action, he had to do it now.

Tyler strode around the house and heard the clatter of dishes. Karen. His heart started to pound. He swallowed back his sudden nervousness and stepped into the kitchen just as she turned to look at the doorway.

Their gazes collided, and Tyler felt the spark hold and hum between them. His skin flushed and tightened. His memory zinged back to that moment he found her in his bed. And how perfect she had looked there.

She had been naked, the thread-bare cotton sheet draping her lush curves, offering tantalizing shadows. Her long red hair had shielded her identity in vibrant waves. His chest had tightened when she flipped her hair back, revealing her beautiful bare face. Karen's blue eyes had widened with surprise. Her full lips parted—

"Where's the aluminum foil?"

"Huh?" Tyler blinked, and shook his head as if that could clear it. His mind landed back in the kitchen with a thump.

Karen was fully clothed in tight faded jeans and a chunky red sweater dotted with snowmen.

"Foil," Karen repeated briskly. "To cover the dishes."

"Next to the sink, left drawer," he answered hoarsely, trying his damnedest to keep his distance before he grabbed. He smiled as she reached for the right drawer. "Other left," Tyler said.

Karen paused and curled her fingers into a fist. "Thanks," she muttered, and hastily grabbed the handle of the left drawer.

He leaned against the counter, trying to look casual as blood roared through his veins. His nerves rattled like the windows against the fierce winds. He wasn't sure how to bring up the subject. He needed to just say it or lose the opportunity. "What do you think about having an affair?"

The rectangle box fell from her hands. "What?" Her voice whipped across the kitchen walls.

Okay, maybe he should have set it up some more. Tyler crouched down and picked up the box. "You and me," he clarified, just in case she had some crazy ideas.

"Have an affair?" she repeated dully. "With *you?*"

That response didn't sound good for him. "Aw"—he flashed her a lopsided smile as he handed the box to her— "when you say it like that, it makes me worried."

She retrieved the box cautiously, as if he'd had time to attach strings to it. If only. "I am dating someone right now," she reminded him.

"Yeah, what's up with that?" He came back to town and found Karen dating a jerk. "Corey isn't your type."

"And you are?" The rip of aluminum punctuated her question.

"Yeah." The lights flickered. He glanced at the overhead light before looking out the window. Snow swirled chaotically around the bowed trees.

"I appreciate the offer," Karen said dryly as she walked back to the bowls and casserole dishes, "but I'm not sleeping with you."

He wasn't going to admit defeat. Tyler went back to leaning against the counter. "Why not?"

She paused. "I'm still dealing with the fallout from the last time I was found in your bed."

"I wondered when you were going to bring that up."

She ripped the foil again with a vicious swipe. "I've tried not to."

Tyler rolled his eyes. "That goes without saying. It's been what?" He shrugged and crossed one ankle over the other. "A year?"

Her hands shook as she covered a bowl. "Valentine's Day," she reminded him with great reluctance.

"And don't you think I've been a gentleman about it?" he asked.

"You?" She whirled around. "A gentleman?"

He flattened his palm against his heart. "I never said a word to anyone."

She jabbed a hand on her hip. "How difficult was that? Everyone already knew, and you left town the next day."

"Yeah," Tyler folded his arms across his chest. "Whoever thought being a gentleman could be so easy?"

Karen pressed her lips together. He couldn't tell if she was trying hard not to laugh or throw the box at his head. "I'm with a *real* gentleman now," she informed him. "And Corey isn't going to appreciate your proposition."

Tyler raised his eyebrow. "It's not him I'm propositioning."

Karen glared at him. "I'm with Corey." She emphasized each word through clenched teeth.

"You should be with me." He knew it, knew deep in his bones that he was right.

"Why do you think that?" She splayed her hands in disbelief. "What do you think you can give me that Corey can't?"

"Sex, for starters."

Karen flinched. Her mouth opened and closed. "Excuse me?" she squawked.

"Come on, it's obvious." Tyler pushed off the counter.

She blushed and turned her back on him. "You don't know what you're talking about."

"Yeah, I do." He crossed the kitchen floor in long, confident strides. "The two of you don't touch and aren't even aware of each other when you're in the same room. I know you guys haven't had sex." And if he had anything to do with it, they never would.

"We've only started dating," Karen said, taking a step away as he drew beside her. "Not to mention he recently broke up with Sherri."

"If I started dating you, we would have been to bed," Tyler predicted, his voice turning husky. "And everyone would know it by the way I watch you. The way I wouldn't be able to keep my hands off of you."

Karen speared him with a withering look. "And how is that different from now?"

A smile tugged at the corner of his mouth. "I would be watching you with satisfaction."

Her eyes glittered, but he didn't look away. Didn't want to. He couldn't keep his eyes off of her. Soon he wouldn't refrain from touching her. He wanted her so much that he shook with it. Tyler didn't care if she knew it as long as she took him out of his misery.

Karen's eyes darkened. Tyler's breath caught in his throat. Was she considering his offer? His heart threatened to hammer out of his chest.

The lights flickered and plunged them into darkness. He heard Karen gasp. His control snapped, and he reached for her, but she wasn't there. "Karen?"

"Hey, Stevens!" Zack called from the other room. His friend's voice scraped at him. "Where are you, man? Looks like we're going to need some flashlights."

Tyler's shoulders sagged as the realization hit him. They were snowbound and in a blackout. How the hell was he going to keep Karen out of Corey's bed now?

* * *

Karen shifted toward the fireplace and read her wristwatch from the faint glow of the dying fire. It just became Christmas Eve. She sighed. Big whoop.

Christmas just wasn't fun when you were an adult, she decided as she fidgeted against the corner she'd claimed her own. She tried to find a comfortable spot. As far as she could tell, there weren't any.

Of course, she could be sharing a bed with Corey right this very moment. Problem was, she wasn't exactly making a run for it. Maybe it was because Corey was sleeping off one too many beers. Might have to do with the fact that she didn't get all quivery at the idea of sharing a bed with him. Or it could be that she was fully aware that Tyler was up there, just a door away from Corey. Maybe it was all of the above.

Karen drew her legs to her chest and rested her chin on her knees. Her gaze fell upon her tidy pile of opened presents. The disappointment punched her in the stomach.

While others received thoughtful gifts or presents about long-forgotten jokes, her gifts were so impersonal they bordered on generic. She knew it was petty and immature to care, but tonight she felt like an outsider more than ever. It was yet another sign that no matter how long she'd lived here, she didn't quite belong.

She might have been setting herself up for unrealistic expectations when she went overboard creating homemade presents, but Karen was grateful for the presents everyone gave her. Everyone but Tyler. She frowned as the tears stung her eyes. He probably thought that any present would hold too many innuendos, but the oversight cut her like a knife.

Tyler. The fates were having a field day with her. She'd finally landed a family guy who not only was a part of this town but whose ancestors were the founding fathers, and Tyler returned wanting to start an affair with her.

Karen shook her head wearily. Tyler Stevens, the one guy she wanted the moment she saw him but knew better than to go after him.

And he'd made it clear tonight that he wanted her to go after him. Before he'd gone upstairs to bed, he'd given her a look that curled her toes. Her body still tingled with excitement. But she didn't want Tyler to excite her. She didn't want Tyler.

No, that wasn't true. She didn't *want* to want Tyler. He was not a small-town family man. He wanted to roam, and she wanted to stay put. Karen would find someone to share the kind of life she wanted to lead. Tyler wasn't that guy, and she made a point of steering clear of him.

Of course, she had been so busy avoiding Tyler that she managed to trip over some guys who didn't deserve a second glance. Like her high school sweetheart who told everybody about their sexual escapades in detail.

Or more recently, her ex-boyfriend Max. She had been prepared to do whatever it took to make their relationship work. When they hit a really rough patch, she went to great lengths of adding some spice to their sex life. Like when her boyfriend went to a wedding on Valentine's Day she couldn't attend because of work. She planned to give Max a last-chance sexy Valentine's surprise.

But the surprise was on her. Who knew that she would get lost and break into the wrong room? That she would wind up in Tyler's hotel bed instead. That Tyler would have moved the remaining wedding party to his room when the bar closed.

Max missed the incriminating scene because he was getting it on with a tipsy bridesmaid, but only Karen's reputation suffered. After all, everyone knew the men in Max's family were loyal and steadfast. All they knew about Karen were the stories they heard.

And while everyone might frown on her reputation, Corey was different. He didn't care what people thought about her. If only . . . Karen tried to keep the thought at bay, but it was no use. She couldn't hide from the truth. She wasn't attracted to Corey.

Damn, maybe Tyler was right. Karen buried her face in her

hands. No. No, he wasn't. He couldn't be. He was just messing with her mind.

She would not give up. She could be attracted to Corey. She needed to give him a chance, Karen decided as she rose from the floor. She could have anything she wanted if she worked hard enough for it. *If I wanted to have sex right now, right this very minute, nothing would stop me.*

She would seduce Corey and put their relationship on a new level. Her pulse jittered from the decision. Karen decided that it was from excitement and not a sense of doom. She crept out of the room, hoping she wouldn't wake up the others sprawled on the floor and furniture.

Karen couldn't see a thing in the hallway. She stubbed her toe as she tried to find the stairs. When she climbed the steps, every creak screamed in her ears.

Pausing at the landing, she squinted, trying to make out the closed bedroom doors. Since this was Zack's house, he would be in the master bedroom with his girlfriend. When Tyler arrived in town, Zack offered him one of the extra rooms.

But which one was Corey in? She vaguely remembered Zack and Tyler helping Corey upstairs. What did they say? First door on the left, that was it.

She wavered, swamped by indecision. For a second she felt lost. She couldn't remember right or left, up or down. Karen gripped the banister until the wooden edge bit into her palm.

Keep your cool. Don't let what Tyler said interfere. Don't let that man come between you and your dreams.

Karen squeezed her eyes closed, hanging on to the last of her courage and turning the corner. She faced the closed bedroom door and raised her fist to knock.

She froze before her knuckles hit the wood. What was she doing? She didn't need to knock. All she had to do was waltz in there and pounce.

Anyway, knocking would mean waiting for an answer. It would give Corey an easy way out. That didn't go with her plans.

Karen silently opened the door and slipped into the room. It was darker than the hallway, if that was possible. She blinked several times, but her eyes didn't adjust to the thick darkness.

She listened and heard Corey's steady breathing. Okay, good. She'd already passed the first test. He hadn't ordered her out the minute she got in. Karen shuffled her way to the bed and stumbled over what felt like a rug.

She caught herself before she kissed the floor. Her heart stuttered as she heard Corey shift. She exhaled shakily when it was apparent he hadn't awoken from the noise. Either he had more to drink than she realized or he was a sound sleeper.

Karen quickly removed her clothes. By the time she stripped off her bra and panties, she was shivering from the cold. At least she hoped that it wasn't nerves that made her teeth chatter.

She slid under the blankets and found the bed sheets icy cold. Karen curled against Corey and felt his warmth immediately. She drew back, startled, when she felt the soft T-shirt and sweatpants he wore to bed. Why it surprised her, she had no idea. There was a blizzard going on out there.

But where did he get the clothes? Obviously Zack or Tyler had loaned him something. Probably Tyler since Zack was built like an ox. Tyler was sleek and—

Don't think of Tyler. Keep him out of your mind. Do not *let him do this to you.*

With renewed determination, Karen pressed herself against Corey. She tilted her face up and grazed her lips against his whiskered jaw.

When she felt him awaken, panic shot through her. Visions of her tossed out of the bed, tossed out of the room, filled her head. Karen knew there was only one thing she could do. She had to seduce Corey's brains out and never give him a chance to say a word.

Tyler sighed and stretched as he felt the voluptuous heat against him. His dream about Karen was revisiting, but something was different about this dream. He frowned, trying to figure it out.

Usually in his fantasies, he would see her in full living color. Karen would be violently needy and would rip off his clothes. She'd punctuate her actions with urgent whispers of how much she wanted and loved him.

This time he couldn't see a thing, and she moved shyly against him. Karen was never shy. Never hesitant. And never more real.

Whoa! Someone else was in the bed. Tyler jerked up and stared into the darkness. "Uh . . ."

Fingertips fumbled against his mouth. "Ssh," Karen whispered. "Let's talk later."

Karen? What was going on? Karen Price was in his bed? That couldn't be right, he decided as her hands drifted to the back of his neck, tugging him insistently.

Tyler tumbled down against her nude body. All of his senses went into overdrive. He inhaled her scent as his hands reverently brushed her soft skin.

He couldn't believe his dream was coming true. He'd thought he blew it, but instead he'd convinced Karen to give them a chance. He wasn't sure how he'd managed that, but he wasn't going to question it.

His mouth brushed against hers, and he tasted Karen for the first time. His heart skipped a beat as his body grew heavy. Karen was right. Talking could wait.

Chapter Two

Karen was surprised at the excitement swirling in her chest. When Corey pressed his mouth against hers, she knew they were going to be great together. It didn't make sense why she already felt achy and needy when Corey's kisses usually inspired nothing more than lukewarm affection.

She wasn't going to question it now. She wasn't going to wonder if it was because she couldn't see Corey. If it meant she was destined to make love in the dark, so be it. Whatever worked.

Slipping her hands under his T-shirt, Karen let out a satisfied murmur when she felt the crisp hair scattered along his sleek chest. She had no idea Corey was this toned. The guy had to stop hiding behind baggy chinos and sweaters. He should dress more like Tyler.

Tyler. A vision suddenly formed of Tyler above her, his muscles rippling, sweat glistening from his tanned skin. She tingled, the image so strong that she could inhale his scent of soap and peppermint.

Karen forced the thought aside as she shoved Corey's shirt past his hard chest and pulled it free. She gasped and shivered as his hot skin pressed against her breasts.

Corey's kisses grew intense, and Karen felt it deep in her body. She arched into him as her nipples stiffened and stung.

Karen loved the strong and solid feel of his shoulders, and she clung to him, pulling him closer.

He embraced her tightly, fitting her against him. She felt defenseless, yet protected. Small but powerful. Swept away but grounded.

Dropping her hands down his shoulders, she smoothed her fingertips over the hard planes of his back. The latent strength, the power under his hot skin, made her stomach clench with anticipation.

His hands dug into her loose ponytail, stripping the scrunchie from her hair. As he devoured her with another kiss, Karen felt the wildness unleashed inside her.

Corey's hands were everywhere on her. He caressed her with wonder, like a man who had found paradise. The touches from his insatiable fingers zinged through her heated blood. She explored his body with delight. Each slope, each dip, was like a new world to her.

The uneven, mingled breaths echoed in the cavernous room as the salty tang of his skin danced on her tongue. But it wasn't enough. If only she could see him! Darkness shrouded her. She couldn't see shapes or shadows.

She yanked down his sweatpants, and her fingertips fanned the sculpted curve of his buttocks. She scored his hard flesh with her nails, and his moan skipped along her. Karen smiled, feeling very feminine and powerful. She knew Tyler's face tightened with pleasure.

Her heart skipped a beat, and she froze. *Tyler?*

No, Corey, she admonished herself, breathing uneasily as the panic loosened from her chest. *C-O-R-E-Y. Get it straight.*

Corey's mouth trailed down her breasts. She quivered as his tongue darted against her skin. His teasing mouth tormented her until she was ready to beg.

She bucked against his hand as he cupped her sex. The contained heat was almost unbearable. Gasping as Corey dipped his fingers into her wetness, her need brightened, grew hotter. Stronger. She felt it could consume her.

Karen moaned and writhed as he demanded pleasure from her body. Corey nipped and grazed down her stomach, his warm breath billowing against her dewy skin. She felt branded by the trail he left.

Excitement skittered across her hips as Tyler lowered his head between her legs. He invaded her with his mouth and fingers, and Karen surrendered instantly, overwhelmed by the intense pleasure. When he took her clit in his mouth, a keen cry burst from Karen's lips. She scraped her nails along his shoulders, his groan meshing with hers.

Karen hooked her knees over his shoulders and clenched her hands into his hair. She pressed him closer, desperate for more, desperate for Tyler to plunge his tongue as deep into her as possible.

Not Tyler. Karen pressed her lips together until they burned. What was wrong with her? She hoped she didn't do something as dumb as calling out the wrong name.

Corey felt her hesitation and drew back. Her protesting whimper fizzled in her throat as he cupped her bottom. He flipped on his back and carried her with him. The only place she could go was straddling his face.

She held herself away from him. "What—?"

"Ride me," Corey ordered her in an urgent, hoarse whisper. His voice sounded rougher, different, but his next command distracted her. "Ride my mouth."

Karen shivered as she imagined the deep pleasure he could give her. She lowered herself on him, his unshaven jaw scratching the soft flesh of her thighs. The first flick of his tongue resonated deep in her body.

Flattening her palms against the wall, Karen gently rocked against Tyler's mouth. His nose rubbed hard against her clit as her hips rolled.

The sensations swept inside her, building, building until her hips moved in a blur. She arched and swayed as Corey's hands flew over her curves, seeking her hips, her legs, her breasts. He squeezed her breasts until she thrust deep in his mouth. He awarded her for the audacious move by pinching her nipples hard.

The climax she sought tingled in her toes and rushed up her legs until it exploded deep in her hips. She pitched forward, slamming against the wall as the climax shattered inside her.

She felt Tyler's hands cradling her back as he gently lowered her on the bed. Karen gulped air as he parted her shaking legs and surged into her.

She forgot to breathe as he burrowed inside her. He stretched and filled her, each move hammering the deep-seated longing that had been a part of her forever.

Karen stared into the darkness, overwhelmed by the sensation of being claimed. Taken. She never felt like this. Didn't know if there was even a name for it.

The sensations and uncertainty pounded down on her as Tyler claimed her mouth as he thrust into her. She felt the last thread of thought hanging over the edge, ready to plunge into the unknown, knowing that no matter what happened, she would never be the same.

Tyler's rough and untamed moves triggered her release. Her body clenched his as her hips lurched off the bed. Light showered behind her eyes as he stiffened and plunged one last time.

His sweat-slicked body collapsed onto her spent body, and Karen gratefully accepted the warmth. Tears pricked her eyes as he gathered her close and shielded her from the cold. She heard the heavy thud of his heart and allowed herself the pleasure of curling her arms around him.

Karen stared in the darkness, her heart pounding, her body throbbing. She pressed her lips together and blinked away the tears. Because she knew she couldn't feel like this again. She couldn't be with Corey. Ever. She didn't deserve it.

Because the whole time she had been imagining Tyler.

Karen winced the next morning as the blinding sunlight leaked through the shades. She frowned in her sleep and snuggled deeper under the blankets. Her leg bumped against something solid as her toes rubbed against the crisp hair covering a very masculine leg.

Corey. Karen froze and struggled to keep her eyes closed. Struggled not to leap out of bed. She had to wake up and face him, knowing full well that she'd had sex with him while thinking of Tyler. Knowing she had to break up with Corey and not tell him the real reason.

Her mind felt shattered as she tried to come up with a plan to sneak out of the bed undetected. Any half-baked idea evaporated as Corey's arm tightened around her waist and held her close against him. Her eyes shot open as his thick cock nestled against her bottom.

Longing drifted lazily to her womb like fat, feathery snowflakes. The need gathered until it weighed heavily on her. Karen rocked against him, giving in to the undeniable sensation.

"Karen," he murmured against her ear. The husky tone skittered across her skin.

She stared at the wall as if her life depended on it. Karen wanted to melt into him, but she had to be strong. She was feeling particularly vulnerable and weak because she hadn't had sex for such a long time. Hadn't been held with such tenderness. Possessiveness.

"We need to get up." Her voice came out as a croak.

His hand flattened against her stomach. Could he tell how it somersaulted? Did he know how much last night had affected her? She forgot to breathe as he captured her earlobe between his teeth.

"Kiss me first," he urged her.

A kiss. Okay, she could do a kiss. One last kiss. She just had to control it before it got out of hand like last night.

Don't remember last night. Purge it from your memory. Just turn around and give Corey a kiss.

Only Corey wasn't patient about it. She felt him nibbling down her jaw. Karen closed her eyes in anticipation. She swiped her tongue across her lips right before his mouth met hers.

His lips were warm and demanding. Karen responded without hesitation, greedily kissing him back. She dug her fingers into his hair and drew him closer as she dipped her tongue into his mouth.

Okay, so much for just one last kiss, but she couldn't help it. Tyler's kisses were so addictive. No, not Tyler. *Corey.* Sheesh. Why couldn't she get it straight?

Corey rolled on top of her, his chest crushing her breasts. She was surrounded by a mesmerizing heat that drugged her senses. Karen parted her legs, welcoming his hardness. She wanted Tyler inside her. Now.

Damn, she was doing it again. *Corey.* She was kissing *Corey.* And the kiss was getting out of control. She had to pull away. She had to do the right thing, even if it wasn't the easiest.

Karen reluctantly withdrew her mouth from his and opened her eyes. "We have to . . ." She stumbled into silence when she saw Tyler above her.

Oh, noooo. Her fingers tightened against his skull. She was getting worse. Now she was hallucinating!

But her vision of Tyler was unlike anything she imagined before. His short black hair was mussed and sticking up. His brown eyes were bleary with sleep and desire.

Dread pulled at her in all directions. Why was she imagining him like this? Why did he seem all too real, right down to the ruddy color under his tanned complexion?

Tyler gave her a slow, knowing smile that turned her inside out. "We have to what?" he asked, lowering his head for another kiss.

Karen's breath lodged in her throat. She parted her lips. And screamed.

Tyler clapped his hands over her mouth. "Holy shit, Karen." What had gotten into her? She hadn't made this much noise when she was coming.

She tried to wiggle from his hold. "What are you doing here?" His hand muffled her voice.

His ears were still ringing. Maybe he didn't catch the entire question. "This is my bedroom."

Karen slapped his hands away. "Where's Corey? What did you do with him?"

Why was she asking him? Do what to Corey? "Are you always like this first thing in the morning?" He heard of people being disoriented when they woke up, but Karen was seriously confusing him.

She looked around the bedroom. "Oh, my God."

"What's wrong?" He knew his room was a mess, but it wasn't that bad.

Karen covered her face with trembling hands. "Oh, my God," she whimpered. "Oh, my . . . God."

Something was definitely wrong. She should be chanting this right before he brought her to an orgasm, not on the morning after. "Karen?"

"I need to get up."

She looked pale. Tyler backed away in case she was sick, but the way she bolted from the bed showed remarkable athleticism. "What the hell is going on?" he asked as she went straight to her pile of clothes.

"This isn't happening again," she said, snatching a scrap of lace. She turned away, shielding her body from his gaze.

Her words whirled around in his head. His stomach clenched. "Again?"

"I thought . . ." She dipped her head, her fingers motionless against the hooks of her bra. "I thought Corey was sleeping here."

Her confession hit him hard. She hadn't been trying to seduce him. She had been trying to seduce . . . "Corey," he repeated.

"It was dark and . . ."

"You thought I was Corey." Her wild responses, her adventurous sensuality, had been for Corey. The mind-blowing sex she just gave him was meant for that jerk.

She froze at his biting tone and cautiously looked over her shoulder. "It was an honest mistake."

Tyler fell back against his pillow, a burning feeling eating away at his gut. He wanted to puke. He finally got Karen Price in his bed, and it turned out to have been a mistake.

"I am really, really sorry about this," Karen said almost breathlessly as she threw on her clothes.

He didn't answer and stared at the ceiling. If she was expecting him to apologize, she was in for a long wait.

"It would be best if we just forget last night."

Not going to happen.

Tyler sensed her pausing. He could feel her gaze on him. He braced himself for whatever she had to say.

"And," she added in a soft voice. "I would really appreciate it if you didn't tell anyone about this."

He slowly turned and glared at her. What kind of guy did she think he was? Tyler thought it would be in everyone's best interest if he didn't ask out loud.

She busily grabbed her socks off the floor before stuffing them in her jeans pockets. Apparently she couldn't stand the sight of him as long as it took to put on her socks. She halted when her gaze clashed with his. "Please?"

Tyler propped his head against his hand. "Why would I want anyone to know that you keep showing up in my bed hoping I'm a different guy?"

Karen winced. "Tyler, it's not like that. You're a great guy and—"

If she said something about being a good friend, he was going to jump naked into a snowbank. He frowned when he saw her backing up to the door. "Where are you going?"

She shot a pleading look skyward. "Somewhere as far away from here as possible."

That would be the worst course of action. He knew the house would be crawling with people. Nosy people who couldn't keep a secret if their lives depended on it. "I wouldn't go out there if I were you. At least not alone. Let me come with you."

"Are you crazy?" she hissed. He could see her knuckles

whiten as she gripped the doorknob. "Why would I want to incriminate myself like that? It's better if I sneak out."

"Someone will see you." And if there was something he knew about this town, it was that if you acted guilty about anything, your neighbors would eat you alive.

"I doubt it. And the sooner I'm way from this"—she fluttered her hands in the general direction of the bed—"the better."

"Karen!" He lunged for the door, but she slipped away. Damn, he had to follow her. No way would he repeat *his* mistake. He was going to be at her side, whether she liked it or not.

Karen closed the door gently behind her, her heart clanging against her ribs. She had to get downstairs fast. The last thing she needed was to have everyone know she wound up in the wrong bed again. She would never live it down.

She didn't realize she had been holding her breath until she saw Corey walk out the door from across the landing. Her lungs shriveled on the spot. Karen hesitated and immediately ruined her getaway.

"Karen?" His voice echoed in the hallway.

She plastered a smile onto her face, furious at herself for that telltale guilty pause. "Hey, Corey." From his red eyes and washed-out skin tone, Karen could tell that he was suffering from a horrendous hangover. "How are you feeling?"

He ignored her question. "Where've you been?" His eyes squinted with suspicion.

"Um . . ." Her answer trailed off as Zack walked out of the bathroom. She hoped the guy would distract Corey so she could escape.

"Morning, all." Corey winced from Zack's booming voice. Karen saw her opportunity. She wasn't going to mess it up this time.

"Hey, Karen, don't get lost again," Zack teased. "That's Tyler's room."

She never had appreciated Zack's humor. Even more so at this very moment. Especially with Corey looking at her as if she'd sprouted another head. What could she do other than play stupid? "Is it?" She took another step away from the door.

Corey wasn't buying her act. "You and Tyler?"

Okay, stupid wasn't getting the job done. "What?" She made a face. "No, I was looking for you."

Corey's eyes narrowed into slits. "Where'd you sleep last night?"

A movement on the steps caught her attention. She saw a few heads bobbing. Great, more spectators. Like she wasn't feeling crowded in already.

"Karen," Corey repeated as if she was a belligerent child. "Where did you sleep?"

"Uh . . ." She didn't have a good answer. She looked at the audience and knew she had to come up with something. "Where'd you sleep?" she shot back at Corey. From the look on their faces, she could tell her tactics weren't working in her favor.

"Okay," Zack said, his voice rolling across her spent nerves like thunder. The guy had no concept of indoor and outdoor voices. "Let's put it this way. How long were you in Tyler's room?"

Great, why not notify everyone else in the house to come watch the show upstairs? Karen was ready to give up and commit social suicide by telling him to mind his own business. It would be just as bad as a full confession. Probably worse.

The door behind her opened. Karen felt as though her entire world came crashing down as she watched everyone's faces sag with shock. Time skidded into slow motion as she heard Tyler step out of the bedroom.

Just keep walking. Walk right by me. Let the folks know there's nothing to see here.

She felt him stop at her side. Karen refused to look at him.

She knew he was guided by some twisted sense of chivalry, but she could strangle him right about now.

"Hey, sweetheart," he said as he encircled her wrist with his large fingers, "I found this under your pillow." He stuffed her hair scrunchie into her limp hand.

Karen stiffened when he wrapped his arm around her waist and placed a tender kiss against her tangled hair. If the obvious display of ownership didn't get the message across, the fact that Tyler wore a pair of unbuttoned jeans and nothing else should clobber the idea into everyone's head. She was surprised he didn't work in the scratches she put on his back.

"Hey, guys," Tyler said as if he just noticed the crowd in the hallway. "I don't know about you all, but I'm starving."

No, Karen decided as she ground her back molars, strangling was too good for him.

Chapter Three

Karen cracked the bathroom door open and saw that the coast was clear. After Tyler's untimely appearance, she had hurried into the bathroom and left him to the wolves. He seemed to have done just fine without her and managed to herd the other guests downstairs.

Stepping outside the bathroom, she absently wrapped the scrunchie in her hair. Karen nibbled her bottom lip with indecision. She wasn't sure where to go.

Even though she was ashamed of her cowardly dive into the bathroom, Karen wished she could have locked herself in until the snow melted. But the fact was, she was freezing and desperately needed to stand in front of the fireplace. So she would withstand the censorious glares and stage whispers. Anyway, she had no room to hide away from everyone, so she might as well get it over and done with.

Huh, that's strange. Karen considered that as she crept toward the landing. She usually wanted to hide within the crowd, not avoid them.

Karen jumped when she saw someone standing in the shadows. "Corey!" She slapped her hand over her thumping heart.

"You want to tell me about it now?" Corey stepped into the light, his words and movements clipped with anger. "There's no audience this time."

"I'm so sorry." She took an instinctive step back and struggled to look him in the eye. "It was an honest mistake."

Corey didn't seem to care about her reasons as he blocked her way to the stairs. "Did you sleep with him?"

Karen stalled. Would it be wise to say that she thought it was him? She had a feeling that Corey wouldn't appreciate the case of mistaken identity.

Corey's expression pinched as her silence grew longer. "I guess that answers my question."

She squeezed her eyes shut. "I didn't mean to go into Tyler's room."

"Right." His voice dripped with sarcasm. "Like you didn't mean to be in his bed at Farmer's wedding."

Her shoulders dipped in defeat. "I know it's hard to believe," she admitted quietly. She hoped that someone, anyone, would believe her, but that was asking too much. "And I understand if you don't want to speak to me anymore."

Corey drew back in surprise. "Nonsense," he replied, the anger disappearing from his voice in a flash.

He was being nice, Karen realized. That was probably how gentlemen handled these situations. She squared her shoulders back, prepared to say the necessary words. "We need to break up."

His eyes widened. "We've barely started dating," Corey argued. "You should give us one more chance. Come on, Karen. It's Christmas."

Karen was already shaking her head before he finished. She wasn't going to hang on to a guy because it was the holidays. "That would be a bad idea."

Corey frowned. "I don't think you understand the predicament you're in . . . ."

A movement on the staircase distracted her. She darted a look past Corey's arm and spotted Tyler standing at the bottom step. Karen felt a blush zoom up to her face when she saw Zack's girlfriend behind Tyler. Other houseguests crowded behind her, listening intently.

At least everyone but Tyler was trying to hide their presence. From the tension shimmering off his body, Tyler looked as if he was waiting for an excuse to barge in. She waved him off, hoping Corey didn't see her move. From the way Tyler's eyebrow arched, she sensed she aggravated his bad mood.

". . . but I'll stand by your side until the gossip blows over," Corey finished, his promise grabbing her attention.

Karen hesitated, and she glanced into his pale eyes. It was incredibly tempting to take Corey up on his offer. She wouldn't mind someone backing her up, but she knew it wouldn't be right.

And, if she was going to be completely honest with herself, she wanted Tyler to be the one backing her up. But she couldn't rely on him. He was never around long enough. She knew that, but she also knew no one else would do. She'd handle whatever came her way alone. There were no other options.

"That's generous of you," she told Corey, "but I would feel uncomfortable about that. It's understandable why we won't see each other anymore."

"No." He grabbed her wrist, and she jerked back.

"Corey, we're through," she said, trying to shake off his hold.

"You need me." His fingers bit into her flesh.

She winced. "What does that mean?" she asked as she heard footsteps pounding up the stairs.

"What it really means," Tyler interrupted, suddenly standing next to her, "is that he needs you more than you need him."

Corey dropped Karen's wrist. "Go to hell, Stevens."

"See?" Tyler asked her, motioning at the other guy. "He doesn't deny it."

Karen rubbed her forehead. She was cold, hungry, and worn out. She wished she was back home, in her own bed, and far, far away from all this.

"And no one would deny my right to take a swing at you for sleeping with my woman," Corey said with a snarl.

"From what I just heard, you were barely dating, so how could she have been your woman?" Tyler's arms hung loose, but the atmosphere around him crackled with menace.

Corey stood toe to toe with Tyler. "From what I understand, any man could claim her as his woman."

It all happened in a blur. Karen barely had time to gasp from the verbal slam when Tyler shoved Corey. Before she knew it, Tyler had him pinned against the wall.

"That's enough, you guys!" She tried to sound firm but knew they weren't listening to her. She wasn't going to get any help from the spectators who stormed the stairs, cheering the men on.

Karen tugged at Tyler's bare arm. She felt the strength flow underneath her hand and knew there was no way she could pull him off. "Tyler, please don't do this. Please leave."

He didn't spare her a glance as he held his quarry immobile. "Sure, sweetheart. Right behind him."

"Why should I leave?" Corey spat out. "You're the one interrupting a *private* conversation with my girlfriend."

Tyler's nostrils flared. "Non-girlfriend."

"Ex-girlfriend," she automatically corrected. She sighed and dragged her hands through her hair. "This is all my fault and I can't tell you how sorry I am."

"Don't be sorry," Tyler ordered. "At least, not for Corey. This works perfectly for him."

"Shut up," Corey warned.

"What's going on?" She caught the look between the men as the group fell into an expectant silence. She knew what that meant. She was left out again. On something important. Something about her. "Tyler, tell me."

She saw the muscles in his jaw bunch. "Going to visit Corey's parents for Christmas?" he asked, the tone of his voice soft and lethal.

Karen frowned at the off-topic question. "I was," she answered cautiously as she tilted her chin up with pride. "What of it?"

He sliced an enigmatic look at her. "Ever wondered why? Since you guys only 'just started dating'?"

She swallowed roughly as the bitter taste of dread filled her mouth. "No." She looked at Corey, who glared at his captor.

"It appears Corey's heart still belongs to Sherri," Tyler revealed, his fists tightening on the man's wrinkled sweater, "but she didn't pass his family's approval. So he decides he'll show how great Sherri is by dating the one woman his family would disapprove of on the spot."

"Me," she said in a broken whisper. She should have seen that one coming. Karen had wanted to believe the family invite was a sign of acceptance. But from the uncomfortable silence behind her, everyone knew she had been invited because she would have received a cold reception.

She had been wrong, Karen realized as the numbness bled through her body. Corey did care about her bad reputation. Just not in the way she had expected.

"And that's why he's not ready to call it off yet," Tyler explained. "His plan is incomplete."

"I see." A cynical smile flitted across her lips. It served her right. The one time she dated a guy for a reason other than love. Karma was definitely turning around and biting her back.

Through her disenchanted haze, she saw Tyler's concerned frown. He quickly let go of Corey. "Karen?"

She couldn't handle his pity, especially now. Damn this snow day. Whoever dreamt for a white Christmas was insane. Completely, freaking insane.

"Karen?" Tyler repeated sharply.

"I need to be alone," she said, and rushed into the closest room. It didn't matter which one it was, as long as it offered an escape from the sympathetic looks. She slammed the door right before Tyler reached her.

Sliding the lock home, Karen ignored his insistent knocking. She rested her forehead on the cold wood, horrified by her actions, knowing there was no way to repair the damage.

Turning, she glanced around the room, wondering if there was another way out.

Her eyes widened with horror when she discovered she was back in Tyler's room. Karen slid to the floor and stared at the unmade bed. What else could go wrong today?

"What are you doing out here?" Tyler called out to Karen as the back door swung shut behind him.

Karen looked over her shoulder. "What does it look like?" she asked as she scooped more snow with the shovel and tossed it to the side.

Tyler strode over to her. The cold slapped and burned at him. He huddled deeper into his coat, wondering what possessed Karen to be outside. "We don't need a clean sidewalk to the shed."

Karen shrugged and resumed shoveling. Tyler glanced around the backyard. From the looks of it, Karen had removed the snow from all the sidewalks and steps. If he didn't stop her, she'd be heading for the alley. He shook his head at the sight. Well, as long as she took her anger out on the snow and not at his head. . . .

"Corey left," Tyler abruptly informed her. "He decided the trek was more appealing than staying here."

"Corey lives six blocks away," she said matter-of-factly as the snow crunched against her shovel. "I would hardly call that a trek."

"Yeah." Tyler noticed that she wasn't exactly distraught over the breakup. He also noticed that he was much too satisfied about the fact. "But since he was your ride, I'll drive you home once the streets are cleared."

She paused, "Thanks."

He watched her scoop up the snow, wanting to wrestle the shovel from her hands and haul her inside. But he had a feeling she was out here because of him. He needed to fix it. "Uh . . . and I want you to know that I'm sorry."

"Sorry?" Karen turned, her face bright pink. Her blue eyes that haunted him glistened from the cold. "About what exactly?"

"Not about last night," he clarified hotly. No matter how it happened, he was not going to regret having Karen in his bed. The next step was showing that he wanted to share more than a bed with her.

"Then sorry about what?" She brushed away the vibrant red hair from her face.

"Telling you about Corey's plan. When you were hiding in the bathroom, Debbie told me what she heard from Sherri. I shouldn't have told you in front of everyone." He shook his head and raised his arms in apology. "I'm sorry."

"Don't be." Her mouth twisted in self-disgust. "I should have figured it out on my own."

Tyler studied her expression. If she wasn't upset about that, he could slip in the other thing while she was in a forgiving mood. "And I'm sorry about walking out of the bedroom when you asked me not to. I could hear those guys and—"

"Okay"—Karen pointed an accusing finger at him—"that you should be sorry about. I know why you did it, but it still pisses me off."

"Can't you feel that way inside?" He gestured to the house.

Karen let out a sigh, her breath a smoky white puff against the icy cold. "I rather stay out here."

He rolled his eyes. Karen could be too stubborn sometimes. "I'll stay out of your way," he promised. He wouldn't like it, but he'd do it.

She flashed a surprised look at him. "It's not you I'm worried about."

Tyler glanced toward the house. The kitchen curtains twitched. "Those guys?" He admitted one or two got on his nerves, but in a town as small as this one, friends were decided on by age, not by personality. "Why do you care what those guys think?"

"You wouldn't understand." She returned to shoveling the walk.

"Try me," Tyler said with a trace of exasperation.

He thought she was going to ignore his request when she finally muttered, "You don't know what it's like being an outsider."

Her comment startled him. He'd never thought of her as one. "I got a taste of it," he admitted, "but didn't stay in one place long enough for it to matter. Why do you stay?"

"What's going to make another town different?" She grunted as she tossed snow into the pile. "I'm still going to be an outsider."

"This town doesn't have much to offer for you."

Karen seemed to take offense at his opinion as she whirled around to face him. "So I should leave? No way. I decided that this place in the world is my territory."

This was his birthplace, and while it was close to his heart, he wasn't that passionate about it. "Why here?"

"Why not here?" She stabbed the shovel into the snow as though she was claiming a mountain with a flag. "I'm not bailing out because it's hard. I'm not leaving. I'm going to dig in and make it work."

Tyler's heart flip-flopped as he took it all in. Would she feel the same about him? Would she lavish him with the same passion, the loyalty, the love?

He was making a lot of decisions over a long shot, but if she ever fell in love with him, he would spend a lifetime to prove that he was worthy of her. Tyler smiled with anticipation. All this time he had been seeking adventure and endless possibilities, and it was right next door packaged as a redhead who couldn't tell her right from her left.

"What?" She placed her hands on her hips and glared at him. "Why are you looking at me like that?"

He knew better than to tell her now. She wouldn't believe a word he said. "No reason."

Her eyes narrowed into slits. "Whatever. You probably don't understand what I'm talking about. You left the moment you could and stayed away for as long as possible."

"But I'm back now."

"Yeah, for how long?" she tossed back at him. "You didn't move back home when you got out of the army. Nothing changed as far as I know."

Everything changed the moment he saw her in his bed.

"After all," she continued, "what's keeping you here? You have no family and no job to tie you down."

"Maybe I want to claim my corner, too," he said with quiet certainty.

Tyler saw the flare of recognition in her eyes. He met and held her gaze. He could tell what she thought. She had a sense she was that corner.

She broke eye contact and looked down at the sidewalk. "I think I'm done." She made a show of stretching her back and shoulders. "Here, you can finish it up."

He looked at the shovel and grabbed it with a short jerk. Just as he hoped, she lost her balance and fell against him. Tyler curled his arm around Karen and kissed her before she got away.

She should have stopped him, Karen realized as she nibbled his mouth, tasting him and wanting more. She suckled his bottom lip, drawing him in, listening to his ragged breath. Come to think of it, she should probably pull away now.

After all, she knew better than to kiss Tyler. Instead she closed her eyes and returned the kiss with an uncontrollable hunger that frightened her.

Karen vaguely heard the shovel falling into the snow. She didn't care where it landed as she wrapped her arms around Tyler's shoulders. She needed to get closer, feel his skin, melt into his body.

Need, hot and urgent, rolled inside her, gaining momentum, gathering strength. But it was the underlying sense of belonging that made her want to crawl into him. It drew her into his arms and kept her there. It urged her to get closer and discover the source she'd been seeking all this time.

She explored his mouth. Her pulse skipped as her blood turned thick and slushy. Tyler braced his legs as she moved closer.

Karen clung to his shoulders, wanting to climb all over him. Tyler slid against the wet sidewalk, and he reeled back. She held on tight as they fell.

Snow sprayed around them. Tyler cradled her head as they landed. His gentle, protective touch nearly undid her. She looked into his dark eyes and shivered.

"I want you so much," Tyler confessed before he claimed her mouth again.

Karen paused, her lips clinging to his, snowflakes burning her skin. *Want*. The word bounced around in her head. He wanted her.

What was she thinking? He desired her, nothing more. She'd been desired. She was looking for something to go along with it. Adored would be a good start. Cherished would do. Love . . .

Staring at Tyler sprawled in the snow, Karen felt as if she had been hit in the head with the shovel. Love? No, she didn't want to love Tyler. She definitely didn't want to be loved by him. That would be trouble. Inconvenient.

And so right.

No, no. It couldn't be right. She pulled away and got up quickly, her moves awkward and ungainly. "Being wanted is not enough for me."

"Karen." He reached for her.

She dodged his hand and brushed the snow from her clothes. "Despite what the evidence suggests, I am not an easy lay."

Tyler slowly stood up. "Believe me, I'm fully aware of that."

She flipped her hair out of her eyes with an irritable move, the wet snow spattering her hot cheeks. "And I have *not* slept my way through this town's phone book."

"Who says you have?" His gloved hands bunched into fists. He looked ready to take on anyone who would suggest such a thing.

"What exactly do you want from me, then?" She couldn't figure it out, and it was driving her nuts.

The look he gave made her weak in the knees. She felt as if he saw her, all the layers she hid from others as well as herself, and found her lovable. Loved all the scars and shadows because they were a part of her.

"I want to make you mine," he said in a soft growl.

Karen ignored the warmth flooding her veins. She was doing it again. Hearing what she wanted to hear. She couldn't afford that luxury. "Your what?"

He shrugged as he searched for the right word. "Everything."

That particular word held a wealth of meaning, and yet, it said nothing at all. "Right," she said harshly. "I don't believe you."

He stiffened. "Why not?"

"I have heard every ploy to get me in bed," she revealed bitterly.

"I'm not trying to get you into bed." His voice echoed in the barren outdoors.

"Because you already got me there?" She turned and stomped back to the house. "That's no guarantee that I'm going to show up again."

"I don't want you in my bed."

Karen skidded to a stop. What a liar! She whirled around, ready to call him on it.

He approached her with slow, sure strides. "Not until . . ."

Ah, a catch. She should have known. Karen silently admitted she was disappointed. She'd thought Tyler was different. "Until what?"

Tyler stood beside her and lowered his head. She stood still to prove that she wasn't affected by his close proximity. Prove that she wasn't worried. That she was in total control.

"When you show up in my bed again," Tyler said softly in her ear, "it will be because you want to be there with me. Because you want *me* and can't live without me."

Her jaw dropped. "Are you saying?" She spluttered and tried again. "Of all the—"

"That's right, Karen," Tyler said as he walked away. "I'm not letting you back in my bed until I know that you mean it."

Chapter Four

Karen felt her good behavior was hanging on by a thread. It was already night, and the power still was out. She was thankful that the roads were now cleared or there was no telling what she would have done.

She had done everything she could to keep busy, keep warm, and keep away from Tyler. She couldn't say she succeeded, but she'd done her best. She'd like to think she put on a good act that nothing was the matter, but Zack's girlfriend shattered that belief when she hugged her goodbye.

"Don't let the guys bug you," Debbie whispered in Karen's ear. "It's about time you and Tyler got together."

She froze. "What?"

"And don't worry, Zack is staying over with me tonight, so you can have the whole house to yourself."

Karen drew back. "You don't understand. We're not a couple." It was bad enough for her to hope, but she didn't want her friends to expect something to happen.

"Not yet, but you will if Tyler has anything to do with it," Debbie predicted as she headed for the open door, the cold wind snagging at the festive decorations. "Merry Christmas!"

Karen weakly repeated the wish and waved Debbie goodbye. From the corner of her eye, she saw Tyler waiting at the door. Karen could feel his gaze on her. It was tempting to glance in his direction. Too tempting.

"I'm going to help them get their cars out of the snow," Tyler told her.

"I'll come with you." Karen avoided looking at him as she went for her boots.

"No, you've done enough shoveling for one day," he decided as he stepped outside. "Stay here. I mean it."

"Fine." She shrugged. It would make it easier to stay away from him.

When Tyler closed the door, Karen drifted to the window and watched. She could see Tyler's silhouette in the car headlights as he helped their friends. She couldn't stop staring as the need tugged deep at her.

Karen turned away, wishing the feeling would disappear. She needed more than an affair. More than sex. Mind-blowing, amazing sex . . . *Stop thinking about it!*

She jumped into action and tidied the living room. With the blazing fire in the fireplace her only source of light, it was a slow job that gave her too much time to think. She wanted Tyler, but was she willing to risk everything for him?

If an affair was all she could have with Tyler, Karen decided as she folded a blanket, maybe that would be enough. And when he left like he always did, she would know what it felt like to belong with someone special. The aching loss had to be much more soothing than the nagging bite of yearning.

The bang of the door jerked her to full attention. "Hey, Karen?"

She would do it. The decision made her feel jittery. She would launch herself into a relationship with Tyler. And if wanderlust hit him, she would follow.

Wow. Karen gripped the blanket. She couldn't believe she just decided that, but it was true. It would be difficult, but she knew the sacrifice would be worth it.

All this time she struggled not to feel like a stranger in her hometown. But she had been looking in the wrong place. She belonged with Tyler, no matter where they lived.

She heard him walk into the room. "Karen? What's that smile about? Thinking of me?" he teased.

"Maybe." She looked at him and felt edgy all of a sudden. Scared and excited. Alive and ready to take a leap. "You look cold. I'd make you something warm to drink, but the lack of power kind of makes it difficult."

"No problem. You can keep me warm in other ways." He wagged his eyebrows with exaggeration.

She pressed her lips together, refusing to encourage him. "First I have to tell you something."

Tyler exhaled and looked at the fire. "What?" he asked reluctantly, lines bracketing his mouth.

She swallowed nervously. "Last night, I might have thought it was Corey"—she was almost too embarrassed to admit it, but she knew she had to tell him—"but I kept thinking of you."

He did a double-take. "Say what?"

Oh, God. He was going to think she was the most horrible person. "What you said made me worried that something was wrong with Corey and me," she rushed to explain. "And something was wrong. I liked him, but I didn't love him. I'm not attracted to him, either. I never was."

Tyler stuffed his hands in his pockets and rocked back as he studied her. "So you were going to lie on your back and think of me?"

"I didn't *plan* to think of you!" She glared at him and noticed the sly twinkle in his eyes. Her glare deepened. "When I realized what I was doing and how wrong it was, I knew I had to call things off with Corey. Then I woke up and found you next to me."

"Have you ever thought that winding up in my bed wasn't an accident?" he asked with a knowing smile.

"Because that's where I want to be anyway?" She couldn't

believe her confession was going straight to his head. "You're stretching it, Tyler."

"Wait a second. Let me get this straight." He held up a hand. "You didn't break up with Corey because you slept with me—"

"It was a factor!"

He continued as if she hadn't spoken. "But because you want to be in my bed."

She hesitated and took the risk. "Because I want to be with you."

He stiffened as if he was afraid to move. The intense look he gave rooted Karen to the spot. Only when his eyes slowly brightened with hope did she find the courage to continue.

"No matter what," she added, her heart taking a free fall. It was exhilarating, in a make-you-feel-nauseous sort of way. "I avoided the truth long enough. I knew we wanted very different things, and I kept my distance from you. But now it's more important for me to be with you, even if you leave again."

"Don't you know?" he asked with a small smile. "I'm here to stay."

"You are?" She dropped the blanket as her heart hit the brakes midair. "Why?"

"I came back for you."

She was afraid to believe it. "You're just saying that," she said softly, taking a step back.

"No, I'm not." Tyler followed her. "It's weird, I've always thought about you over the years. What you would have said about something. When I remembered something about this place, you were always front and center."

"Really?" His words washed over her. Was she hearing what she wanted to hear? If it wasn't what she thought, she would crash and burn and not be able to pick up the pieces this time.

"I thought it was because we're friends, but then I noticed I didn't think about the others as much. Never dreamt about them." He reached out and cupped her shoulders. "And every time I was in town, whether it was for an hour or a week, I'd look for you. Made excuses, some really pathetic ones, just to be around you."

"No you didn't." Her chest felt tight as hope pressed against her ribs.

"I didn't realize I was doing it," he said, gently drawing her closer. "I didn't understand it until Farmer's wedding when I saw you."

She winced as the memory flashed in her mind. "Do you have to bring that up?"

"Yeah"—the word came out in a seductive growl—"because when I saw you in my bed, I knew you were meant to be there."

She slicked her tongue across her lips. "Then why did you leave?"

"Because I knew the truth and it freaked me out," he admitted as his hands skimmed down her spine. "But I'm back now. For good."

She flattened her hands against his chest and felt the powerful beat of his heart. "What was true?"

He dipped his head until his mouth brushed hers. "That I love you, Karen."

Her mouth trembled as she kissed him back. She knew there was no way to misinterpret his words. She heard them loud and clear.

Urgency invaded her with such speed that she gasped in surprise. She pulled at his shirt, grasped his hair, and greedily took his mouth in hers. She needed to show him how she felt, how much those words meant to her.

Tyler seemed to understand, feeding her fierce emotions with wild, hot kisses. His hands roamed her body, shoving up her sweater and sliding his fingers under her bra to cup her breast.

She pulled off her sweater and unhooked her bra. Standing

in the firelight Karen didn't feel vulnerable as she shucked off her jeans and panties. She wanted Tyler to watch her, to take pleasure from her body.

"Let me help you with this," she told him as she unbuttoned his jeans. Tyler yanked at his shirt with clumsy fingers. By the time he got it off, Karen had already unzipped his jeans and dropped to her knees.

She removed his thick penis from its confinement. Desire fizzed in her as she gripped him at the base. He was hot, smooth, and sleek. She stroked his length, one hand after the other.

"Karen—" Tyler's voice sounded strangled. She glanced up. His male beauty made her feel weak. The firelight glowed against his harsh lines and sharp angles. She couldn't wait to feel those lines and angles against her. In her.

She leaned forward and took his penis in her mouth. Karen flicked her tongue along the weeping tip. She murmured with delight as he clasped his hands against the back of her head.

She took him deeper into her mouth, tasting him, inhaling his scent. As she cupped and squeezed his balls, Tyler's firm hands guided her into a rhythm. His rasps and fragmented words excited her, and she drew him deeper.

"I can't take anymore," Tyler said as he roughly withdrew from her mouth. Dropping to his knees with such force that the wood floor vibrated, he grabbed her hips and pulled her to him.

She fell back, her elbow colliding against the stone hearth. She had no time to gasp as he settled between her legs and tested her wet arousal with demanding fingers. "I love you, Tyler."

He paused and looked into her eyes. With a triumphant groan, he claimed her with a deep, surging stroke.

Tyler stirred against the cold hardwood floor. He couldn't move much as Karen's head was lying on his outstretched arm.

He nestled against her, cradling her back against his chest. When he pulled the blanket to their shoulders, he realized it was too bright for nighttime.

Cracking one eye open, he saw the Christmas trees twinkling. The lamps and overhead lights glared in his eyes. More importantly, he felt a whisper of heat.

"Karen," he said as he nudged her awake. "The power is back on."

"About time," she muttered sleepily and yawned.

"Merry Christmas," he whispered in her ear.

She turned her head and kissed him. The gentle touch overflowed with love, leaving him breathless. "Merry Christmas."

Karen settled back against him, sighing with contentment. She fit so perfectly against him that he was about to protest when she lifted her head. "What's that?"

"What?"

The blanket swept down her as she moved away. Distracted by the curves he finally saw in full light, he didn't notice her reaching under the tree. "There's a package here. Someone must have forgotten it. Hey! It has my name on it."

He recognized the dark green wrapping paper, and his gut twisted. "Uh, Karen . . ."

She glanced over her shoulder, her eyes shining with excitement. "It's from you."

Panic attacked him with one swipe. "Don't open it!" He made a grab for the package.

Karen held it out of his reach. "Oh, now I have to," she said as she tore the paper.

I am going to be in deep sludge. "It's not a good time to do that. Now that the power's on . . ." He trailed off as she lifted the lid.

He waited, but Karen didn't say anything. She looked up at him, her eyebrows almost reaching her hairline.

Deep, deep sludge. "It seemed like a good idea at the time."

She pursed her lips as she reached in. "A compass?"

Maybe she wouldn't notice the words "left" and "right"

engraved on the back. "It was a joke. Okay, maybe a reminder of what happened, and—"

Her hands shot out, and Tyler was ready to take cover. Karen's whoop of joy startled him. When she threw her arms around him, he was at a complete loss.

O . . . kay, Tyler thought as he held her tight. Whatever made her happy. That he was the one who did it was a bonus.

Karen kissed him with an enthusiasm that made him wild. He couldn't keep up with her mouth. His body tightened as he surrendered to her wild kisses.

"Tyler," she said breathlessly as she pulled away.

The tension shimmering inside him was unbearable. "Yeah?" His voice sounded rough to his ears.

She looked into his eyes. "Take me to bed."

He smiled as the white heat kicked into his blood. "Lead the way."

We don't think you will want to miss Lori Foster's
JUST A HINT—CLINT,
coming in October 2004, from Brava.
Here's a sneak peek.

A bead of sweat took a slow path down his throat and into the neckline of his dark T-shirt. Pushed by a hot, insubstantial breeze, a weed brushed his cheek.

Clint never moved.

Through the shifting shadows of the pulled blinds, he could detect activity in the small cabin. The low drone of voices filtered out the screen door, but Clint couldn't make out any of the slurred conversation.

Next to him, Red stirred. In little more than a breath of sound, he said, "Fuck, I hate waiting."

Wary of a trap, Clint wanted the entire area checked. Mojo chose that moment to slip silently into the grass beside them. He'd done a surveillance of the cabin, the surrounding grounds, and probably gotten a good peek in the back window. Mojo could be invisible and eerily silent when he chose.

"All's clear."

Something tightened inside Clint. "She's in there?"

"Alive but pissed off and real scared." Mojo's obsidian eyes narrowed. "Four men. They've got her tied up."

Clint silently worked his jaw, fighting for his famed icy control. The entire situation was bizarre. How was it Asa knew where to find the men, yet they didn't appear to expect an interruption? Had Robert deliberately fed the info to Asa to embroil him in a trap so Clint would kill him? And why would Robert want Asa dead?

Somehow, both he and Julie Rose were pawns. But for what purpose?

Clint's rage grew, clawing to be freed, making his stomach pitch with the violent need to act. "They're armed?"

Mojo nodded with evil delight. "And on their way out."

Given that a small bonfire lit the clearing in front of the cabin, Clint wasn't surprised that they would venture outside. The hunting cabin was deep into the hills, mostly surrounded by thick woods. Obviously, the kidnappers felt confident in their seclusion.

He'd have found them eventually, Clint thought, but Asa's tip had proved invaluable. And a bit too fucking timely.

So far, nothing added up, and that made him more cautious than anything else could have.

He'd work it out as they went along. The drive had cost them two hours, with another hour crawling through the woods. But now he had them.

He had *her*.

The cabin door opened and two men stumbled out under the glare of a yellow bug light. One wore jeans and an unbuttoned shirt, the other was shirtless, showing off a variety of tattoos on his skinny chest. They looked youngish and drunk and stupid. They looked cruel.

Raucous laughter echoed around the small clearing, disturbed only by a feminine voice, shrill with fear and anger, as two other men dragged Julie Rose outside.

She wasn't crying.

No sir. Julie Rose was complaining.

Her torn school dress hung off her right shoulder nearly to her waist, displaying one small pale breast. She struggled against hard hands and deliberate roughness until she was shoved, landing on her right hip in the barren area in front of the house. With her hands tied behind her back, she had no way to brace herself. She fell flat, but quickly struggled into a sitting position.

The glow of the bonfire reflected on her bruised, dirty face—and in her furious eyes. She was frightened, but she was also livid.

"I think we should finish stripping her," one of the men said.

Julie's bare feet peddled against the uneven ground as she tried to move farther away.

The men laughed some more, and the one who'd spoken went onto his haunches in front of her. He caught her bare ankle, immobilizing her.

"Not too much longer, bitch. Morning'll be here before you know it." He stroked her leg, up to her knee, higher. "I bet you're getting anxious, huh?"

Her chest heaved, her lips quivered.

She spit on him.

Clint was on his feet in an instant, striding into the clearing before Mojo or Red's hissed curses could register. The four men, standing in a cluster, turned to look at him with various expressions of astonishment, confusion, and horror. They were slow to react, and Clint realized they were more than a little drunk. Idiots.

One of the young fools reached behind his back.

"*You.*" Clint stabbed him with a fast lethal look while keeping his long, ground-eating pace to Julie. "Touch that weapon and I'll break your leg."

The guy blanched—and promptly dropped his hands.

Clint didn't think of anything other than his need to get between Julie and the most immediate threat. But without giving it conscious thought, he knew that Mojo and Red would back him up. If any guns were drawn, theirs would be first.

The man who'd been abusing Julie snorted in disdain at the interference. He took a step forward, saying, "Just who the hell do you think you—"

Reflexes on automatic, Clint pivoted slightly to the side and kicked out hard and fast. The force of his boot heel caught the man on the chin with sickening impact. He sprawled flat with a raw groan that dwindled into blackness. He didn't move.

Another man leaped forward. Clint stepped to the side, and like clockwork, kicked out a knee. The obscene sounds of breaking bone and cartilage and the accompanying scream of pain split the night, sending nocturnal creatures to scurry through the leaves.

Clint glanced at Julie's white face, saw she was frozen in shock, and headed toward the two remaining men. Eyes wide, they started to back up, and Clint curled his mouth into the semblance of a smile. "I don't think so."

A gun was finally drawn, but not in time to be fired. Clint grabbed the man's wrist and twisted up and back. Still holding him, Clint pulled him forward and into a solid punch to the stomach. Without breath, the painful shouts ended real quick. The second Clint released him, the man turned to hobble into the woods. Clint didn't want to, but he let him go.

Robert Burns had said not to bring anyone in. He couldn't see committing random murder, and that's what it'd be if he started breaking heads now. But in an effort to protect Julie Rose and her apparently already tattered reputation, he wouldn't turn them over to the law either.

Just letting them go stuck in his craw, and Clint, fed up, ready to end it, turned to the fourth man. He threw a punch to the throat and jaw, then watched the guy crumble to his knees, then to his face, wheezing for breath.

Behind Clint, Red's dry tone intruded. "Well, that was efficient."

Clint struggled with himself for only an instant before realizing there was no one left to fight. He turned, saw Julie Rose held in wide-eyed horror, and he jerked. Mojo stepped back out of the way, and Clint lurched to the bushes.

Anger turned to acid in his gut.

Typically, at least for Clint Evans and his weak-ass stomach, he puked.

Julie could hardly believe her eyes. One minute she'd known she would be raped and probably killed, and the fear had been all too consuming, a live clawing dread inside her.

Now . . . now she didn't know what had happened. Three men, looking like angelic convicts, had burst into the clearing. Well, no, that wasn't right. The first man hadn't burst anywhere. He'd strode in, casual as you please, then proceeded to make mincemeat out of her abductors.

He'd taken on four men as if they were no more than gnats.

She'd never seen that type of brawling. His blows hadn't been designed to slow down an opponent, or to bruise or hurt. One strike—and the men had dropped like dead weights. Even the sight of a gun hadn't fazed him. He moved so fast, so smoothly, the weapon hadn't mattered at all.

When he'd delivered those awesome strikes, his expression, hard and cold, hadn't changed. A kick here, a punch there, and the men who'd held her, taunted her, were no longer a threat.

He was amazing, invincible, he was . . . *throwing up*.

Her heart pounded in slow, deep thumps that hurt her breastbone and made it difficult to draw an even breath. The relief flooding over her in a drowning force didn't feel much different than her fear had.

Her awareness of that man was almost worse.

Like spotting Superman, or a wild animal, or a combination of both, she felt awed and amazed and disbelieving.

She was safe now, but was she really?

One of her saviors approached her. He was fair, having blond hair and light eyes, though she couldn't see the exact color in the dark night with only the fire for illumination. Trying to make himself look less like a convict, he gave her a slight smile.

A wasted effort.

He moved real slow, watchful, and gentle. "Don't pay any mind to Clint." He spoke in a low, melodic croon. "He always pukes afterward."

Her savior's name was Clint.

Julie blinked several times, trying to gather her wits and calm the spinning in her head. "He does?"

Another man approached, equally cautious, just as gentle. But he had black hair and blacker eyes. He didn't say anything, just stood next to the other man and surveyed her bruised face with an awful frown that should have been alarming, but wasn't.

The blond nodded. "Yeah. Hurtin' people—even people who deserve it—always upsets Clint's stomach. He'll be all right in a minute."

Julie ached, her body, her heart, her mind. She'd long ago lost feeling in her arms but every place else pulsed with relentless pain. She looked over at Clint. He had his hands on his knees, his head hanging. The poor man. "He was saving me, wasn't he?"

"Oh, yes, ma'am. We're here to take you home. Everything will be okay now." His glance darted to her chest and quickly away.

Julie realized she wasn't decently covered, but with her hands tied tightly behind her back, she couldn't do anything about it. She felt conspicuous and vulnerable and ready to cry, so she did her best to straighten her aching shoulders and looked back at Clint.

Just the sight of him, big, powerful, brave, gave her a measure of reassurance. He straightened slowly, drew several deep breaths.

He was an enormous man, layered in sleek muscle with wide shoulders and a tapered waist and long thick thighs. His biceps were as large as her legs, his hands twice as big as her own.

Eyes closed, he tipped his head back and swallowed several

times, drinking in the humid night air. At that moment, he looked very weak.

He hadn't looked weak while pulverizing those men. Julie licked her dry lips and fought off another wave of the strange dizziness.

Clint flicked a glance toward her, and their gazes locked together with a sharp snap, shocking Julie down to the soles of her feet.

He looked annoyed by the near tactile contact.

Julie felt electrified. Her pains faded away into oblivion.

It took a few moments, but his forced smile, meant to be reassuring, was a tad sickly. Still watching her, he reached into his front pocket and pulled out a small silver flask. He tipped it up, swished his mouth out, and spit.

All the while, he held her with that implacable burning gaze.

When he replaced the flask in his pocket and started toward her, every nerve ending in Julie's body came alive with expectation. Fear, alarm, relief—she wasn't at all certain what she felt, she just knew she felt it in spades. Her breath rose to choke her, her body quaked, and strangely enough, tears clouded her eyes.

She would not cry, she would not cry . . .

She rubbed one eye on her shoulder and spoke to the two men, just to help pull herself together. "Should he be drinking?"

Blondie said, "Oh, no. It's mouthwash." And with a smile, "He always carries it with him, cuz of his stomach and the way he usually—"

The dark man nudged the blond, and they both fell silent.

Mouthwash. She hadn't figured on that.

She wanted to ignore him, but her gaze was drawn to him like a lodestone. Fascinated, she watched as Clint drew nearer. During his approach, he peeled his shirt off over his head then stopped in front of her, blocking her from the others. They took the hint and gave her their backs.

Julie stared at that broad, dark, hairy chest. He was more

man than any man she'd ever seen, and the dizziness assailed her again.

With a surprisingly gentle touch, Clint went to one knee and laid the shirt over her chest. It was warm and damp from his body. His voice was low, a little rough when he spoke. "I'm going to cut your hands free. Just hold still a second, okay?"

Julie didn't answer. She *couldn't* answer. She'd been scared for so long now, what seemed like weeks but had only been a little more than a day. And now she was rescued.

She was safe.

A large lethal blade appeared in Clint's capable hands, but Julie felt no fear. Not now. Not with him so close.

He didn't go behind her to free her hands, but rather reached around her while looking over her shoulder and blocked her body with his own. Absurdly, she became aware of his hot scent, rich with the odor of sweat and anger and man. After smelling her own fear for hours on end, it was a delicious treat for her senses. She closed her eyes and concentrated on the smell of him, on his warmth and obvious strength and stunning ability.

He enveloped her with his size, and with the promise of safety.

She felt a small tug and the ropes fell away. But as Julie tried to move, red-hot fire rushed through her arms, into her shoulders and wrists, forcing a groan of pure agony from her tight lips.

"Shhhh, easy now." As if he'd known exactly what she'd feel, Clint sat in front of her. His long legs opened around her, and he braced her against his bare upper body. His flesh was hot, smooth beneath her cheek.

Slowly, carefully, he brought her arms around, and allowed her to muffle her moans against his shoulder. He massaged her, kneading and rubbing from her upper back, her shoulders to her elbows, to her wrists and still crooning to her in that low gravely voice. His hard fingers dug deep into her soft flesh, working out the cramps with merciless determination and loosening her stiff joints that seemed frozen in place.

As the pain eased, tiredness sank in, and Julie slumped against him. She'd been living off adrenaline for hours and now being safe left her utterly drained, unable to stay upright.

It was like propping herself against a warm, vibrant brick wall. There was no give to Clint's hard shoulder, and Julie was comforted.

One thought kept reverberating through her weary brain: *He'd really saved her.*

Meet the men of the Smithson Group—five spies whose best work is done in the field and between the sheets. Smart, built, trained to do everything well—and that's everything—they're the guys you want on your side of the bed. Go deep under-cover? No problem. Take out the bad guys? Done. Play by the rules? I don't think so. Indulge a woman's every fantasy? Happy to please, ma'am. Fall in love? Hey, even a secret agent's got his weak spots...

Bad boys. Good spies. Unforgettable lovers.

Episode One:
THE BANE AFFAIR

Alison Kent

"Smart, funny, exciting, touching, and *hot*."—Cherry Adair

"Fast, dangerous, sexy."—Shannon McKenna

Get started with Christian Bane, SG–5

Christian Bane is a man of few words, so when he talks, peo-ple listen. One of the Smithson Group's elite force, Christian's also the walking wounded, haunted by his past. Something about being betrayed by a woman, then left to die in a Thai prison by the notorious crime syndicate Spectra IT gives a guy demons. But now, Spectra has made a secret deal with a top scientist to crack a governmental encryption technology, and Christian has his orders: Pose as Spectra boss Peter Deacon. Going deep undercover as the slick womanizer will be tough for Christian. Getting cozy with the scientist's beau-tiful goddaughter, Natasha, to get information won't be. But the closer he gets to Natasha, the harder it gets to deceive her.

She's so alluring, so trusting, so completely unexpected he suspects someone's been giving out faulty intel. If Natasha isn't the criminal he was led to believe, they're both being played for fools. Now, with Spectra closing in, Christian's best chance for survival is to confront his demons and trust the only one he can . . . Natasha . . .

Available from Brava in October 2004.

Episode Two:
THE SHAUGHNESSEY ACCORD

Alison Kent

Get hot and bothered with Tripp Shaughnessey, SG–5

When someone screams Tripp Shaughnessey's name, it's usually a woman in the throes of passion or one who's just caught him with his hand in the proverbial cookie jar. Sometimes it's both. Tripp is sarcastic, fun-loving, and funny, with a habit of seducing every woman he says hello to. But the one who really gets him hot and bothered is Glory Brighton, the curvaceous owner of his favorite sandwich shop. The nonstop banter between Glory and Tripp has been leading up to a full-body kiss in the back storeroom. And that's just where they are when all hell breaks loose. Glory's past includes some very bad men connected to Spectra, men convinced she may have important intel hidden in her place. Now, with the shop under siege, and gunmen holding customers hostage, Tripp shows Glory his true colors: He's no sweet, rumpled "engineer" from the Smithson Group, but a well-trained, hardcore covert op whose easy-going rep is about to be put to the test . . .

Available from Brava in November 2004.

Episode Three:
THE SAMMS AGENDA

Alison Kent

Get down and dirty with Julian Samms, SG–5

From his piercing blue eyes to his commanding presence, everything about Julian Samms says all-business and no bull. He expects a lot from his team—some say too much. But that's how you keep people alive, by running things smooth, clean, and quick. Under Julian's watch, that's how it plays. Except today. The mission was straightforward: Extract Katrina Flurry, ex-girlfriend of deposed Spectra frontman Peter Deacon, from her Miami condo before a hit man can silence her for good. But things didn't go according to plan, and Julian's suddenly on the run with a woman who gives new meaning to high maintenance. Stuck in a cheap motel with a force of nature who seems determined to get them killed, Julian can't believe his luck. Katrina is infuriating, unpredictable, adorable, and possibly the most exciting, sexy woman he's ever met. A woman who makes Julian want to forget his playbook and go wild, spending hours in bed. And on the off-chance that they don't get out alive, Julian's new live-for-today motto is starting right now . . .

Available from Brava in December 2004.

Episode Four:
THE BEACH ALIBI

Alison Kent

Get deep under cover with Kelly John Beach, SG–5

Kelly John Beach is a go-to guy known for covering all the bases and moving in the shadows like a ghost. But now, the ultimate spy is in big trouble: during his last mission, he was caught breaking into a Spectra IT high-rise on one of their video surveillance cameras. The SG–5 team has to make an alternate tape fast, one that proves K.J. was elsewhere at the time of the break-in. The plan is simple: Someone from Smithson will pose as K.J.'s lover, and SG–5's strategically placed cameras will record their every intimate, erotic encounter in elevators, restaurant hallways, and other daring forums. But Kelly John never expects that "alibi" to come in the form of Emma Webster, the sexy coworker who has starred in so many of his not-for-primetime fantasies. Getting his hands—and anything else he can—on Emma under the guise of work is a dream come true. Deceiving the good-hearted, trusting woman isn't. And when Spectra realizes that the way to K.J. is through Emma, the spy is ready to come in from the cold, and show her how far he'll go to protect the woman he loves . . .

Available from Brava in January 2005.

Episode Five:
THE MCKENZIE ARTIFACT

Alison Kent

Get what you came for with Eli McKenzie, SG–5

Five months ago, SG–5 operative Eli McKenzie was in deep cover in Mexico, infiltrating a Spectra ring that kidnaps young girls and sells them into a life beyond imagining. Not being able to move on the Spectra scum right away was torture for the tough-but-compassionate superspy. But that wasn't the only problem—someone on the inside was slowly poisoning Eli, clouding his judgment and forcing him to make an abrupt trip back to the Smithson Group's headquarters to heal. Now, Eli's ready to return . . . with a vengeance. It seems his quick departure left a private investigator named Stella Banks in some hot water. Spectra operatives have nabbed the nosy Stella and are awaiting word on how to handle her disposal. Eli knows the only way to save her life and his is to reveal himself to Stella and get her to trust him. Seeing the way Stella takes care of the frightened girls melts Eli's armor, and soon, they find that the best way to survive this brutal assignment is to steal time in each other's arms. It's a bliss Eli's intent on keeping, no matter what he has to do to protect it. Because Eli McKenzie has unfinished business with Spectra—and with the woman who has renewed his heart—this is one man who always finishes what he starts . . .

Available from Brava in February 2005.